I0728150

Book 6 in the Amber Ridge Series

unfinished

NYSSA KATHRYN

UNFINISHED
Copyright © 2026 Nyssa Kathryn Sitarenos

All rights reserved.

No part of this book may be used, stored, or reproduced in any form or by any electronic or mechanical means, including information storage and retrieval systems, without written permission from the author, except for use of brief quotations in book reviews.
This book is for your personal enjoyment only.
This book may not be resold or given to other people.
This is a work of fiction. Names, characters, places, and incidents are the product of the author's imagination or used fictitiously, and any resemblance to actual persons, living or dead, business establishments, events, or locales is entirely coincidental.

An NW Partners Book
Cover by Deranged Doctor Design
Developmentally and Copy Edited by Kelli Collins
Line Edited by Jessica Snyder
Proofread by Amanda Cuff and Jen Katemi
Cover Photography by Briquelle Kayanne Photography

❈ Created with Vellum

ACKNOWLEDGMENTS

Thank you to Kelli, Jess, Amanda and Jen for helping me get this story ready for the world to see. I am so lucky to have each of you on my team.

Thank you to my PA Alana and my ARC team for reading and reviewing and giving me the confidence to let the world read my story.

And thank you to my amazing husband and girls. Thank you for your endless love, patience and belief in me.

PROLOGUE

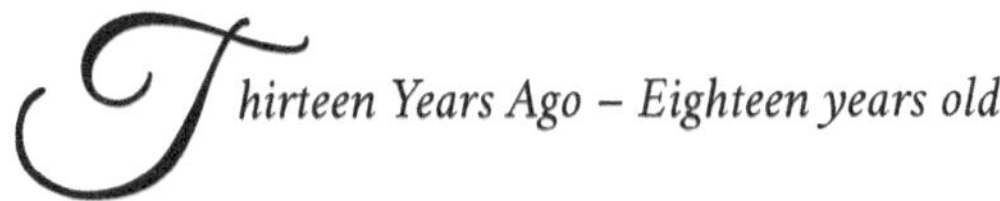

BONNIE HAYES'S heart thrashed against her ribs. Hard, violent hits that made her entire body tremble.

Dead. Her parents were dead. She'd just attended their funeral. It didn't feel real.

She swiped a tear from her cheek, wanting to go back in time. God, she'd do anything to go back two weeks when she'd had living parents. Back when life had made sense and the hurt in her chest hadn't felt like it would swallow her whole.

But she couldn't. Her parents were gone. And she'd never see them again.

She parked at the lookout and the second she was out of the car, she threw up, her entire body convulsing.

Her fault. Her entire world was collapsing and it was all her fault. She shouldn't have gone out that night. Her parents had *told* her to stay home. After everything with Dean and his family, they'd wanted her with them so they could make sure she was okay.

But she hadn't listened. And now she'd never be okay again.

Stupid. Selfish. The words repeated in her head. *Had been* repeating for weeks.

She *had* gone out that night. Not to anywhere in particular, just to try to escape the hate this town was shooting at her from every direction.

And they'd come for her. Her parents had gotten into their car to bring her home…only they hadn't made it home.

She stumbled into the forest, tears filling her eyes, blurring the ground beneath her feet. The tears on Indie's cheeks flashed in her head. Her sister had cried during the entire funeral. Loud, anguished tears that would haunt Bonnie for years to come. While Noah had just stood there, so still she hadn't seen him take a single breath. Like the shock and grief stole his ability to function.

Bonnie, on the other hand…she hadn't been able to shed a single tear. There'd been too much self-hate. She hadn't *deserved* to cry. Not at the funeral, not when so many people were hurting because she'd made the wrong decision.

But now? In the dead of the night when there was no one to see her break…she felt it all. The pain. The guilt. The claws that were shredding her insides.

She'd never hear her father's voice again. She'd never feel her mother's healing hugs.

Pain squeezed at her ribs, so tight it felt like her bones were breaking. She doubled over, wrapping her arms around her middle like that could somehow dull the ache and hold her together.

A few months ago, she'd been numb. Chasing the ability to feel something, *anything*.

Now? Now her chest, her *entire body*, had been cracked wide open, and she'd do anything to go back to before.

She started to heave, the very act of breathing feeling too hard. The shake in her limbs was so violent it made remaining on her feet a challenge.

Breathe. She needed to breathe. But she couldn't. Dean was dead. The town blamed her. Called her a murderer. Graffitied her car. Now her parents, the only two people in the world who had loved her unconditionally, were gone too.

She scrunched her eyes, like that could somehow make it all stop.

But that was a stupid thought. It would never stop. This would always be her fault. Her reality.

Her phone rang from her pocket. It had been going off since she'd left the funeral.

She pulled it out, having to blink three times to make out the words on the screen.

Noah.

She couldn't answer it. How was she supposed to talk to him? How was she supposed to talk to *anyone*? All she did was hurt those around her.

There were texts too. A couple from Maisie. Her best friend had been trying to reach her for weeks, but after what happened that night with Dean, she had zero desire to go to her. And then there was a text from Carlos, Dean's father. A man who hated her so fiercely that he seemed to take joy in her pain.

She wasn't sure why she hadn't blocked his number yet. Maybe because some part of her had been waiting for him to reassure her that Dean's death wasn't her fault. She wanted him to tell her that she was only eighteen, and it had not been her responsibility to get their son home safely from that party.

She skimmed the text, certain familiar words glaring at her.

Murderer. Gone. Your fault.

The words hit her in the stomach like bullets.

Air started to thicken, no longer making it to her lungs. She couldn't breathe. This town, this moment, the losses, were suffocating her.

Out. She needed out. Out of Amber Ridge. She needed to find somewhere she wasn't drowning.

CHAPTER 1

resent Day

BONNIE HAYES WRAPPED her jacket tightly around herself, the cool morning breeze chilling her as she walked. How had she forgotten how cold it got in Montana? Or maybe she'd just gotten used to the San Francisco sun.

Thirteen years. She'd been away from Amber Ridge for thirteen whole years. Away from her brother. Her sister. Her cousins and aunt and friends she'd gone to high school with.

Friends? No. People she'd *thought* were friends. But then Dean had died and everything had changed.

She checked the road before crossing.

It was strange how a town could simultaneously feel different and also exactly the same. The buildings were the same. The parks and the houses. But the locals were older. The businesses more modern. Some painted. Others with new owners.

She swallowed the lump in her throat and sped up.

The town wasn't the only thing that had changed…she was different, too. Wiser. Stronger. And she was going to make this work.

Two women on the other side of the road stopped and looked at her. She didn't return their gazes. She didn't need a repeat of what had happened last week, when Dean's high school buddies had harassed her outside of The Tea House. They weren't the first and they wouldn't be the last. A lot of people didn't want her here. Apparently, thirteen years did nothing to change the narrative that Dean's death was her fault.

When the two-story women's shelter came into view, relief relaxed the muscles in her shoulders. The shelter was a converted older house that had been painted a pale green. There was a big privacy fence that surrounded the building and required a code to gain access. The front and back doors were always locked.

There wasn't a parking lot, but that was fine for her because she'd sold her car in San Francisco and hadn't replaced it yet. She'd had a rental last week when she was running around town buying things for the apartment, but now she was back to walking, at least until she bought a new one.

The shelter didn't have any signage, which wasn't unusual. These women were often fleeing terrible circumstances, usually from abusive ex-partners or friends or family members. They didn't need a big sign to tell everyone where they were.

She tapped the code into the gate and used her key for the front door. A couple of women were eating breakfast at the table while Chett, a five-year-old boy, sat in front of the TV. His eyes lit up at the sight of her. He jumped to his feet and raced over, then threw his little arms around her legs.

"Bonnie! Mommy's letting me have morning TV as a treat."

Bonnie widened her eyes, feigning excitement. "Wow. What a special day. What are you watching?"

"*Bluey*."

"Oh my gosh. You be careful though. Too long watching that and you'll start speaking with an Australian accent."

The five-year-old's nose wrinkled. "What's an accent?"

She chuckled. "Sorry, bud. Sometimes I forget you're only ten."

He gasped. "I'm not ten."

"Twelve? Fifteen?"

"I'm five!"

She laughed again, messing up his hair. "Have fun watching *Bluey*."

He raced back to the TV, and she waved to the women at the table.

One of them smiled, but the other didn't look up. Not a surprise. This was only Bonnie's second week, and trust didn't come easily or quickly to women who'd been hurt.

But that's why Bonnie had gotten into this work. Thirteen years ago, helping others had been the only thing that made her feel even remotely okay—like each good deed could stitch shut a piece of the damage inside her.

Now, she did it because it gave her something deeper —purpose.

Down the hall, she stepped into her office. It was small and there were still boxes stacked against the wall. She hadn't had much of a chance to unpack because work had started on day one and it hadn't stopped.

The second she lowered into her seat in front of the laptop, she sighed. Even though she hated to admit it, the walk to work— a walk anywhere—made her nervous. That someone would see her and openly hate her. That she'd run into the White family.

She massaged her temples. She was going to see them eventually. Would they still hate her? Blame her?

"Bonnie."

She jumped and turned. "Shelley. Good morning."

Shelley was both the shelter manager and a counselor. She was nice but also seemed a bit…cold for a counselor. But maybe that was because the counselors at the shelter in San Francisco had been so warm and friendly that *anyone* would feel cold in comparison.

"How are you doing with the program?" Shelley asked, all business.

As the program coordinator, it was Bonnie's job to organize activities for the women and apply for funding and grants. "Good. I've organized some art therapy for this afternoon. There's also a series of life skills workshops, focusing on cooking, budgeting, and cleaning. And I'm going to run a session on rental applications and the process of searching for housing on Friday."

Shelley nodded, not even a hint of a smile on her face. "Okay. What about something physical to get the women active?"

"Well, I've been trying to find a yoga and breathwork instructor, but there doesn't seem to be many options in Amber Ridge. I'm going to widen my search and see if there's anyone in Bozeman who'd make the drive."

Shelley frowned. "You're sticking within budget, right?"

The budget was small. "Uh, yes, but I'm also applying for grants."

"Good. It sounds like you're off to a good start." Shelley went to step away, only to suddenly turn back. "Oh, I ordered a couple of pies from The Tea House for the women. I need you to pick them up."

Bonnie internally cringed, but that was stupid. She'd moved back to this town. That involved going places. But then, picking up pies wasn't exactly in her job description. Though it felt too early to be telling her boss that. "Sure. When do you need me to go?"

"Now. Thanks." Then she was gone. Which was probably a good thing because she missed the way Bonnie's entire body recoiled at the request.

It was fine. The Tea House was only a fifteen-minute walk. The problem was, The Tea House seemed to be where *everyone* congregated in this town these days. Plus, in the week she'd been here, she hadn't seen her brother or sister yet. Noah had been asking.

Would any of her family be there? Or Dean's family?

She shook her head. It didn't matter who was there. She was a grown-ass woman, and she'd see them all eventually. She grabbed her cell and shoved it into her back pocket before moving out of the office.

She'd just stepped outside when she heard it—crying.

Where was that coming from?

She frowned as she rounded the side of the building to see Sarah, Chett's mother. Her shoulders were hunched, and her was head down as she looked at her phone screen.

"Sarah?"

The woman spun and quickly straightened.

Bonnie tried to gentle her voice. "I'm sorry. I didn't mean to scare you. I heard you crying and wanted to check on you."

The woman scrubbed the tears from her cheeks. "It's fine. I'm jumpy at the moment."

"Is everything okay?"

"Not really. But that's what happens when you have a child with a psychopath."

Bonnie frowned. "He doesn't know you're here though, right?"

"He shouldn't. And he's in jail. But old fear is hard to shake… especially when I have Chett to protect."

Bonnie nodded. She'd come across lots of women like Sarah. Mothers fleeing domestic violence. Women who were doing everything they could to protect themselves and their children.

"You're safe here," Bonnie pushed gently. "No one gets in without the code."

Sarah nodded quickly.

"I'm here every day if you need someone to talk to. Right now, in fact, I'm going to pick up some pies from The Tea House. Would you like to come? Chett could join us too."

Sarah shook her head. "But thanks."

"You're welcome. Offer's open to talk anytime."

"Thank you."

Bonnie stepped onto the street, her heart hurting for the women in the shelter. God, she hated that so many of them were in such awful situations.

Her phone suddenly rang and she pulled it from her pocket to see Noah's name on the screen. A genuine smile curved her lips. "Hey."

"I can't believe you've done this."

She frowned as she crossed the street. "Done what?"

"You tease me with the fact that my little sister is in town but then don't give me your address or organize a time to meet up."

She wrinkled her nose. It was true. "I'm sorry. I only just moved into my apartment, and my new job's been busy."

It wasn't a lie. Shelley had high expectations and kept throwing extra tasks her way that weren't even in her job description.

"What about tomorrow?"

Her heart stuttered. "Um, tomorrow I might be working late. But I have Wednesday morning off, if you want to meet for a coffee at The Tea House?"

Meeting in a public place felt safer. Less chance of blubbering like a baby.

"Wednesday morning works for me," he said.

"You don't have to work?"

"I can get it off."

"Noah—"

"I can get it off, Bonnie. This is important. I need to see you."

She swallowed. She was nervous, but she also really wanted to see him too. "Okay. Wednesday."

"How's ten?"

"Ten's great. I'll see you then?"

"I'll see you then. And Bonnie…I hope you're ready for the biggest damn hug you've ever had."

Emotion clogged her throat. "I am."

When she hung up, there were tears in her eyes. She was finally going to see her big brother. A big brother she'd deserted thirteen years ago, who didn't seem to hate her for it. Something she was unbelievably grateful for.

She was just pushing her cell into her pocket when two people rounded a corner down the street.

She froze. A whole-body, couldn't-walk-another-step kind of freeze. Because she recognized both of them—Dean's mother, Jane, and Bonnie's ex-best friend, Maisie.

Yes, a few minutes ago, she'd told herself she could handle anything. It was a lie. At least, right now it was. She couldn't handle them. She couldn't even handle them seeing her.

Quickly, she pushed inside the business on her left. The second the door closed, she leaned her back against the wood and closed her eyes, trying to both breathe and still her racing heart.

There had been a time when Dean's mother had liked her. That was before she'd left Dean at that party. Then she'd openly blamed Bonnie for her son's death, telling anyone and everyone that it was her fault.

She scrunched her eyes, counting down the seconds, not sure how many she needed to remain where she was, when a deep, gravelly voice suddenly sounded.

"Are you okay?"

Bonnie's eyes flew open. Then she looked up, first at a shirtless, muscled chest with thickly veined muscles. The chest moved quickly, like the man had been working out, and there was a sheen of sweat on his skin.

Then her gaze continued to lift until they met the deepest blue eyes she'd ever seen. Eyes she'd seen before. Because she'd met this man. He'd saved her outside The Tea House when Dean's friends had harassed her.

And just like then, there was a whole new reason for her heart to race.

CHAPTER 2

Zane Merrick reared back his fist before letting it fly forward and hitting the tan leather bag hard. It trembled under the violence. He did it again and again, yet that pit in his gut didn't go away.

Hitting a bag had once brought him peace. It had allowed his mind to quiet and the world around him to disappear.

That hadn't happened for over a year. Since before everything had gone down with Monty.

He punched the bag harder, the thump of his fist hitting leather the only sound in the quiet gym. *His* gym. The Pit. The place didn't open for another hour. Exactly why he liked to work out now…because he liked the quiet. The noise of an open gym didn't compete with the noise in his head.

He jabbed the bag then lifted his leg to kick it, rage sitting in his gut like a rock. The same rage that had been there since Monty, his cousin, a man who was *family*, had done the unthinkable.

Zane had been through a lot in his thirty-five years. His time as an Army Ranger almost broke him. Then his years in the UFC had tested him both physically and mentally. He'd fought world champions and won. But this last year…fuck, it had been hard.

Punch, punch, kick.

Sweat beaded his forehead, the muscles in his shoulders aching. He didn't stop. He didn't even *think* about stopping. He wanted to feel so damn exhausted that he had nothing left.

Jab, hook.

Air soared in and out of his lungs. Six months. That's how long it had been since that asshole was sentenced. Now Monty would spend the rest of his worthless life behind bars—like he deserved.

Just because Monty was locked up didn't mean he didn't have access to the outside world though. He had money, and money bought things a person behind bars shouldn't have.

The next punch was so powerful, the bag swung wide.

Zane caught it. Steadied it. Then he pressed his temple to the leather and breathed. It was hard. But he was used to hard. Good at hard.

When he eventually stepped away from the bag and pulled the wraps off his hands, his gaze went to the window that overlooked the street.

It felt good to be out of Billings. To be somewhere people didn't know what he'd been through and the media didn't hound him. Thankfully, all that shit had only made local news…and that's where it would stay—in Billings.

He'd just dropped the wraps when he heard the click of the door opening.

His head swung around. A wall separated the hall from the rest of the gym, so he couldn't see the person, and when no one stepped around, he frowned.

Who the hell was it?

He moved toward the hall, only for his frown to deepen at the sight of a woman leaning against the door. She was short, with long brown hair that had blond streaks through it. Her eyes were closed. Not just closed—squeezed tight. And her palms and back were flush against the door.

She didn't seem to hear him as he closed the distance between them. Because her chest was heaving?

Was she scared? Was she hiding from something? Or someone?

"Are you okay?"

Her eyes flashed open. Beautiful hazel eyes. And so fucking expressive that a million emotions passed through them. Shock. Confusion. Recognition. "Hi."

Her soft voice was kind of breathless. From whatever she was hiding from? Or him?

He'd seen her at The Tea House a week ago. Two assholes had tried to mess with her, and he'd been a second away from stepping in, but she hadn't needed saving. She'd thrown one of the jerks onto his ass and saved herself.

He checked the window beside the door, then returned his gaze to her. "I'm Zane."

"Bonnie."

Bonnie. It fit. Pretty. Simple. Different. "Is everything okay, Bonnie?"

She swallowed and glanced over her shoulder at the wooden door before looking back at him. "I just need somewhere to hide for a second. Is that okay?"

"Are you in danger?"

"Not the physical kind. At least, I don't think the physical kind. But what's out there could definitely hurt me."

What the hell was she talking about? Whatever it was, for some damn reason, if this woman needed shelter, he wanted to give it to her.

She glanced down at his chest, and there was the smallest flaring of her eyes before her gaze shot back up.

He stepped back. He was big. Big enough to come across as a threat. "Stay as long as you need."

He headed back toward his bag.

The soft pad of footsteps sounded behind him. "This is the place you mentioned? Your gym?"

He paused, their conversation the week prior coming back to him. After those assholes had messed with her, he'd offered to let her train here. "This is it."

"It looks great. Actually, it looks like the kind of place my brother and cousins would like."

He turned. "Who's your brother?"

"His name's Noah. He was a Marine. And my cousins are all badass military guys too."

Zane lifted his bag to his shoulder. "I've met Noah."

"You have?"

"Yeah. We went a round in the ring."

Her focus flickered to the octagonal ring before flinging back to him, an emotion he couldn't place crossing her face. Longing? Why the hell would that be her first emotion at the mention of her brother?

"Have you been in a ring before?" he asked.

"Once or twice. I've done a lot of self-defense classes." Her brow creased. "Have you ever offered any kind of classes?"

"No. This place isn't really built for that."

She nodded almost absently, and when she glanced out the window, she gasped and stepped back so the hallway wall covered her.

He followed her gaze to two women crossing the road outside the gym, one older and one maybe early thirties. He looked back at Bonnie. It wasn't fear in her eyes. Apprehension? "You know them?"

"Knew them. I haven't seen them since the last time I was here."

"Was that a long time ago?" Why the fuck did he ask that? It wasn't his business, and he shouldn't care. He *didn't* care.

"Thirteen years." She looked at the window again, even though the women were gone.

"That's a long time to be gone, considering you have family here."

"It took me longer than I thought it would to come back. Guess we're not all built with courage."

She thought she didn't have courage?

She continued to frown at the window. "It feels different…the town. I mean, I knew it would but—" She suddenly stopped and shook her head. "Sorry, you don't care about this."

That was the thing—even though he'd just told himself he didn't care, for some goddamn reason, he did.

The door suddenly opened. "Yo, boss, the door's unlocked. Did you—" The twenty-one-year-old stopped at the desk at the end of the hall. "Oh. Sorry, I—" He frowned at Bonnie. "Hey. You look familiar. Do I know you?"

Her eyes widened.

"Yeah." Stetson moved closer. "You dated my cousin."

She swallowed like she was suddenly nervous. Why would she be nervous of Stetson? He was like a puppy dog.

"I'm Stetson. Dean's little cousin. Although, I'm not eight anymore." He laughed. "I didn't know you were back."

"I got here a couple weeks ago." Anxiety. It wove through her words.

What the fuck had happened between her and this Dean guy?

Stetson shook his head. "Sad what happened to my cousin. But just so you know, I never bought into *anything* my aunt and uncle said about you. Even at eight, I was too smart for that."

"Thanks. I, um, should go." She looked up at Zane. "Thanks for letting me hide in here."

He dipped his head.

She smiled, and fuck, that hesitant curve of her lips did something that it absolutely shouldn't. It felt like a kick to his gut.

She disappeared into the hall, and there was a quiet click of the door closing.

"I can't believe she's back," Stetson said, almost to himself. "I wonder if Jane and Carlos know."

"Jane and Carlos?"

"My aunt and uncle. Awful people." Stetson looked at Zane's raised brow. "You think I'm joking? I'm not. They made a lot of money on some good investments and it went straight to their heads. Think they're right all the time when they're not. But their son died, so Mom and Dad think I should cut them some slack."

"So this Dean guy's dead?"

"Yep. Died thirteen years ago."

Thirteen years ago…when Bonnie had left.

"Do you want—"

"No." Zane cut the kid off. He knew exactly what Stetson was going to ask. If he wanted the story. He didn't. Or at least, he shouldn't. Because he should mind his own damn business. He checked the window one last time, but she wasn't there. "I'm going to shower."

"You got it, boss."

His lips twitched. This is why he'd hired the kid. Stetson wasn't great at the bag or in the ring, but he was likable and worked hard, two things Zane valued.

In the changing room, before getting into the shower, he lifted his cell and texted Ethan. The man wasn't just a childhood friend from their hometown of Deep River, he was also a former Navy SEAL who'd made a business out of finding information that most couldn't.

Zane: He's still there, right?

The response was immediate.

Ethan: He's in there for life, Zane. He's not going anywhere.

The same response Zane always got. And yeah, Monty *had* been put away for life. He *should* spend the rest of his days rotting in Montana State Prison.

So why did Zane feel so fucking uneasy?

CHAPTER 3

The thumps of Bonnie's heart were loud and hard in her chest as she walked to The Tea House. And there was a tremble in her fingers that had been there since she'd woken that morning.

This was it. She was finally going to see Noah and Indie after thirteen years of nothing. What would she even say? *Sorry for deserting you right after our parents died, when we needed each other most? Sorry for not answering your calls? Sorry for completely cutting you off because I hated myself for a while?*

She swallowed the hard lump in her throat and quickened her pace.

There were no words she could give that would make it better. The truth was, she'd been eighteen and hurting.

So she'd left. Run. Tried to escape it all. Because at eighteen, she hadn't known what else to do.

But that wasn't the worst part. The worst was remaining gone for so long. At eighteen years old, she could be forgiven for making bad choices. But years had passed, and she'd remained in San Francisco. She hadn't reached out. She hadn't apologized. Because every year that passed had made the mountain that she'd

19

put between herself and her family feel that much higher. It had taken Noah reaching out to *her*, and showing her a kindness she hadn't felt she deserved, for Bonnie to finally reconnect.

But she was here now. And she was ready to start making amends.

Well, at least she thought she was. Until The Tea House came into view. Then her heart raced again.

No. She could do this.

She stopped at the door and took one deep breath.

It will be fine. Everything will be okay. The words whispered in her head before she pushed inside.

He was the first person she saw. The only person.

Noah. He was so much older. No longer the twenty-one-year-old brother she remembered. There were lines beside his eyes. And God, his shoulders were wide. But that smile...it was so achingly familiar.

He rose from the booth. She didn't even feel like she had control of her feet, they just started moving.

"Hey, Bon-Bon."

Tears suddenly welled in her eyes, and she threw her arms around his shoulders. His strong arms wrapped around her, holding her as she cried into his chest.

"How is it possible that you feel the same?" she whispered. Not just felt the same. Smelled the same. Sounded the same.

His arms tightened. "I know what you mean."

She breathed him in. It felt like a part of her had suddenly been returned. Like she hadn't even realized that piece was missing, but now that she had it back, she felt a bit more whole.

When they finally separated, Bonnie swiped tears from her cheeks. "You look good."

One side of his mouth lifted, showing a familiar dimple. "Right back at you."

"Is Indie here?"

There was the smallest hesitation from Noah.

And suddenly she knew. "She's not coming."

"Morning sickness. It's been pretty rough for her. It has nothing to do with you. She wanted to be here."

Bonnie nodded, wanting to believe him.

He gestured to the booth. "Sit. We have a lot to catch up on."

She lowered, unable to take her eyes off him. The last time she'd seen him, he'd only been in the military for a couple of years. He hadn't been as big or strong or…hardened.

"How are you?" she asked.

"Good. Great, actually. We had some hiccups at the park that caused us to close for a while, but we've reopened, and it's been busy."

"That's great. And what about the woman you're dating. Addie, was it?"

His eyes softened, the affection so immediate that she almost felt his love for her. "She's amazing. I don't know how I got so lucky with her. She sees my flaws and she loves me anyway."

Noah's smile made *her* smile. Of course Addie loved Noah—he was the best guy she'd ever met. "Maybe I'll get to meet her soon."

"You'll definitely get to meet her. She wanted to come today but also wanted to give you and me some time first."

An older woman stopped by the table. "Hi, Noah. Your usual?"

He smiled at the woman. "Thanks. Mrs. Gerald, this is my youngest sister, Bonnie. Bonnie, Mrs. Gerald. She's the fabulous owner of this place."

Mrs. Gerald scoffed. "I'm not sure about fabulous."

Bonnie looked up at the woman. "Your coffee is amazing."

"Thank you, dear. That means a lot to me. What can I get you?"

"I would love a dirty chai with almond milk."

The older woman frowned. "You might have to explain that one to me. I've become pretty clued in on most drinks, but I haven't heard of a dirty chai."

She almost forgot she wasn't in a big city anymore. "It's an almond milk chai latte with a shot of espresso. But if you don't serve that—"

"No, I can do it. It's good for me to learn new things." The woman grinned before walking away.

One side of Noah's mouth lifted. "Fancy."

"No. Not fancy. Nothing about me is fancy."

His smile softened. "I can't believe you're home."

"Me neither."

"Tell me about your job."

She lifted a shoulder. "It's similar to my last. I organize the programs for women at the shelter."

"How'd you get into that?"

"I started by working night shifts at a women's shelter in San Franscisco. I got some certificates and became the program manager. I was there for my entire time in San Fransico."

He shook his head. "I've missed so much."

Pain cut into her chest. Her fault. It was her fault he'd missed her life. And her fault she'd missed his. "I'm sorry." Two words she'd wanted to say so many times over the years. "I'm sorry I ran. I'm sorry I stayed away for so long. I'm sorry for so many things."

He reached over and slipped his large warm hand over hers. "Why did you run?"

How many times had she played this conversation over in her head? So many that she should have her answer worked out by now. She didn't. "Because when Dean died, everyone said it was my fault. Strangers were coming up to me in the street and yelling at me. One person threw their drink at me. Another spat on me, and someone spray-painted my car."

The muscles in Noah's forearms visibly contracted.

"It was so constant that I started to believe them. Then Mom and Dad died on their way to pick me up after they'd told me not to go out, and it just…it broke me. I *hated* myself, and I suddenly couldn't stand to be in this town. I felt like I needed to tear off my own skin. Like I wanted to be in another body. So I ran from the memories that lined these streets. It felt like survival."

The expression on Noah's face was almost one of pain.

He leaned forward. "You realize that none of those deaths were your fault though, right? Dean made the decision to get into a car and drive while under the influence of alcohol and drugs. *He* sealed his fate that night. And Mom and Dad…that was just something really shitty that happened. The road was icy. Dad hit the brakes too late. The car slid. It *wasn't* your fault."

She scrubbed a tear from her cheek. "Does Indie hate me for leaving?"

"No. She's got some big feelings, but hate isn't one of them."

She pressed her nails into her thigh under the table. Even before Bonnie left town, she and her sister hadn't gotten along. Indie had been the sweet, organized, polite daughter. The one who did as she was told. Never talked back to her teachers or parents and got straight As in class.

Whereas Bonnie had been none of those things. And that had created friction between them.

"Tell me everything else I've missed," Noah said gently.

She smiled and started talking about her apartment in San Francisco. The retro coffee shop she'd visited regularly, sometimes twice daily. She told Noah about her attempt at keeping a fish alive—attempt because it hadn't lasted long. And Noah told her about his life. About his time as a Marine. About Addie and the park.

It felt so good to catch up with him. She'd almost forgotten about that sibling bond. The one that was so different from any other relationship. A built-in person who shared this special history with you that no one else shared or understood.

She was just finishing her latte when she glanced up to see a man standing by the counter. Wait…those broad shoulders were familiar.

Zane.

Her heart gave a little kick.

Two days had passed since she'd stumbled into his gym. Okay, not stumbled. Shot inside like she was being chased. And she'd thought about him both of those days. About the deep rumble of his voice. The way that he really seemed to listen when she spoke.

Suddenly he turned. He didn't look surprised to see her. Because he'd already noticed her? One side of his mouth lifted, making him look just a bit less dangerous...slightly softer. She smiled before quickly looking away.

Oh God, she felt fifteen again.

Noah frowned. "You know him?"

"Not really. We've run into each other a couple of times, that's it. He said he knows *you* though."

"He's built a good gym here."

"You don't like him." It wasn't a question.

"I don't *know* him. He helped Indie when she got into a bad spot not long ago, so seems like a good guy."

A good guy with impossibly broad shoulders and laser blue eyes? Sounded like a dangerous combination.

Something behind Bonnie had Noah straightening.

"What?" She turned her head—and her entire stomach dropped to her feet.

Carlos White...Dean's father. He was standing by the door like he'd just stepped inside. He was looking straight at her, and he did *not* look happy.

This was it. This was the moment she saw her deceased boyfriend's father again. And despite the time that had passed and the healing she'd done, every inch of her suddenly wanted to be anywhere but here.

She pushed her mug away. "I should go."

"Bonnie—"

She rose from the booth, but it was too late, Carlos was marching toward her.

Shit, shit, shit.

"*You,*" Carlos growled.

Noah rose from the booth, but when he tried to step in front of her, she pressed a hand to his chest. If she wanted to stand on her own two feet in this town, she couldn't let her big brother fight her battles.

"Hi, Carlos."

His eyes spit fire. "You dare show your face here after you *killed* my son?"

"*Hey.*"

At Noah's shout, she stepped in front of him and gave her full attention to Carlos. "I'm back because this is my home. But I understand that my return might be a shock for you, so I'm going to leave."

"You sure as hell are going to leave."

"Not Amber Ridge," Bonnie clarified. "This café. This town is my home, Carlos. And I'm here to stay. I know it might take a while for you and Jane to get used to—"

"A while to get used to? I'm not going to drink fucking coffee beside the woman responsible for my son's death! The best thing you ever did was leave, and if you know what's good for you, you'll do it again."

Then he stormed straight back out of The Tea House.

A rush of air Bonnie hadn't realized she'd been holding rattled out of her chest. Her heart beat like it was trying to punch out of her body. And maybe it was. Maybe it wanted to run as much as the rest of her.

"Are you okay?" Noah's words were quiet, but there was also an edge to them. An anger. Like he was right on the verge of going after Carlos.

She turned and looked at him, trying hard to keep her voice steady. "He didn't do anything."

Noah eyes narrowed like he didn't agree. "You should have let me put him in his place."

"His son died. He's still hurting. And I'm thirty-one now. I don't need my brother throwing punches for me." She swallowed the lump in her throat. "I'm going to go."

"I'll walk with you."

She shook her head. "No. I just...I need some time to think." She reached out and pulled her brother into a hug. "Thank you. For coming today and welcoming me home. And for being on my side."

His strong arms were tight around her. "I'll *always* be on your side, Bon."

They parted, and she smiled once more before turning. But before stepping outside, she caught a glimpse of Zane. He was still at the counter but standing straighter now, watching her. And he looked as angry as her brother. Maybe angrier.

Angry on her behalf? He didn't even know her.

One thing she knew for absolute certainty—the White family still placed the blame for their son's death squarely on her shoulders.

CHAPTER 4

"Hi, Zane. It's *so* good to see you."

No. Too eager.

Just because he had that unfair combination of strength and symmetry like someone had built him out of spare Greek god parts, it *did not* mean she needed to bat her lashes over him.

She watched her reflection in her bathroom mirror as she practiced again. "Zane. Hey. I was wondering if you had a minute."

Better. More professional.

She stepped out of her bathroom, grabbed her cell from the top of the dresser, and moved out of her bedroom.

Her apartment was small. One bedroom. One bathroom. And the tiniest living and kitchen area. But it was what had been available. And it was also in an apartment building, which meant a key was needed to get inside.

It wasn't that she was expecting someone to come and harass her at her front door…

Oh, who was she kidding? She had no idea what to expect from this town anymore. And Carlos's little speech last week had just confirmed that nothing was forgiven or forgotten.

She grabbed a granola bar from the kitchen and shoved it into her pocket before stepping into the hall. When she hit the still-dark street outside, because it was too dang early, her mind flicked back to Zane.

"Good morning, Zane. I was wondering if I could ask you a favor?"

No. It wasn't a favor. It was a job. They were different.

She opened her granola bar and had taken one bite when a text came through on her phone. She assumed it was Noah, because he was the only one who ever texted her.

It wasn't.

Her jaw dropped, crumbs of granola slipping from her mouth.

Indie: Hey. I'm sorry I couldn't make our catch-up last week. This pregnancy nausea has been kicking my ass these last few weeks and I really want to be fully present when we see each other. How have you been?

Indie was texting. Her sister, who Bonnie hadn't had a proper conversation with in *years*, was messaging her.

She started responding, then shook her head and deleted it. Then she wrote more words. Again, she deleted them.

Crap, she was nervous. With good reason. Indie was the person she'd hurt the most by leaving, and Bonnie wanted to make things right. She just had to figure out how.

Bonnie: That's okay. Noah told me about your morning sickness. I'm good. Just figuring out this new job. Are you feeling any better today?

She hit send, swallowing the granola in her mouth.

Indie: I'm currently debating whether ginger tea or death is a better option. But also loving that I'm pregnant. Pregnancy's weird.

Bonnie grinned.

Bonnie: Once the baby comes, I bet you'll forget all about the nausea.

Indie: You're right. But right now, I'm living on dry crackers.

The three dots popped up, then disappeared. And yeah, Bonnie wasn't sure how to respond either.

Indie: I'm really looking forward to seeing you.

Her belly gave a little kick.

Bonnie: Me too.

She wanted to write more. She wanted to ask Indie when they might meet. Maybe Bonnie could pop over to Indie's house, or Indie could visit her apartment. But she kind of wanted Indie to initiate it because she wanted her sister to be in control of this reunion.

Indie: I've got to go. Colt's telling me I need to eat breakfast. That man does not like me skipping meals, but then, neither does baby. Chat again soon?

Bonnie: I'd love that.

She shoved her cell back into her pocket. Texting was progress. It was a start.

She looked down at her granola bar, no longer even the tiniest bit hungry.

When she reached The Pit, the lights were on. Good. According to the website, the place wasn't supposed to open for another ten minutes, which, considering it was still pretty dark, felt far too early for Bonnie.

But she wanted to talk to Zane before getting to the shelter. Shelley had been riding her ass about physical activity for the women.

She pushed inside and walked over to the desk, only to frown. There was no one here. She scanned the gym. Empty.

"Hello?"

No one answered. So no one was here? But then why was the front door unlocked?

Her gaze caught on the closed door near the back beside a hall. An office? Could he be in there?

She shot her gaze to the entrance. She should leave. The place wasn't open and no one had answered her call. She could come back another time.

But she really wanted to lock this in so she could report back to Shelley.

She crossed over to the closed door and knocked, only then realizing it wasn't completely closed, but ajar. Her knock pushed it a bit more open.

She ducked her head in. "Hello?"

Also empty. There was a desk in the center of the room and a hip-level filing cabinet opposite the door. Her gaze caught on some framed photos above the cabinet.

Like her feet had a mind of their own, she crossed over to the pictures. All of Zane. Most looked like they were taken after a fight. Some of him with other fighters. There was even one of him in the ring.

She focused on a photo of Zane with an older woman. He looked younger in that photo. Maybe early twenties. And the woman was old enough to be his grandmother.

She tilted her head. They both looked so happy.

She was about to leave when a photo poking out of a folder on top of the cabinet caught her eye. It was printed on a piece of paper, and the only reason she looked twice was because it was clearly a mug shot of a man with narrowed black eyes and a bald head.

Something about his photo made her shudder. Maybe because he looked so…hardened? And angry. Definitely angry.

Without thinking, she slipped it out from beneath the pile and read the heading: "Active Monitoring File." There was an inmate number and a name.

"Monty Cruz," she read quietly.

"What the hell are you doing?"

She gasped and spun, her hip hitting the cabinet and the paper slipping from her fingers. "Zane."

He stepped forward, looking big and angry, almost predatory. "Bonnie, I'm going to ask you again. What are you doing?"

Her mouth opened and closed. Shit. This looked bad. This looked like snooping.

Well, it looked like snooping because it *was* snooping. "I came to talk to you. The front door was unlocked, but I couldn't find anyone."

"So you came in here to go through my stuff?"

"I can see how it would look that way." Bad…it was bad. "I came in here looking for you, but then I saw the photos on the wall, and I…" She what? Got closer because she was nosy, then decided to be *more* nosy and look at a document that was none of her business?

"You need to leave." He turned and started walking—no, *storming* away.

Crap, crap, crap. Not the way she'd rehearsed this morning.

"Wait, I'm sorry." She took off after him.

He didn't stop, slow, or answer, just went straight to the front desk. A door somewhere else in the building opened, then Stetson walked out of the hall. "We better not miss trash day. Those trash cans are filling up." Stetson grinned at her. "Bonnie, you're back."

"You left the front door unlocked," Zane called from behind the front desk, eyes on the computer screen.

Stetson cringed. "Sorry, boss."

Bonnie stopped on the other side of the desk. "Zane, please. I'm really sorry."

"You need to go."

"But I need to ask you something." She wrinkled her nose, because now was *not* the right time to be asking for something— but dammit, she was going to do it anyway.

* * *

ZANE HELD on to his frustration by a thread. A single fucking thread. She'd been in his office alone. Looking at Monty's damn file.

"The place is about to open," he said through gritted teeth. "So unless you're going to ask to hit a bag, which, based on the heels, I'd say no, you need to go."

He was angry because in that document was information he shouldn't have. And information he sure as hell didn't want Bonnie to have. On Monty's activity in prison. Every little thing Zane had been able to get his hands on to make sure Monty was staying exactly where he was.

He was logging on to the computer when Bonnie suddenly reached over the desk and placed her warm palm on his hand. The second she touched him, something happened. He didn't even know what. It was like this low hum under his skin that took the edge off the anger.

"Please," she whispered, voice soft. "Just hear me out."

He should say no. But fuck, her hand was still on him and her eyes were wide and vulnerable. "What do you need, Bonnie?"

"I'm the program coordinator at the local women's shelter. It's my job to organize empowering activities to help the women get on their feet again and feel safe."

Right away, he knew exactly where this was going. "I'm not the person for that."

"You don't even know what I'm going to ask."

"So you're not about to ask me to run self-defense classes for the women at the shelter?"

She deflated.

Bingo.

"Okay, maybe you did know," she rushed out. "But we'll pay you, albeit not much because the budget is small, but you'll be helping the most vulnerable women."

"I'm a former UFC fighter. I'm not trained to teach self-defense."

"You know how to fight. Heck, you were an Army Ranger before you got in the ring. You have so much you could offer."

He scrubbed a hand over his face, because the pleading in her eyes was doing something to him it absolutely shouldn't be.

He was just lowering his hand when someone at the window had him frowning.

Who the hell was that? The guy had a laptop bag strung over his shoulder, and his face was literally pressed to the glass like a fucking stalker. He wasn't looking at the gym, him, or even Stetson, who was busy setting up for the day.

He was looking at Bonnie.

The fuck?

Finally, Bonnie pulled her hand away. "How about instead of giving me an answer right now, you think about it. Please?"

He looked back at Bonnie. "I'll think about it."

Her hazel eyes lit up, and she fished a card from her jeans pocket. "Great. I'll give you my card. It's got both my work number and email, and"—she reached across the desk like she owned the place and grabbed a pen—"here's my private cell." She scribbled down the number before handing him the card. "I'm really looking forward to hearing from you."

By the excitement in her voice, you'd think he'd said yes.

He took the card. "Thanks."

The door to the gym opened, and the guy with the laptop bag stepped in and crossed straight over to the desk.

"Can I help you?" Zane asked, not in the mood for more surprises this morning.

But the guy barely spared him a glance. "No thanks." He stopped in front of Bonnie. "Bonnie Hayes, right?"

Apprehension crossed her face. "Who are you?"

He reached out a hand and smiled, but the expression was too polished. "Abernathy Koch, but you can call me Abe."

"And how do you know my name, Abe?"

"It's my job to know." He dropped his hand, not seeming put

off that she didn't take it. "I'm a reporter for the *Amber Ridge Chronicle*, and I'd love to interview you about what happened to Dean White."

Color left Bonnie's face.

"I've been searching the town for you for a couple of days," the reporter continued. "Then, on my way to get coffee, here you are. So, what do you—"

"No," Bonnie interrupted.

"Come on. His parents think you're responsible for their son's death. Don't you want your side of the story told?"

"What I want is for you to leave me alone."

She went to step around him, but he moved into her path, blocking her.

"Hey." Zane shot around the desk and shoved the guy in the chest. "Get out of her way."

The reporter's bag slipped from his shoulder, and he pulled it back up before fixing a strand of hair behind his ear. "Look, I'm just trying to do my job."

"She said no."

"This story has been circulating for thirteen years. She's back now and can tell us what really happened the night of her graduation party."

Zane stepped closer. "What part of 'no' do you not understand? Now get the fuck out of my gym."

"But—"

He took up all of the guy's personal space, towering over him. "Either walk yourself out or I'll do it for you."

Koch's eyes narrowed, his chest puffing up. Was he really considering challenging Zane? Was he that stupid?

"I'm not someone you want to piss off."

Zane almost laughed. "You think *I* am?"

"What I *think* is you'll regret getting in my way."

"I'm shaking. *Leave.*"

The reporter's jaw visibly clenched, and he spun and left.

Zane turned back to look at Bonnie. She was still pale.

"He wants to write a story on Dean's death," she said in almost a whisper.

"If you don't talk to him, he'll have nothing to write."

She laughed, but there was no humor behind the sound. "He'll get his information from other sources. Lots of people in this town will be willing to tell him what a villain I am." She looked back at him. "Thank you for kicking him out."

"He was a tool. I'd do it again."

"I should go." She touched his arm. "Thank you for considering my request. It would help so many women."

He dipped his head before watching her leave. He hadn't been planning on calling her. Hell, he'd been fully prepared to forget the request entirely.

But the sadness in her eyes, the way it turned them a dull sand color…it made him want to make things better. Do whatever she damn well asked. And he had no idea why.

CHAPTER 5

$\mathcal{H}$oly heck, it had been a long day. Fires needed putting out left, right, and center, and Shelley had dumped a million jobs on Bonnie that weren't hers to do.

Now it was eight, she was still at work, and the grant application that she was only just finishing had a deadline that closed in thirty minutes.

But the good news? She was done.

Submit. Thank God.

She leaned back in her seat and rubbed her eyes. Shelley, of course, had taken herself home hours ago. But then, Shelley was the boss and could apparently do whatever she wanted.

As the laptop shut down, she packed her things, groaning at the darkness outside through the window. Great. She'd be walking home in the dark.

She was passing the bathroom in the hall when she stopped and frowned. What was that? It sounded like someone was in there breathing so heavily she could hear it from the hall.

She pressed her ear to the door. The sound got louder.

Her gaze lifted to the hall, then back to the door. There was a counselor here somewhere. But she wasn't sure where; they might be with one of the women.

Gently, Bonnie knocked on the wood.

The breathing quieted.

"Hello? This is Bonnie, the program coordinator. I just wanted to check that you were okay."

Another beat of silence. It stretched so long she thought no one was going to answer. Then the door creaked open. It was the same woman from a couple of weeks ago. "Sarah?"

The other woman's brows flickered. "Bonnie."

"Are you okay?"

It took Sarah a moment to answer. "I-I'm fine. I'm just having a bad day with everything."

"Is this about your ex?"

The woman's eyes flared. "I think he tried to call me today."

"You think?"

"I had a missed call from the prison." Her breathing sped up.

Bonnie stepped forward. "Hey. Why don't you breathe with me for a second?" She sucked in a deep breath and held it for a few seconds before easing it out.

Sarah copied her.

"There you go." She repeated it, and so did Sarah. They continued to breathe in silence until Bonnie was sure the other woman was steadier. "Feel better?"

Sarah gave a small nod.

"You don't have to answer any calls you don't want to," Bonnie said firmly.

"I know. But just seeing the call scared me. It made me think that he's never going to let us go. I didn't let Chett leave my side all day. I'm so scared for him all the time."

"I can understand that. But you're both safe here."

She nodded again.

"Is there anything I can get you?" Bonnie asked gently.

"No. I'm okay. Really. I should get back to Chett. He's asleep."

Bonnie didn't want to leave her. But at the same time, she couldn't do much to help. Sarah *was* safe here. Her ex was in prison. It would just take time for her to trust that. "Call the counselor on shift if you need anything."

When Sarah headed upstairs, Bonnie stepped out of the building, and as soon as she did, she groaned. It was so dark. And now she had to walk home. She *really* needed to buy a car. She was moved into her apartment, settled in at work, so she had no excuse not to.

Wrapping her jacket tightly around her body, she started walking, fast steps to get her home as quickly as possible. There was no one on the street, and she wasn't sure if that made her feel safer or not. Every time a car passed, she sucked in a deep breath like she was preparing for them to stop and harass her.

Jesus. *That's* what her life had become here. But it would get better. People would get used to her being home. She just had to have faith.

A car turned onto the street, and she shot a glance over her shoulder…only to frown. Why were they driving so slowly? Were they doing it on purpose to tail her? Scare her? Who?

She almost laughed because there were so many possibilities. Dean's parents. The reporter. Anyone in this town who had a fight to pick with her.

The sudden ringing of her phone made her jump. She pulled it out to see Noah's name on the screen, and as soon as she put it to her ear, the car sped past.

"Noah."

"Hey." There was a short pause. "Are you okay? You sound shaky."

"I'm fine." Not really true. But then, she hadn't really been fine since returning to Amber Ridge. She'd been riding the highs of being close to family and the lows of the harassment. "I'm just walking home from work."

"Now? It's dark out."

"I had to work late."

"Where are you? I'll pick you up."

Even though her brother couldn't see her, she was shaking her head before he finished speaking. "No. I don't live far. I'm almost home."

She actually would have loved for Noah to pick her up. What she *wouldn't* love was to be a big fat inconvenience.

"Bonnie—"

"Did you call to tell me something?" She rounded a corner.

Noah sighed. "I called to check in and see how you're doing."

"I'm good. Work's been…busy. Though I've been waiting for a call from Zane all week that hasn't come." Maybe she just needed to accept that he didn't want to do the classes. He'd *told* her he didn't want to, and she couldn't make him.

"Why have you been waiting for a call from Zane?"

"I asked him to do some self-defense classes for the shelter out of his gym."

"Does he offer self-defense classes?"

"Well, no, but he could." And she was pretty certain he'd be good at it. She rounded another corner. "What are you doing tonight?"

"Actually, that's the other reason I called. I'm heading to the bar with some of the family. Come."

She stumbled over a bump in the sidewalk. The thought of stepping into a busy bar made fear curl in her belly. Stepping into *any* busy place felt hard. That probably made her weak, didn't it?

"I'm kind of tired, Noah."

"Come on. Jesse and Becket too."

So basically, all the men in her family would be there to protect her. But the thing was, she didn't want to be protected. "Maybe in a few weeks, when I'm more settled." And a bit braver.

"Okay. Another time. Are you sure you don't want me to pick you up?"

"I'm only a street away from my building."

"Stay safe."

"Thanks."

She hung up just as the door to a Chinese restaurant on her right opened. Her jaw dropped, because there in front of her was her high school best friend, Maisie, and Dean's older brother, Damien.

"Maisie. Damien."

Maisie's eyes widened. "Bonnie."

"Hi, Bonnie." Damien slipped an arm around Maisie's waist.

Bonnie glanced down at the arm then back up. "You two are together?"

"Married, actually." Maisie lifted her hand to show a wedding and engagement ring.

Holy crap, they were *married*? Damien had always been so serious and driven and competitive...the complete opposite of Maisie.

Was it because he came from money?

No. Maisie didn't care about money, did she? Well, Bonnie didn't really know much about her. Not now. And as it turned out...not in high school, either.

"Congratulations," Bonnie finally said.

"Thanks." Maisie swallowed. "I heard you were back. How have you been?"

She lifted a shoulder, because honestly, she didn't feel like baring her soul to the person who once upon a time was supposed to be her best friend.

"Come on, Maisie." Damien tugged her toward the street. "It was good to see you, Bonnie."

Bonnie nodded and continued walking, only to stop at the rustle of footsteps behind her.

"Bonnie."

She turned to see Maisie heading her way, while Damien waited by a car, looking impatient.

Maisie stopped, and when she spoke, her voice was low. "I've always wondered…why didn't you tell anyone?"

"I think the bigger question is, why didn't you?" She glanced around Maisie. "At least, it *was* the question. I guess now I know the answer."

Maisie's eyes widened, and when she didn't respond, Bonnie turned and continued walking.

Maisie didn't call her back a second time.

When she reached her apartment building, she was frazzled and, in her head, that night at the party played over and over again. There was a good reason Bonnie had left Dean at the party that night. And it had everything to do with what she'd seen Dean and Maisie doing in a bedroom.

After unlocking the door, she stepped inside her building. Her head was still down as she jogged up the stairs and stepped onto her floor. And that's when she collided with a big, broad chest.

Her eyes widened as a what-the-hell-is-going-on kind of shock wiped through her system. "Zane? What are you doing here?"

He frowned. "I live here."

* * *

ZANE'S FINGERS wrapped tightly around his beer, the music loud in the bar.

Bonnie lived in his apartment building. Fuck, she didn't just live in it, she lived on the same damn floor, across the hall, two doors away.

He tipped back the beer and downed a third of the bottle. At first, he'd thought she'd somehow figured out where he lived and had come to get an answer to her request in person.

Honestly, he wasn't sure if that would have been better or worse.

But then she'd revealed she'd leased the apartment down the

hall, and it had taken everything in him not to lose his damn mind. Because there was something about her. About the sweet scent that followed her. The lyrical notes of her voice…all of it toyed with him. And now he could run into her every day.

He checked his watch. Nine. Where the hell was Ethan? He was never late.

He checked his phone to see if his friend had made contact. He hadn't.

The door to the bar opened, but it wasn't Ethan who stepped in. It was Bonnie's brother, Noah. With a couple guys behind him, one being the town sheriff.

Great.

Noah saw him looking, and Zane dipped his head and glanced away, draining the rest of his beer. What Ethan was doing for him wasn't exactly illegal. But it also wasn't something Zane needed the sheriff's office knowing about. Thankfully, they headed toward the back of the bar.

Another few minutes passed and he checked his watch again. It *really* wasn't like Ethan to be late. He lifted his phone and sent a text.

Zane: Everything okay?

He'd just hit send when someone stepped up beside him. It wasn't Ethan.

"Hey."

Zane looked up. "Noah, right?"

The man nodded. "Yeah. How are you doing?"

"All right."

When the bartender stopped in front of Noah, he ordered three beers before looking back at Zane. "I heard my sister's asked you to run some self-defense classes for the shelter."

"She has."

"Are you gonna do it?"

"I'm still thinking about it." A damn lie. The less time he spent with Bonnie, the better.

"You should. She's been through a lot. And you saw what Carlos did to her in The Tea House the other day. She needs some good in her life."

Zane could have laughed. "I don't know if I'm the good she needs."

Noah lifted a shoulder. "You don't seem like a bad guy. And this is important to her." He clapped Zane on the back. "Have a good night."

Shit. Now he felt guilty. The few interactions he'd seen of Bonnie with locals, they *had* been awful to her.

He shouldn't do it. He knew he shouldn't.

He lifted his cell and sent a text.

Zane: I'll do it.

The three dots immediately popped up.

Bonnie: Zane?

Zane: Yeah. I'll run sessions for the women in your shelter. Five sessions, and the women need to come to The Pit.

Bonnie: Oh my gosh. Thank you so much. I'll call to organize tomorrow.

He was going to regret this. He already lived in the same building as the woman, he didn't need more of her. Not when he wasn't in a place to date and the woman was so fucking dateable.

But right now, he didn't care.

"Texting someone important?"

He looked up. Ethan was just as tall and built as him, with light brown hair and a permanently serious expression on his face. "Where the hell have you been?"

"You know how long the drive is from Deep River?"

"Two hours."

"Yeah, so cut me some slack."

Zane shook his head. They'd been friends for so long, they knew each other well. "How are things at home?"

"Not the same town we grew up in."

"Why? What's going on?"

Ethan laughed, but there was no humor in the sound. "One name—Sheriff Ward. Lazy asshole. And under his leadership, or lack thereof, crime rates are up. Someone went missing in the mountains last week and he did damn near nothing."

"What about your search and rescue team?"

Ethan scoffed. "It's full of elderly volunteers. They don't know what the hell they're doing."

"Shit. What are you gonna do?"

"There's not a lot I *can* do as one person with no support." He pushed a folder across the bar. "Your first quarterly update."

For a moment, Zane just stared at the manila folder. They were doing this in person because Zane didn't want a trail.

"It's all in there," Ethan said. "His daily activities. Meetings with his lawyer."

"Anything I should be concerned about?"

"Not in the folder."

Zane looked up, frowning at his friend. "What does that mean?"

"There's a rumor that he's planning something."

"Planning *what*?"

"I don't know yet. My source is looking into it though."

"But I should be worried?"

Ethan's eyes narrowed. "Officially, no. Unofficially...you should be worried."

"It's perfect. It's exactly what I need and such a good price."

She probably shouldn't be saying that to this man. Heck, it went against every "how to buy a car" guide out there. But the red Santa Fe really was exactly what she needed and smack dab in her budget. It had low miles and looked like it was in great condition.

"I can put a deposit down right now and come by with the rest of the money tomorrow," she added.

The middle-aged man with graying hair lifted his brows. "Great. Wait here, I'll go get the missus and let her know."

Bonnie grinned. "Thanks."

She'd finally have a car. Thank God. Because she was sick of getting around everywhere on foot. Don't get her wrong, she was glad her apartment was so central, but a car would be easier, especially when she was staying late at work so much.

As the guy disappeared into the house, she ran her fingertips over the hood. The test drive had been so smooth, and she'd paid a mechanic to have it checked while she was at work this afternoon.

She'd come here straight from work because the thing had only popped up on Facebook Marketplace this morning.

She pulled her phone from her pocket, a little of her excitement fading at the empty screen. No response from Indie. They'd been texting every day, and this morning, Bonnie had finally mustered the courage to invite Indie over. But her sister hadn't responded. It was the first text that she hadn't received an immediate response to.

The door to the house opened, and Bonnie shoved her cell back into her pocket.

She looked up and smiled. "Hi."

The woman stopped a few feet out the door, a frown cutting between her brows. "I know you."

Shit. The tone of her voice told Bonnie that was *not* a good thing. "I'm Bonnie."

"Yeah. You're that Hayes girl who left Dean White at the party, even though you were his ride."

Her belly rolled.

"What are you talking about, Magna?" her husband asked.

The woman glared at Bonnie. "Dean, Billy's friend. Crashed that car the night of the graduation party because *she* left him there. She was supposed to drive him home."

Bonnie swallowed. "Look, I'm just here to buy a car."

The woman crossed her arms. "Price is eighty thousand."

Bonnie's eyes bulged out of her head. "That's three times the listed price." Hell, they were less than forty thousand brand new. She could buy two of them for that price and have change.

"Decided I want more. Eighty thousand. Take it or leave it."

Bonnie looked at the guy beside her. But even though he seemed shocked, he clearly wasn't about to jump in and save her. She turned back to the woman. "Come on, that's not fair."

"No? What's not fair is that Jane, one of my best friends, had to bury her son thirteen years ago because the kid's girlfriend couldn't be bothered to take him home."

Bonnie shook her head. She was wasting her time. "I'm leaving."

"Good. Don't come back."

Bonnie stormed down the street, hating the angry tears that gathered in her eyes. She shouldn't care that Jane and Carlos had told everyone Dean's death was her fault. Once upon a time, she'd thought that too. It wasn't true. She knew that now. It should be enough.

But God, she should also be able to buy a car without being made to pay a guilt tax.

A tear fell down her cheek and she swiped it away.

No. She was not going to cry. They didn't deserve her tears. Not that woman. Not the Whites. Not anyone.

What she needed was a dirty chai from The Tea House and a long walk.

She turned onto the next street, only to groan. Because there, only a few yards away stepping out of a shop, was Carlos White.

Good God, could this day get any worse?

Quickly, she crossed the street, not in the mood for another confrontation.

"Hey."

She ignored him and sped up.

"Hey. I'm talking to you."

Loud footsteps thumped behind her.

She didn't glance over her shoulder, but she didn't need to do so to know he was close.

"Why are you still here?" Carlos shouted.

"Leave me alone."

"Leave *you* alone? You come into *my* town, a walking reminder of the worst thing that's ever happened to me, and you want *me* to leave *you* alone?"

Bonnie walked so fast she was almost jogging. And she hated that. She hated having to run from this man.

"Did you think we'd all forget?" Suddenly, he grabbed her arm and spun her, strong fingers digging into her skin. Then he got so close, she could feel his breath on her face. "I will *never* forget. And I will never let this *town* forget."

"I don't want to hurt you, Carlos, but if you don't release my arm, I will."

"I will follow you. *Torment* you. Ensure every move you make is so uncomfortable that you wish you'd stayed away."

Her skin chilled, and for a moment the threat paralyzed her. The rage in the man's voice. The way he said the words with such conviction.

"Get the fuck off her!"

She jumped at the fury in the new voice. New but familiar. Zane.

He appeared beside her, but Carlos didn't release her arm.

"Stay out of this, boy," Carlos seethed through gritted teeth.

Zane inched closer to Carlos, almost stepping between them. "You have two seconds to release her before I break your wrist." He said the words slowly, firmly, the threat alive in the air.

Carlos's chest rose and fell, and for a moment, anger blackened his eyes. Then, finally, he let go of her and stepped back.

He glared at Zane before turning back to her. "Remember what I said."

Zane watched the back of him until Carlos crossed the road, then turned to her. "Are you okay?"

No. She wasn't close to okay. She was angry and sad and frustrated all at the same time. "I'm fine."

Zane touched her arm, right where Carlos's fingers had been. But where that man's grip had been hard and painful, Zane's was soft, almost soothing.

He lifted her arm and trailed his thumb over the red marks. His expression darkened, rage settling over his face. "I'm going to kill him."

He started to turn but she grabbed his arm. "No. Please don't."

"Then I'll call the sheriff's station. Make a report."

"What will that do? Carlos doesn't care about getting into trouble, he just wants me gone. Besides, I can't report everything that everyone in this town does to me. I'd be there every day."

Suddenly, she questioned *everything*. Her reasons for coming back. The vision of her life if she stayed here. Heck, she wasn't even able to buy a car.

"Hey."

Zane's voice pulled her back to him.

"Come inside the gym."

She frowned in confusion, and that's when she realized she was right outside The Pit. "No, it's getting late. I should go."

She turned, but this time Zane touched her waist. Again, it was gentle but also firm. "Bonnie...come inside with me."

Did she look the mess she felt? Because she *did* feel a mess. A stone's throw away from breaking. Between Indie not responding, the woman who refused to sell her that car, and now Carlos, it was all piling on top of her, feeling like this immoveable weight.

"Okay." The word was so quiet she wasn't even sure it crossed the distance.

He slipped a hand to the small of her back and led her inside.

As she walked in, the only thing holding her together was the warmth of Zane's touch. And maybe he knew that. Maybe that's why his hand lingered.

* * *

IT WAS TAKING every part of Zane, every fraction of self-restraint he possessed, to follow Bonnie inside the gym and not go after the asshole who'd touched her. *Marked* her. Even *thinking* about the fucker made his hands ball into fists like he was going to hit something.

He forced himself to cross the gym to the small bar fridge in the kitchen and grab two beers. He cracked them open, and when he reached Bonnie again, he handed one to her. "Here."

"You're giving me a beer?"

"It's alcohol or hit something. I thought this would be your preference."

Her gaze flicked to the closest bag. "Why not both?" She slipped the beer from his hand and downed a quarter of the bottle before moving over to the leather bag.

Why the fuck did he find the combination of Bonnie, beer, and a leather bag so hot?

He tipped back his own bottle, letting the alcohol burn his gut before following. "Who was he?"

"I dated his son through high school."

"Dean? The guy who died?"

"Yep. Dean got drunk at our graduation party, took his friend's keys, and tried to drive himself home." She ran her fingers over the bag. "He didn't make it."

"How's that your fault?"

"I was supposed to drive him."

The fact that she hadn't made him think there was a good reason. "Still doesn't sound like it's your fault."

"They needed someone to blame. And that someone became me."

"That's why you left town?"

"No. I left because one day I was this numb teenager who did stupid things in an attempt to feel something, and the next, I felt *everything*…and I wanted to claw out of my own skin."

"Just from Dean's death?" He didn't buy it. There was more to this.

"Well, Dean died, the town blamed me. Then my parents died while coming to pick me up after asking me not to go out."

Fuck. She really *had* had it tough. He didn't even want to say sorry, because that felt fucking stupid.

Zane moved to the equipment box and pulled out gloves.

Then, without a word, he took her beer, set it aside, and fit the gloves onto her hands. "Have you hit a bag before?"

"Once or twice."

When the straps were tight around her wrists, he stepped back. "Show me."

One side of her mouth lifted, only to slip again when she turned to the bag.

Her stance was good—left foot forward, chin slightly down, elbows tucked in tight.

She gave the bag one solid strike, her torso twisting.

He watched her throw more punches. Each hit was hard and filled with heavy, loaded emotion.

He watched one more before stepping behind her and gripping her hips.

She gasped. "What are you doing?"

"You've got good form, but you need to twist with your hips, not just your torso." He guided her hips to show her. "And after the hit, you need to unwind your hips and return your hands to guard."

She nodded.

He guided her hips forward a second time, then back. "That's good."

"I thought you said you weren't a teacher?"

"You're not a beginner, so this isn't really teaching."

"Then what is it?"

An excuse to touch her? A strange need to get close? And fuck, why did she smell so good? All florals like he was in the middle of a fucking garden.

He must have taken too long to respond, because she glanced over her shoulder and there was something in her eyes. The sadness from moments ago was gone, replaced with...desire?

He told himself to take his hands off her, to step back. He fucking screamed it. But he didn't listen, because he was weak.

He stood so still he wasn't even breathing, needing to know what she'd do next.

Her gaze lowered to his lips, and that desire in her eyes shifted. Darkened.

Her breathing quickened, her gaze rising to his eyes again.

He was a damn fool. Because even though every part of him knew that he shouldn't, he didn't listen.

He lowered his head and kissed her.

It felt like a gut punch. But the good kind. The kind that felt like he was breathing fresh air for the first time in years. Sweet fucking air that filled his lungs.

She turned the rest of her body, and he only released her hips for a second before gripping them again and tugging her into him. When her chest hit his, she gasped, and he slipped his tongue inside.

And the taste of her…shit, it was like an assault on his senses. So sweet he could drown in her. He swirled his tongue around hers. His hands were just slipping up her sides, getting lost in her softness, when she pressed her gloved hands to his chest and pushed.

It took more willpower than it should have, but he forced himself to step back. Her eyes were hazy and her chest was heaving.

"That was…unexpected," she breathed, voice barely a whisper.

What was? The kiss? Or the way it shifted something between them?

"Can you…" She lifted her hands.

He unstrapped her gloves, and the second they were off she took two steps away.

"Well, I, uh…should be getting out of here." Her next step almost caused her to stumble over a box.

He grabbed her arm. "Do you need a ride home?"

"No. Nope." She stepped away again, his hand dropping. "I'm good. I'm, uh, completely…very good. Yes. Okay. Bye."

She almost raced out of the gym.

His lips twitched. She was nervous. Because the kiss had been as good for her as it was for him?

He was just packing up when the door opened and footsteps sounded. He turned, thinking she'd come back in.

She hadn't.

"What the hell are you doing here?" Zane growled.

Abe Koch, the reporter, stepped into the room, brow lifted. "That's no way to greet a potential customer."

"You're not a customer, because you're not welcome here. Get out."

"Lucky for me, I'm not here to work out. I'm here for my story."

"Bonnie's not here for you to harass."

"Actually, I've shelved that story for now. I found something better."

A slow burn crawled up the back of Zane's neck, like a warning under the skin. "What does that have to do with me?"

"Well, I found some pretty interesting information. About you and your cousin from Billings. There was a murder, right? Your prints were found on a gun at a party? Then there was that guy a few months later that you—"

Zane was across the gym in a second, grabbing Koch by the shoulders and shoving him against the wall. "You so much as print my name in your paper, you'll regret it."

The asshole laughed, and it made Zane's hand twitch to hit the guy. "Go on, hit me. I'll add it to the story."

The door to the gym opened again, and seconds later, two men came around the wall. Noah and the town sheriff.

The fuck?

"What's going on here?"

Zane wasn't sure which man spoke—he only had eyes for the asshole reporter. It took five seconds to let him go. To step back.

And he immediately regretted it because of that smug look on the asshole's face.

The sheriff stepped closer. "I'm Sheriff Hayes and I'm going to ask again—what's going on here?"

Koch lifted a brow, leaving space for Zane to answer.

"Nothing." The single word growled from Zane's lips.

"Well, I'll take that as 'no comment.'" The reporter smiled. "Have a good evening, gentlemen."

Zane's stomach curled as he watched the guy leave, wanting to follow him. Threaten the fucker until he agreed to drop the story.

"Hey."

Zane dragged his gaze to Bonnie's brother.

Noah frowned. "Everything okay?"

Not even close. If the reporter had found out what had happened in Billings, if he printed it for the town to read, everyone would know about his past...about what he'd done.

CHAPTER 7

Bonnie turned the passenger van right, her heart giving a little kick when The Pit came into view. Zane was about to hold a class for the women in the bus.

It would require talking to him. And watching him. Standing close enough to breathe in his earthy masculine scent.

It would be fine. So they'd kissed then barely communicated for almost a week. It didn't mean this had to be awkward. They were adults and adults kissed sometimes.

Not all adults. But they had. And it was a good kiss. Filled-far-too-many-dreams kind of good.

She wasn't sure why she hadn't contacted him. Maybe because their emails back and forth about this self-defense session had been so formal. And maybe because she'd been hoping to run into him in the apartment building but hadn't.

She pulled the van over in front of the gym and turned to look at the women. "Ready?"

A few women smiled, the others nodded. Sarah just fussed over Chett, who sat beside her. They'd offered for him to remain at the shelter with a couple of the other kids, but Sarah had wanted to bring him, so Bonnie assured her they'd make it work.

She climbed out and opened the back door. Sarah and Chett were last out.

"Bonnie, Mama packed me huckleberry taffy in my lunch box."

Bonnie's eyes widened. "No way!"

"And I have new Legos!"

"Oh my gosh, you are just the luckiest five-year-old I have ever met."

He beamed at her, and even Sarah's lips twitched. "Come on, Chetty."

Once the van was locked up, Bonnie caught up with Sarah and lowered her voice so Chett couldn't hear. "I've been meaning to check in. How have you been?"

Sarah nodded. "Good, actually. I've been talking to Tanya, and it's really helping calm my nerves."

Bonnie smiled softly. Tanya was one of the counselors, probably the best at the shelter. "That's great."

She moved to the front of the group and pushed the door open, leading the way to the desk. Familiar nerves crawled through Bonnie's belly, but it wasn't Zane who greeted them, it was Stetson.

He smiled from behind the counter, his shaggy blond hair falling into his eyes. "Hey! You made it."

"We did and we're ready to go."

"Fantastic. Follow me. You can put your stuff down at the back while we wait for Zane." They trooped through the gym, and the women were just setting their water bottles down when the creak of a door opening somewhere else sounded.

Bonnie glanced at the hall, and her mouth dried. Desert-level dry. Because not only did Zane step out of the hall looking ridiculously hot in his tight white shirt, his hair was also wet and falling into his eyes.

Holy Jesus, the man was a walking romance novel cover.

Pull yourself together, Bonnie. And absolutely no drooling.

She cleared her throat and straightened as he crossed over to her. "Hey."

"Hi, Bonnie." He didn't look at her, just turned to the women. "This is my group?"

Oh. Well. She hadn't expected a good-morning kiss or a butt slap, but a simple smile with some eye contact would have been nice. "Yeah. They're ready for you."

"Let's start then."

Not one glance her way. So while she'd been dreaming about the guy and his lips, he obviously had not been doing the same.

She turned to the women. "If I could get everyone's attention." She waited until the room quieted. "This is Zane Merrick. He's a former Army Ranger and UFC fighter. He knows what he's doing and I think we'll all learn a lot from him."

Zane stepped forward. "Thanks for coming. You're going to have to be patient with me because I haven't run a class like this before, but hopefully everyone gets something out of this."

Bonnie moved to Chett's side as he sat on the floor and worked on his Legos, but her gaze remained on Zane.

His deep, gravelly voice slid over her skin as he spent the first twenty minutes talking about situational awareness and verbal assertiveness. He explained how empowering it can be to know how to protect oneself. And everyone listened. Even Chett stopped playing to focus on Zane.

When it came to the warm-up, Bonnie joined in. They did jumping jacks and a few dynamic stretches.

The first skill was the palm heel strike, which, according to Zane, was safer than a fisted punch because there was less risk to the hand. Because there were an even number of women, Bonnie sat out of that activity.

Which was fine. It allowed her to work on her don't-stare-at-Zane strategies. They all sucked. She stared at him far too often.

After twenty minutes, Zane demonstrated the knee strike.

The women did great. And not only that, they seemed to be

having fun. More fun than at the yoga session she'd organized a few days ago. But then, Bonnie would choose this over yoga too.

When Zane called the group back together again, Bonnie was so deep in her own head that she missed her name being called.

"Bonnie?"

Her gaze shot up to Zane. "Yes?"

"I asked if you'd like to help demonstrate a wrist grab escape?"

"With you?" Shit, why was her voice so high-pitched?

"Yes. With me."

She nodded, probably far too vigorously. "Yes. Sure. Of course." She crossed over to the front of the group.

"You're okay with me being the attacker?" he asked, his eyes finally on her. "That way the women can see how to get out of the hold of someone bigger than them."

Zane touching her. Yeah, she could do that without turning to a puddle on the floor. "Absolutely fine."

"Okay, I'm going to grab your right wrist with my left hand." He reached out and wrapped his fingers around her wrist. His touch was warm, fingers overlapping.

"If someone grabs you like this," Zane said to the group, "it's important to stay calm."

Calm? While he was touching her? Ha. That was like asking her to remain calm in the middle of a hurricane.

He looked at her again. "Keep your feet shoulder width apart, knees soft and no panic. The thumb side of the attacker's grip is the weakest point. You want to rotate your wrist so *your* thumb points toward the attacker's thumb. Do it quickly, then step back to add body weight to the movement."

Bonnie twisted her arm and stepped back. Zane immediately released her.

He nodded. "Good. Again, but faster."

The second his fingers wrapped around her, she twisted her wrist and stepped back.

"Good." He faced the women. "Then you get your ass the hell out of there. Pair up."

Bonnie bit her bottom lip as she watched everyone get back into pairs. She could still feel the imprint of Zane's fingers on her wrist. Her skin felt hot and tingly, and it was taking everything in her not to run her finger right over where he'd touched her.

* * *

DON'T LOOK AT HER. *Don't fucking look at her.*

The words had been on repeat in Zane's head since Bonnie stepped through the door. But listening to those words was killing him. She wore this skintight white top and leggings that showed every damn curve. But it was her eyes that stole his fucking sanity. That beautiful hazel that had a million emotions running through them.

He needed to stop. Stop thinking about her. Craving her. Dreaming about that damn kiss.

He couldn't kiss her again. Not right now. Not while Monty was planning something from his cell, and certainly not when that fucking reporter had threatened to write his story.

His phone rang, and he pulled it from his pocket to see Ethan's name.

Finally.

He moved over to Stetson. "I just need to take a call. Are you good here?"

"Yeah, I'm good. I'm actually enjoying this."

He squeezed the kid's shoulder before moving down into the small kitchen off the hall. "Ethan, you got a number and address for me?"

"I do. Texting them to you now."

His phone vibrated but Zane didn't lower the cell from his ear.

"I haven't been able to find any dirt on the reporter though," Ethan continued. "The guy's the cleanest I've seen."

"It's fine. I'll just have to go in the old-fashioned way." Find the guy and scare the shit out of him.

"Don't do anything that could get you into trouble."

"Thanks for the information, Ethan."

"Zane—"

"You don't need to worry about me. We'll talk again soon." He hung up and opened the text to run his gaze over the cell number and address. "Got you, asshole."

"That doesn't sound good."

He swung around to see Bonnie just inside the kitchen. Shit. He hadn't heard her come in. "Is everything okay?"

"I was going to ask you the same question. Are you avoiding me?"

Hell yes, he was. "Why would I do that?"

"It might have something to do with our kiss."

It had *everything* to do with their kiss. "It was a mistake."

She pulled back like he'd hit her. Then blinked as if physically trying to recover. "It didn't feel like a mistake."

No. It hadn't. It had felt raw and explosive, like a sucker punch to the ribs stealing the air from his lungs. "I should get back out there."

He moved to step around her, but she grabbed his arm. "Wait. Tell me why. Why do you think it was a…mistake?"

Even her fingers wrapped around his arm somehow both steadied and unraveled him at the same time. "Because now isn't a great time."

Her brows flickered. "For you or me?"

"For either of us. You've got enough going on. You don't need my shit too."

"You've got something going on?"

He'd had stuff going on for a long time. "Bonnie…I need to get back to the class."

"Okay, but before you go, I just want to say…thank you."

"For what?"

"The other night, before the kiss. With Carlos. You stood up to him for me. You brought me in here. You made that day suck a little less. Thank you."

"I wasn't going to stand back and let the asshole touch you like that. I'm not that guy."

One side of her mouth lifted. "If you say things like that, you're gonna make me catch feelings, Merrick."

Why did it feel too late for him? "You should stay away from me."

"I'm not sure if I can."

He exhaled like he'd been holding his breath for too long, but before he could respond, she squeezed his arm and left the kitchen.

How was it possible that she was gone, and he could still feel her fingers on his arm?

Shit, he was screwed.

He opened the fridge and grabbed a bottle of water, then downed half before heading back out.

Stetson had started a cooldown. Good. They were almost finished.

As he walked around the room, he heard it. A laugh. Soft and lyrical. He turned his head, and it was a fucking mistake.

Bonnie. She was crouched next to the boy playing with Legos. Her head was back, and if he'd thought she was beautiful standing in that kitchen frowning at him, that was nothing compared to the sight of her now. Her lips were curved, her eyes scrunched—like her world lit up.

For a single fleeting second, he wondered if it would be so selfish to kiss her again. To say to hell with caution and just chase what he wanted.

But then two people passed the gym outside. Guys who looked about his age. They didn't stop or point, but the way they looked at her…like they hated her when they probably didn't even know her.

When she saw them, the corners of her lips froze, and something passed through her eyes. Something dark and heavy. Something that made her shoulders sag.

He was a step away from walking out there and asking the jerks what the hell they wanted, but they were already walking away.

Bonnie's smile didn't return.

And that right there was why he couldn't start anything with her. Because she was already trying to regain this town's trust. Trying to convince them she wasn't the villain they thought she was.

So what would happen if the town learned *his* history? If he became the villain, and she was tied to him?

She'd go down with him.

CHAPTER 8

Zane sat in his car outside a newer multistory apartment building. According to Ethan, Abe left every morning at eight a.m. It was ten past.

Where are you, Abe?

Was he expecting Zane? Or did he think he was safe?

To assume he was safe after the threat he'd sent Zane's way would be a huge fucking mistake. You don't poke a bear without expecting retaliation.

Zane strummed his fingers along the door. How had the reporter gotten his information? Had he dug up local news reports from Billings? Spoken to locals? Law enforcement?

The door to the building opened, and Zane's eyes narrowed on Abe stepping out.

Gotcha.

Zane pulled on his cap and climbed out of his car. Keeping his head down, he followed Abe toward the tenant parking lot.

Slowly, he closed the distance between them. Abe didn't even look back. But as he rounded the building, Zane saw him start to reach into his bag.

He saw the pepper spray before Abe had a chance to lift the

can. He grabbed Abe's wrist, easily taking it from his grasp and throwing it to the ground.

Abe gasped and stumbled back. "What do you want?"

"You should know the answer to that, Abe." He stood close enough to emphasize their size difference. To instill just a bit of fear in the reporter.

Abe swallowed, straightened the strap of the bag on his shoulder.

"I want to talk about that article you're thinking about writing," Zane said, inching closer.

"It's already written. You're too late."

"See, that doesn't really work for me." Zane was so close he could almost feel the asshole. "But if it's true, your best course of action would be to trash it before it's printed."

"Yeah? And I think you should get away from me."

Zane almost laughed. "That's not happening. Where'd you get your information from, Abe?"

"I followed up old articles. Then found some first responders who were willing to talk."

"Well, just like you, I know how easy it is to get information others want to hide. It's how I got your address. It's how I know you're one of three siblings and your parents live in Kentucky. It's also how I know you're divorced and have a five-year-old daughter in Missoula."

His eyes flared. "Are you threatening my kid?"

He wouldn't hurt innocent people. No way in hell. But this guy didn't know that. "I'm saying, I was found innocent of both charges. And I went to a lot of effort to move away from the gossip. So I wouldn't look favorably on someone who leaked my story."

Fear crept into the guy's eyes, and he straightened. "Fine. I'll see what I can do."

"Good. Don't forget about the things I've done to protect

myself." He lowered his head so his mouth was near the guy's ear. "People who cross me *always* wish they hadn't."

Abe paled, the fear looking like it was going to swallow him whole.

Good.

When Zane reached his car, he saw the reporter shoot his head around the corner of the building, sighting Zane. Good. He'd know Zane wasn't leaving right away. It would push the narrative that he was watching. And that Abe was vulnerable.

Zane's phone vibrated with a text.

Bonnie: So I know you said no to any more kisses, but what about a friendship?

He frowned at the text. Friendship? He couldn't be friends with her. He could barely talk to her without that consuming need to touch her.

Bonnie: Because the thing is, I don't have many friends. I haven't even seen my own sister since coming back to town. And when I talk to you, I feel like my old self again. Something I haven't felt for a while.

He'd barely finished reading the text when another came through.

Bonnie: I just read that back...I've made myself sound completely and utterly pathetic, haven't I?

Bonnie: Did me admitting that make it even worse? Okay, I'm stopping now. If you don't reply, I might just dig a hole of embarrassment to die in. That's it. Bye.

He scrubbed a hand over his face. Because how the fuck was he supposed to say no to that? And he liked talking to her too. She made him smile, and he hadn't done a lot of that lately.

Zane: I'll come by your apartment tomorrow morning and we can go for a coffee.

He hit send. It was a bad idea. So why didn't he regret it?

"WHAT DO you mean a raccoon got stuck in the equipment box?" Bonnie laughed, the cup of chai warming her hands as she walked down the street with her brother.

"I mean, I got to the rock-climbing wall and the little guy's ass was sticking out of a hole he'd chewed through the box."

"What was in the box that he was so eager to get to?"

"Flint left half a taco in there the day before. He was setting up then forgot about it. The raccoon must have smelled it."

"I'm impressed. But I also feel bad for him. How long would he have been there for?"

"No idea. Could have been the entire night. But after Colt and I performed the great rescue, we gave the little guy the stale taco and he scurried off."

"How did you break him out?"

"Broke the box open."

"Wow. That's quite an effort for a wild raccoon."

"We're quite good guys."

She laughed again before shaking her head. "And you know it."

"So…Indie asked about you." Noah sipped his coffee.

"Really?" Her pulse sped up. "I asked to meet but she said she still wasn't feeling great and doesn't want to be throwing up when we see each other."

"Well, good news, her doctor's got her on some new medication to help with the nausea, so I think she'll feel up to an outing soon."

Nerves tickled her spine. "I'd love to see her. I've been too nervous to ask since my last text."

"You? Nervous?"

"I know, shocker. Fifteen-year-old me was fearless. Remember when I jumped on the back of old man Jim's pickup truck because I didn't want to walk to school?"

"You jumped on while it was *moving*. I was so pissed at you."

"So was he. When he finally saw me, he slammed on the

brakes and got out to yell at me, but I jumped off and ran before he could."

"Mom and Dad got quite the earful. But I think they were also kind of impressed by your fearlessness."

Her smile slipped. "Guess I'm not the person I used to be."

"Hey. There's nothing wrong with realizing that jumping on the back of a moving vehicle is a bad idea. There's also nothing wrong with warming up to things with Indie by texting for a while before you see each other. Why don't I ask her about tomorrow morning? It's your day off, right?"

"I actually have plans tomorrow morning." She nibbled her bottom lip.

"Who could possibly be more important than me and Indie?"

"Not more important, just planned first. Zane and I are getting a coffee together."

Noah frowned. "You're hanging out with Zane?"

"Well, tomorrow I am. We're trying for friends. I like him. And after our…" She hadn't told anyone she'd kissed Zane. She hadn't had anyone to tell.

"After your what?" he asked carefully.

"We, uh, kissed."

His brows shot up. "Really?"

"Yeah." She shot a glance at her brother, who was now frowning again. "What?"

"Nothing. It's just that the other night, Jesse and I were passing The Pit and he had some guy up against the wall and looked like he was going to punch him."

She frowned. "What guy?"

"I don't know. Neither of them would tell us what was going on."

"Okay. It's strange but I don't think he would have done that without a good reason. Some people in this town can be pretty painful." She kicked a rock, a few less than desirable moments coming to mind.

"Yeah, just…be careful."

One side of her mouth lifted. "You being my protective big brother?"

"Always."

Her heart gave another kick. Then she rolled her eyes. "Fine. I'll reschedule with him, and you and Indie can come over tomorrow morning. Happy?"

"You don't have to do that, Bon."

"I want to. I need to see Indie. How about nine thirty?"

"That works."

Two women rounded the corner ahead of them.

Bonnie's chest tightened. Maisie and Jane, Dean's mother. Did Maisie only ever spend time with Dean's family?

Maisie's eyes widened, while Jane's narrowed in anger. Then she gasped, *"Bonnie…"*

The older woman marched forward, but Noah stepped in front of Bonnie before Jane could reach her.

"I could *kill* you for coming back here!" Jane shouted, emotion clogging her voice. "You left my son at that party when you were supposed to drive him home. You let him crash that car and die! And now you want to live here again?"

"That's enough!" Noah shouted.

Bonnie glanced to Maisie, but the other woman wasn't looking at Bonnie. Her gaze was set firmly on the ground.

"You need to leave," Jane growled, trying to push her way past Noah like she wanted to hurt Bonnie. "I shouldn't have to see your face around here. Ever!"

"You need to leave," Noah growled. *"Now."*

Maisie touched Jane's shoulder. "Come on, Jane. Let's go."

Finally, Jane stepped away from Noah and let Maisie pull her down the sidewalk. But even when the two women were gone, Bonnie's heart didn't stop thumping. It hit her ribs so hard that it hurt. A physical pain that throbbed through her entire body.

Noah touched her shoulder. "Are you okay?"

She felt like she'd been slapped in the face. What if Noah hadn't been here? Would Jane actually have attacked her? Would Maisie have just watched? Could Bonnie not even exist in the town she grew up in without someone wanting to hurt her?

"I should get home." She wrapped her arm around her waist.

"I'll walk you."

Bonnie shook her head, already taking a step around her brother. "No, I need a few minutes by myself."

"Bon—"

"I'll see you tomorrow, Noah."

She walked away from him, her steps fast, but not as fast as her pulse.

The anger in Jane's eyes, the hate, it was so fierce, and all aimed at her.

How, after all these years, was she *still* blaming Bonnie for her son getting drunk and getting behind the wheel?

Bonnie dipped her chin to her chest, a little scared someone else would recognize her. Attack her. It took her half the time it usually would to reach her apartment building. Her head was still down when she reached the door.

She was pulling out her key when someone grabbed her from behind and shoved her into the wall beside the door.

She cried out, the shock rendering her completely still as a deep, raspy voice growled into her ear. She barely heard it above the blood roaring between her ears.

"Leave. No one wants you here."

Then her head was yanked back by her hair, and her face slammed into the concrete wall.

CHAPTER 9

*L*oud thuds tugged Bonnie from her sleep. Her eyes scrunched and pain cut through her face.

Ouch.

She touched her temple and flinched.

Jesus Christ. It hadn't been a nightmare. Someone *had* threatened her last night. No. Not just threatened, they'd *assaulted* her.

She took a moment to breathe through the nausea in her belly. Nausea and fear and panic all tangled together. And maybe a bit of embarrassment. But she wasn't sure why she felt embarrassed. She shouldn't.

Another bang sounded, this one louder. She frowned, finally registering that someone was at her door.

Then it hit her. Noah and Indie were here.

Oh God, was her temple as bad today as it was last night? Because last night it had looked like she'd been in a fight.

She was about to reach for her phone to text Noah a lie about not being home when a voice sounded.

"Bonnie? Are you there?"

Shit. Not Noah. Zane.

With everything that had happened last night, she'd forgotten to cancel their morning. She scrunched her nose. And her phone was in the kitchen.

Great.

Quickly, she threw off the sheets and crept out of bed. Her steps were slow and measured. Silent. Well, silent until she hit the creaky floorboard in the hall.

Her stomach dropped.

"Bonnie? What's going on?"

He knew she was here now. She had to open it, right?

When she reached the door, she took one deep breath before tugging it open. She didn't even think about the fact that she only wore an oversized shirt and panties. Hell, she didn't even have a bra on.

But Zane didn't seem to notice any of that. All he looked at was her face. His eyes narrowed and a darkness she'd never seen slipped over his features.

Not just darkness—pure rage.

"Who did that?"

The tone of his voice almost made her step back. Or maybe she did, because he stepped forward.

"I don't know," she whispered.

Another narrowing of his eyes.

How bad did she look? By Zane's expression, pretty bad.

"Do you want a coffee? I really need coffee." She turned, not waiting to see if he followed. But the click of the door closing followed by his footsteps told her he did.

She grabbed two mugs from her cupboard before starting her pod machine.

"Bonnie. Turn around."

She stilled, eyes closing for a second before she worked up the courage to face him.

Zane was close. So close she couldn't move without touching him. He boxed her into the corner of her kitchen.

He reached up and grazed a thumb over her temple. "Tell me

what happened so I can kill the person responsible."

All the fine hairs on her neck stood on end. Because the way he said it…she believed him. "I got to our apartment building last night and someone shoved me into the wall beside the door. They told me to leave. That, um, no one wants me here."

Suddenly, and completely unexpectedly, tears gathered in her eyes. Maybe because she hadn't cried last night. Not after she'd been assaulted. Not after she'd stumbled up the stairs and into her apartment. Not even when she'd placed an ice pack on her aching head.

Zane cursed and tugged her into his chest. And suddenly his strength, his warmth, the safety of his arms—they were the only things that kept her upright. The only things that kept her from completely losing herself.

She wasn't sure how long she cried into his chest, but the tears refused to stop. They fell hard and fast, and she felt like she was splitting wide open.

Another knock came at the door, and Bonnie gasped before pulling away. "Oh no. That will be my brother and sister."

"Do they know what happened?"

She shook her head. "No. And it won't be pretty." But then, nothing about this was pretty or easy or felt in the slightest way okay.

"Go. Tell them," Zane said quietly.

He was right. Noah would find out one way or another. It just wasn't the best way for her to see Indie for the first time in years.

She crossed over to the door and pulled it open. The first person she saw was Indie, and for a fraction of a second, she almost made Bonnie forget. About her attacker and the bruise on her face.

God, her older sister looked different. Not in a bad way. She had a small, rounded pregnant belly, but her green eyes were exactly the same.

"Hi," Bonnie said quietly.

Indie's mouth opened, her gaze on Bonnie's temple.

"What the hell?" Noah shouted. Then his attention shifted to something behind her, and for a split second there was suspicion on his face.

She touched his arm. "Zane's here to help."

"What the hell's going on, Bonnie?" he growled. "Why are you crying with a bruised temple?"

She stepped aside and both her siblings stepped inside her apartment. Suddenly the room felt far too full and the air too heavy.

She wrapped her arms around her waist. "Someone attacked me last night."

Indie gasped while Noah's eyes narrowed. "Who?"

She lifted a shoulder. "I'm not sure. I didn't see them. It was a man, that's all I know. They also threatened me and told me to leave town."

Indie touched her shoulder. It was the first time her sister had touched her in years. The feel of her hand was soft and familiar, and she wanted to tug her sister into her chest.

"Did you call Jesse?" she asked softly.

"I called the station last night." Her stomach got a sick feeling at the memory. "A deputy answered. At first he seemed concerned, but then I told him my name and…"

"And what?" Zane asked, voice low.

"He said that because I didn't see my attacker there was nothing he could do. Then he hung up."

"The *fuck*?" Noah yelled.

Zane scowled. "Who the hell did you speak to?"

"I didn't get his name. He wouldn't even make a report."

Indie's hand went to the small of Bonnie's back as she looked at the guys. "Noah and Zane, call Jesse. I'm going to help Bonnie change."

Bonnie led her into the bedroom and Indie closed the door.

When Indie turned, there were tears in her eyes. "Hey, Bon-Bon. What a sucky first meeting."

"But you're here."

"So are you."

Without another word, Indie closed that small distance between them and pulled Bonnie into her arms. And Bonnie just breathed her sister in. A woman she'd grown up with. A woman she hadn't seen in thirteen years.

God, she'd missed her. Her smell. Her voice. Her everything.

* * *

ZANE LEANED against the far wall of the small living room, arms crossed as he watched the town sheriff talk to Bonnie. She told him about the spineless prick who'd attacked her from behind last night. Who'd threatened her. Hurt her.

If Zane had been there, that man wouldn't be walking right now. Hell, he wouldn't be breathing.

It was taking everything in Zane to remain exactly where he was and not go out and find that Dean kid's father. Because this had to be him. He'd already confronted her twice. And that was twice that Zane knew about—there could be more times that Bonnie hadn't shared.

"You didn't recognize his voice?" Jesse asked from his position crouched in front of her.

Bonnie shook her head, her sister sitting on one side of her, her brother standing on the other. "No, but I was in shock and there was a buzzing between my ears, and he growled the words really low. Maybe I did know him. It's all a blur. I'm sorry." She dropped her head into her hands.

Her sister rubbed her back.

"It's not your fault," Jesse assured her. "The guy attacked you like that to hide his identity. Do you have any idea who it could be?"

74

Bonnie scoffed. "It could be anyone. Half the town hates me."

"That's not true," Noah said.

She tilted her head at him. "It is. The Whites have spent the last thirteen years convincing everyone that their son's death is my fault. Anytime I go anywhere, people point at me. Talk about me. Sometimes people come over and say awful things."

"Who?" Noah growled.

"Everyone."

"What about the dad?" Zane cut in, speaking for the first time since Jesse and his deputy had shown up.

Jesse looked up at him before turning back to Bonnie. "Has Carlos done something?"

Bonnie swallowed, a few seconds of silence passing before she took a breath. "He approached me at The Tea House. Noah was with me and Zane was at the counter. He wasn't happy I was here."

"Then outside my gym," Zane added. "He grabbed you. Towered over you and scared you."

Noah's eyes narrowed. "When?"

"Last week," Zane answered.

Noah cursed and turned back to Bonnie. "Why didn't you say anything?"

"If I reported every incident, every time someone said or did something, I'd be calling every day. Sometimes *multiple times* a day."

"Then call every day," Jesse said, steel in his eyes.

"I called last night. That didn't do anything."

The muscles in the sheriff's forearms flexed, and when he spoke there was an edge to his voice. "Tell me about the call."

Bonnie lifted her shoulder. "There's not much to tell. When I got up to my apartment, I called the station. A deputy answered. I told him what happened and he seemed to care. Then I told him my name."

What the fuck was wrong with this town? Zane was going to murder them. *All* of them.

Jesse turned to his deputy. "Who was on last night?"

"Symes was on the phone."

"Drew Symes?" Bonnie asked.

Jesse looked back at Bonnie. "You know him?"

She laughed, but there was no humor in the sound. "He was friends with Dean."

Jesse leaned forward. "I'm going to make sure that doesn't happen again, Bonnie. Okay? If you call the station, you *will* get help. Or just call me directly."

She nodded, fresh tears filling her eyes. "I'm sorry, it's just… it's been so hard." She scrubbed her eyes. "It was probably naive of me to think I could just walk back into this town and things would be okay."

Indie touched her shoulder. "Bonnie."

She looked at her sister.

"This isn't the entire town," Indie said gently. "Maybe it feels like it is right now because a couple of jerks are being really loud. But that's all it is, a couple of people. The good ones and your family, we're all glad you're here. It's where you're meant to be."

New tears filled Bonnie's eyes, and she leaned her head onto her sister's shoulder.

Jesse and Noah started talking about safety. About Bonnie getting a car and not walking places alone.

Zane couldn't drag his gaze from Bonnie, the same damn thing repeating in his head—that he wanted to burn every fucker who'd hurt her to the ground.

CHAPTER 10

*I*t was too dark. And the silence... She'd never understood people who described silence as loud, but right now, she got it. It filled her ears, making her heart beat faster and a prickle run over the back of her neck.

It was stupid. This was her apartment. And a couple of nights ago, she'd been fine. But that was before someone had attacked her. Assaulted her.

She'd had the entire day off work today, but there were always people with her. Noah. Indie. Jesse. Now she was alone, and she felt it.

She rolled to her other side, gaze catching on the clock beside her bed. One a.m. She'd been lying here, staring into the darkness for three hours, and hadn't gotten a minute of sleep. Not a single second.

Come on, Bonnie, you have work tomorrow. You need sleep.

She squeezed her eyes shut, but the guy on her back suddenly felt like he was there again. The breath against her cheek.

Her eyes flashed open, pulse picking up speed.

Maybe she couldn't sleep because her attacker knew where

she lived. And this building wasn't old, but it also wasn't that hard to access. People forgot to lock the downstairs door all the time. Hell, that was how Noah and Indie had gotten in today. And even if the door was locked, residents let random people in and out a lot.

She'd brought it up to the super before, but he was lazy and didn't care in the slightest.

Did her attacker know which apartment she lived in?

She shot up.

Sleep was not happening. At least, not right now.

On the way to the kitchen to make hot cocoa, she stopped in the bathroom to pee. She was about to leave when her gaze caught on the mirror. Air stuttered out of her at the bruise on her temple.

With fingers that weren't quite steady, she touched the purple bruising and flinched. Someone hated her so much that they'd resorted to physical assault.

It made her want to run. Hide. Maybe even disappear. Because that was her default when things got hard.

But she couldn't do that. This was her home. This was where her family lived. And she wasn't willing to lose it all a second time.

Dropping her hand, she stepped back and turned, heading into the kitchen where she grabbed a saucepan from the cupboard.

The only good part of today was that she'd gotten to see Indie again. They hadn't spoken about anything serious, like her leaving or their parents' passing. In fact, Indie and Noah had been really good at keeping all conversation light and fluffy, which had made everything a bit easier.

Zane hadn't stayed long after Jesse and his deputy had left, but he'd messaged throughout the day, checking in. And there'd been this feeling inside her, like maybe he left because he couldn't hold the rage inside him.

But that was silly. They hadn't even known each other for that long.

She was pouring milk into the saucepan when a scratching noise sounded from the living room balcony door.

She spun, the milk carton hitting the edge of the counter and falling from her fingers, spilling all over the floor. She didn't so much as look at it. Her gaze was on her closed blinds.

She was on the fourth floor. No one would be able to get up to her balcony…right?

Right.

She turned to grab a cloth for the spilled milk when she heard scraping noises, this time louder.

She spun again, slipping on the spilled milk before hitting the floor, *hard.*

Bonnie barely stayed there for a second before she was on her feet and racing to the door.

Not caring that she was covered in milk or that it was ridiculously late, she ran straight down the hall to apartment forty-three and banged on Zane's door.

* * *

Loud thuds had Zane shifting from fast asleep to wide awake in under a second. He shot up, immediately opening the second drawer in his bedside table and lifting the false bottom.

When he held the Glock in his grasp, he climbed out of bed, not caring that he only wore briefs. He didn't even stop to flick on a light. It was after one in the fucking morning. He shouldn't have any visitors.

His steps were fast but silent as he moved down the hall to the door. Keeping his body positioned against the wall, he leaned over and looked through the peephole.

The fuck?

He tugged the door open. "Bonnie, what's wrong?"

Just like this morning, she only wore an oversized T-shirt, but now it was wet. And did she smell like milk?

She wrapped her arms around her waist. "I'm sorry! I know it's late. But I couldn't sleep and then I heard scratching against my balcony door and I spilled milk and slipped in it and—"

"You heard scratching against your balcony door?"

"Twice. And it might be nothing—it's probably nothing—but after last night it just…" She scrubbed her face. "It freaked me out."

"Come in."

When she looked up, there was a hint of tears in her eyes. "Really?"

He reached out and set a hand on the small of her back before leading her inside and locking the door after him. Then he led her straight down the hall to the bathroom off his bedroom. "Wait here." He grabbed a T-shirt from the bedroom. "Shower. Change. I'll go check your apartment."

She swallowed, relief darkening her hazel eyes. "Thank you."

He waited to hear the click on the bathroom door before pulling on jeans and a shirt. It was only then that he lifted the Glock again and headed to her apartment. Even though it might be nothing…it also might not be.

Her apartment door was ajar. He tapped it open, keeping his back to the wall as he glanced around. The hall and kitchen lights were on.

He started in her bedroom, checking the window behind the closed curtains. Nothing. And nothing in the room either. Next he searched the bathroom, then the living room.

Every curtain he pulled back showed the dark night and nothing else…until he reached her balcony door.

There was a small tree in a ceramic pot, maybe four feet tall, and every time the wind blew, its branches scratched against the glass.

That's what she'd heard. Even though it was nothing to worry about, he wasn't surprised she'd been scared, not after the events of the night before.

After tidying the kitchen, including the milk on the floor, he found her phone in her bedroom and her apartment key on the hall table, using the latter to lock up before heading back to his apartment.

He expected to find Bonnie still in his bathroom when he got back. She wasn't. She sat on his couch, hair wet, legs tucked beneath her.

His throat fucking dried at the sight of her in his shirt. It was just a plain white shirt, and it drowned her. But for some goddamn reason it made his hands itch to touch her. And some deep, primal part of him felt like he'd just claimed her.

She rose from the couch, her gaze going to the pistol in his hand before lifting back to him. "Did you find anything?" Her voice was small and vulnerable.

It made him want to fight every asshole who'd threatened her. "Your place is empty. The culprit of the balcony noise was your tree."

"Oh my gosh. I'm so sorry! I freaked myself out. Of course it was Evergreen. She's a dwarf but still tall." She shook her head. "I feel dumb. I should go."

She started to leave, but he touched her arm. "Bonnie...stay here tonight."

The flare of her eyes hinted that she wanted to. But then her brows wrinkled. "Are you sure?"

"I only have one bed, but—"

"I can sleep on the couch."

He almost laughed. "No. You take the bed. I'll take the couch."

"It's a two-person couch. It would basically fit your legs."

"I'll survive."

She shook her head. "Absolutely not. Either I take the couch or I'm not staying."

But even as she said the last part, he heard the tremor in her voice. She didn't want to go any more than he wanted her to. "Fine. We'll share my bed. It's plenty big enough."

Her mouth opened in an *O*, and yeah, it was a dangerous idea. But he didn't want her alone. And now that she was here, he didn't want her out of his sight.

"Are you sure—"

"Yes," he interrupted.

Her throat bobbed as she swallowed. "Okay."

He set a hand on the small of her back, letting the heat unravel anything cool beneath his skin, and led her into the bedroom. "Get comfortable. I'll be back in ten."

She stepped into the room. "Zane…"

He turned, getting damn lost in the dark specks in her hazel eyes. "Yeah, Bon?"

"Thank you."

"It's nothing."

One small smile and she headed to the bed. He turned and went back down the hall to the kitchen, where he took out a shot glass and a bottle of whiskey. He shot it back, the alcohol burning his throat, then his gut.

It wasn't enough. But then, would anything be? Would anything help him get through the torture that would be sharing a bed with Bonnie when he wasn't allowed to touch her?

* * *

BONNIE SLIPPED between the silk sheets. God, the bed smelled like Zane. Earthy and masculine and a bit like pine. Somehow the bed was also warm.

She sighed as she closed her eyes. She shouldn't be here. She knew she shouldn't be here. She should be strong and brave enough to be in her own apartment. But somehow, even though she hadn't known Zane for long, he'd become this safe person for her. Maybe because he was just down the hall. Maybe because he'd already protected her more than once.

Whatever it was, she was grateful. And it made her care a little less that she was somewhere she shouldn't be.

She thought sleep would come to her. It didn't. Which was annoying because she was *so* tired. She'd barely slept the previous night, and if she didn't sleep tonight that would be two nights in a row of basically no sleep.

How was she supposed to function at work tomorrow?

She rolled to her left side. A few minutes passed and she rolled to her right.

Nope. Nothing.

The creak of a floorboard sounded behind her from the hall. She nibbled her bottom lip, suddenly nervous. Nervous for Zane to be so close. When he'd answered the door, he'd only worn briefs. Was he going to sleep like that?

The mattress dipped behind her. And if she'd thought the bed smelled like Zane before, that was nothing compared to now. His scent surrounded her, so strong that all she breathed was him.

Go to sleep, Bonnie. Rest.

She closed her eyes again, but the second she did, she felt that hand yanking her hair again. The stranger's breath against her cheek. And those words snarled into her ear.

Her skin pricked with fear, and some of that warmth left her body.

She wasn't sure if her breathing changed or if she'd made some kind of sound, but the mattress suddenly moved behind her, then a warm body pressed to her back.

A silent gasp escaped her throat at the warm hand on her hip. A breath suddenly whispered against her cheek, so different from the one that had just been in her head. Softer. Warmer.

Then four words whispered into her ear. Kind words. Safe words.

"Sleep, Bonnie. You're safe."

And just like that, her muscles relaxed, and she leaned back into Zane's strength. He surrounded her, held her, allowing her to feel secure enough to sleep.

CHAPTER 11

*Z*ane's feet pounded the hard concrete path as he ran, the cold air slapping him in the face. But even the morning chill did nothing to cool his body.

His skin burned. Hell, not just his skin. His blood. His bones. Heat from *her*. From sleeping an entire night with her hot little body pressed against him.

He pushed himself to move faster, arms pumping at his sides.

All night he'd held Bonnie. And fuck, he'd slept well. But then waking with her ass pushed into his cock...it had taken everything, every damn speck of strength he possessed, to not kiss her shoulder. Not roll her over and see if she tasted as good in the morning as she had that night in his gym.

He rounded a corner, passing an elderly couple on the sidewalk.

He felt like a fucking creep. She'd come to him for safety, and all he'd been able to think about was what he wanted to do to her.

So what had he done? He'd gotten his ass out of bed at the crack of dawn and left. Run to the gym like a coward because it was the only way to stop himself from doing something he shouldn't.

He was nearing his gym when his phone rang. He pulled it from his pocket to see his friend's name on the screen. "Ethan, you got what I need?"

"No." There was an edge to Ethan's voice.

Zane stopped. "What's wrong?"

"He's dead."

"Who's dead?"

"My source inside the prison. Cause of death has been declared a fucking suicide. It's bullshit."

Zane scrubbed a hand over his face. This was the last thing they needed. "You think Monty found out he was leaking information?"

"Yes. And had him killed."

Shit. "This is bad. It means whatever he's planning—"

"Is worth killing over."

Immediately, Zane scanned the street. There was no way Monty was here right now. But that didn't mean Zane was safe.

"I'm working on another way of making sure I stay up-to-date on any new information," Ethan said, voice thin and frustrated. "Until I do, keep your head down."

"Always do."

He hung up, mind still on Monty. The guy was his fucking *cousin.* He'd helped Zane. He was the reason Zane had gotten out of the military and into the UFC. He hadn't expected Monty to do what he'd done. But then, he'd obviously never really known him.

He rounded a corner and The Pit came into view. But that wasn't the only thing he saw.

Noah. The guy stood beside his truck, arms crossed and expression unreadable.

"Noah." Zane stopped in front of him. "You're here early."

Noah pushed off his truck. "I just dropped Bonnie at work."

Zane wanted to ask how she was, not just physically but in every way. The only reason he'd been able to leave her alone in his apartment this morning was because he'd known that Noah was taking her to work.

"Is something wrong?"

"Look, it's not my place to say anything, and she'd probably kill me for being here, but with what the town's putting her through and the fact that she stayed at your place last night, I need to ask you something."

Why the hell did a pit suddenly form in his gut. "What?"

"I need you to assure me that you're a good guy. That there's nothing you're hiding that might hurt my sister."

The pit widened, hollowing him out. "I'm a good guy." He didn't answer the second part of the question, and by the frown on Noah's face, he knew that.

Was he going to push? Demand Zane tell him the deepest, darkest parts of his past?

"I like you. And more importantly, *she* likes you. Don't do anything to screw that up."

Noah tapped his shoulder before straightening and heading to his car.

Zane bit back a curse as he stepped into the gym. He didn't want to tell Bonnie about his past. She had enough to deal with. But by not, he was keeping a huge part of himself from her.

Stetson frowned at him as he stepped into the gym. "Everything okay?"

"It's fine." A damn lie. "I'm going to shower, then you can take a break."

"Gotcha, boss."

In the bathroom, Zane stripped down and stepped into the shower, anger still beating at his chest. Anger at himself for having a past even though it wasn't his damn fault. Fury at the asshole who'd hurt Bonnie outside her apartment. And pure fucking rage that Monty had killed Ethan's guy in prison. That he was planning something. And Zane was *still* looking over his shoulder.

He hung his head, letting the heat of the water hit the back of his neck.

Ten minutes later, he stepped out of the shower, threw on clothes, and left the bathroom. He was halfway to his office when a quick scan of the gym had him stopping.

The fuck was *he* doing here?

The thin hold Zane had on his patience snapped. He dropped his bag, stormed across the gym, and grabbed Carlos by the back of the shirt, yanking him away from the bag. "Get out."

Carlos's brows rose. "Excuse me?"

"You heard me. Get the fuck out of my gym, *now.*"

Stetson rushed over. "Zane, this is my uncle. He asked if he could hit a bag this morning, and he paid…"

Zane laughed. "Why the hell would you want to come here?" Then it hit him. "It's because of Bonnie, isn't it? You want to go where she goes so she doesn't feel welcome."

"This is *my* town." Carlos scowled. "And if I want to go to my local gym, I will."

"*My* gym. And I choose who can and can't come here—and you can't."

This time Carlos laughed. The fucker actually *laughed.* "You're serious? You're throwing me out because of her?"

The words had barely left the asshole's mouth when Zane grabbed him by the arm and pulled him toward the door.

Carlos tried to shake him off. "Hey! Get your hands off me!"

Zane didn't stop or pause. He kept dragging the guy, not caring that Stetson and everyone working out had all stopped to stare at him. When he reached the door, he threw Carlos out, watching him stumble.

"You try to come in here again, and things will get a lot less friendly." Zane slammed the door.

"If he brought a bag, throw it out with him," he said to an open-mouthed Stetson. "And don't *ever* let him in here again."

* * *

BONNIE GRINNED as she read the participation feedback forms from the self-defense session. They were good. Better than any other program she'd run.

I didn't know I could feel strong again.

I felt so empowered.

And Sarah's—*I felt like I could breathe again.*

Bonnie closed her eyes and just let the words sit inside her for a moment. This was why she did what she did. To help. To empower. To bring safety back to women's lives.

She'd intentionally ended her day with these forms because all she'd thought about for hours was the fact that she had to return to her empty apartment tonight.

It was fine. She'd be fine. Yes, she'd been attacked outside her building, and no they hadn't caught the perpetrator, but that didn't mean she had to be scared to sleep alone.

The memory of Zane's arms around her last night made heat slip through her belly.

Of course, when she'd woken up, he'd been gone. Which was kind of disappointing. Okay, not kind of. Very.

Sure, he'd left a note telling her he'd had to get to work early, but that had done nothing to dull the disappointment. She'd wanted to wake up in his arms. To see his day-old stubble and feel the warmth of his body around her.

Gah.

She needed to stop. She was lucky he let her sleep in his bed last night.

She logged off her computer and grabbed the box of sports clothing from the storage cabinet. There were leggings and bras and tops and socks. It was amazing what some companies were willing to donate if you asked.

She also lifted a small bag, then moved to the shelter living room. About ten women filled the space. Some in front of the TV, some in the kitchen.

"Hi, everyone. Can I have your attention for a moment?"

They all stopped at her words. Even Chett and another child paused from playing with blocks.

"I have a box of donated workout clothes. Feel free to come and see if anything's your size. I thought these pieces would come in handy for our next session at The Pit."

Smiles curved the women's faces, and they moved toward the box. All but one. Sarah stood to the side of the room, frowning at her. But before Bonnie could go to her, a small hand tugged at her sweatshirt.

She crouched by Chett's side. "Hey, buddy."

"Are there any kids' clothes?"

Bonnie's smile widened. "Well, I actually have this special bag here." She brought it forward and handed it to him. "This is for you and the other kids, and I think you might find a few things in your size. Do you want to go through it and see what you like?"

His little eyes lit up, and he nodded before taking the bag over to the girl he was playing with.

Bonnie rose as Sarah stopped beside her. The other woman touched her arm and lowered her voice. "Are you okay?"

"What do you mean?"

Sarah leaned closer. "I can see the bruise on your temple."

Crap. She'd thought she'd covered it well with makeup. "I'm okay. The incident's been…taken care of." Ha. That was a lie if ever she'd told one. But she wasn't about to share what had happened with any of the women at the shelter.

"So he's been charged?" Sarah asked.

Well, she was hoping that Jesse called her with good news about Carlos cracking and admitting he was the culprit. But that was probably wishful thinking. "You don't need to worry about me, Sarah."

"You worry about all of us."

"That's my job."

Sarah paused for a moment. "Hang on. I've got something."

Bonnie frowned as Sarah disappeared up the stairs. When she returned, she had a small bottle of something in her hand.

"Pepper spray." Sarah held out her hand.

"Oh, I don't need—"

"I have plenty." Sarah pushed it at her.

Bonnie sighed, still wanting to say no but not wanting to offend the other woman. "Thank you. How are *you* doing?"

Sarah smiled. It was the first real smile Bonnie had seen from her. "Really good. The counseling's still helping. I've made some friends and I'm not hovering over Chett as much."

Bonnie squeezed her arm. "I love that, Sarah."

When the women were done grabbing everything they wanted, Bonnie took the almost empty box back to her office and grabbed her purse.

"Bonnie."

She jumped at Shelley's voice suddenly behind her. "Hi."

"Did you take a one-and-a-half-hour lunch break today?"

"Yes, I did. My brother took me to buy a car, which I did. Buy, I mean. But I've stayed later to make up for the time." Which had always been fine at her last job, but by the look on Shelley's face, possibly wasn't at this one.

Shelley's brows pinched. "We don't do that here. Please don't do it again."

Then she left.

Well, goodbye to you too.

What was frustrating was, she'd put in so many extra hours. Taking a slightly longer lunch break and staying late to make up for it shouldn't be problem. Well, it wasn't in Bonnie's eyes anyway.

She turned off the lights in her office and left.

The second she stepped outside, though, her hands twitched

to reach into her bag and touch the pepper spray Sarah had just given her.

She hurried to her new Honda. It was actually secondhand but new to her. And she'd gotten such a good deal. She wasn't sure if Noah had negotiated the price down before they'd gotten there, but it was a steal.

Thank God for Noah. After the first time trying to buy a car, she'd been nervous to try again. With him by her side though, the nerves had trickled away.

As she lowered into her car, her phone vibrated with a text.

Indie: Hey. Just checking in on how you're doing today.

Bonnie's heart kicked at her ribs. It felt so surreal to have Indie back in her life, but in the best way.

Bonnie: I'm good. Work was fine and Noah took me to buy a car at lunch.

Indie: Is it a good car?

Bonnie: It was a bargain, that's for sure.

Indie: Noah must have gotten you a deal.

Bonnie: Thank God for big brothers.

Indie: Let me know if you need anything.

Bonnie started writing a response, but her phone rang mid-text, Jesse's name on the screen. This was the call she'd been waiting for all day. So why did she suddenly feel so nervous?

One deep breath and she answered the call. "Hi, Jesse."

"Hey, Bon. How are you doing?"

"I'm good." Sort of. "Did you talk to Carlos?" She ran her fingers over the wheel, hoping he said yes. That Carlos had admitted to assaulting her. That he'd been charged.

But she also knew that the chances of that happening were slim to none.

"We did speak to him," Jesse said slowly, and just by the tone of his voice, Bonnie knew she wouldn't like what was coming next. "He has an alibi. He was with his brother at the time you were assaulted."

She frowned, not sure what to make of that. "The brother could be lying though, couldn't he?"

"It's possible."

"Or someone else could have attacked me." She dropped her head to the wheel, suddenly feeling deflated and tired and so incredibly over it all.

"I'm sorry, Bon. We're not stopping our investigation though, okay?"

"I know. Thanks, Jess."

There was a small pause. "I also wanted to let you know that Carlos came in today to make a report against Zane."

Her head shot up. "Zane? Why?"

"Apparently, Zane put his hands on him this morning."

What the hell? "Are you sure?"

"Yeah. We talked Carlos down, but I know you two have been spending a bit of time together, so I thought I should let you know."

She scrubbed a hand over her face. "Okay. Thank you."

When she hung up, she lowered the cell to the middle console.

She should go straight home. She knew she should. But she needed to know what happened between Zane and Carlos. And she needed to know if it involved her.

CHAPTER 12

Zane hit the bag. Blow after blow, the call from Jesse still in his head, pissing him the fuck off.

The asshole had an alibi. But it was him. It had to be him. Zane had seen the rage in the jerk's eyes when he'd yelled at her. Had felt the fury in him when he'd grabbed her.

Then the guy wanted to press charges against *him*?

Cross punch, kick.

It really pissed him off that scumbags did shitty things but still got to walk free. It had almost happened with Monty back in Billings. And now it was happening with Carlos.

Jab, jab, cross.

He'd received a warning from Jesse. To stay away from Carlos. To walk in the other direction if he saw him.

Carlos had been in *his* gym though. And if he entered again, Zane wouldn't hesitate to throw his ass out a second time.

Jab, cross, hook.

The gym had closed half an hour ago. He should have already left. But everything was annoying the shit out of him. Carlos. The murder of Ethan's contact. Even Bonnie's brother coming to warn him off this morning.

Three more punches, then the click of the gym door opening sounded. He stopped and turned, his hand wanting to reach for the Glock in his workout bag. The blinds were closed, so he hadn't seen anyone from the street.

Bonnie stepped out of the hall.

The sight of her made a quiet pressure settle on his chest, the air no longer reaching his lungs quite as easily.

She offered a small smile. "Hey."

He swallowed, arms dropping. "What are you doing here?"

"Well, that's a bit like a hello but not."

The memory of holding her all night had him fisting his hands, like he was trying to stop himself from reaching for her. "It's getting late. It's not safe for you to be out at night by yourself."

She glanced at the window, then gave him a look. And yeah, even with the blinds shut, it was clear that it wasn't dark just yet. But he stood by what he said.

She set her bag on the front desk like she was staying. "I want to know what happened between you and Carlos."

Jesus Christ, he did not want to talk about that asshole.

He used his teeth to tear off the wrist wrap of the first glove. "There's nothing to say."

"Except he went to the sheriff's office to report you, which means something happened. What?"

"He came in. I told him to get out. He wouldn't because he's an idiot. So I *dragged* his ass out." He dropped the first glove into his bag before tearing off the second.

"Zane, you didn't need to do that for me."

He almost laughed. "You think I'd let the fucker who bruised you work out in my gym?"

She closed the distance between them. "I don't want you getting into trouble for me."

If she knew the kind of legal battles he'd fought in Billings, she'd realize that someone as small as Carlos was nothing.

"He's not welcome here. He steps into my gym again, I'll do worse."

"No. I don't want you getting into serious legal trouble for me."

"Did you come in here to fight with me?"

She gave a half eyeroll. "And to thank you for last night. You left before I could wake up and say it this morning."

"You don't need to thank me," he said quietly.

She touched his arm. "I feel like I do."

He glanced down at her small fingers on his arm. Not that he needed to see them. One touch and he felt her everywhere. One touch and his body betrayed him. Did that thing where it got fucking hot and his defenses folded like paper in the rain.

Then her gaze lowered to his lips, and he didn't know what the hell happened.

One second, she was in front of him, the next, someone moved—he didn't know who—and they were kissing, their mouths crashing together.

There was no hesitation in the kiss. She parted her lips and he dove right in, letting the taste of her blur out the world that had been pressing on his chest all day.

He swept his arms around her waist and tugged her closer, her front pressing against him. And even that, the small shift of her body into his, caused a complete quieting of every frustration and anger that had been weighing on him.

She silenced it. Dulled it. Changed it.

He lifted her and she wrapped her legs around his waist. She fit so perfectly in his arms, like this was the only place she was meant to be.

Her hair was soft as he slipped the fingers of one hand through her locks. He deepened the kiss, absorbing every moan and whimper that escaped from her throat.

What the hell was it with Bonnie? She made him want her like he'd never wanted anything or anyone else. He burned for her.

Three big steps took them to the desk, where he deposited her. Then he was leaning over her body, her back touching the desk, legs still around his waist.

The slivers of pain from her fingers digging into his shoulders were in complete contrast to everything else she made him feel.

He slipped a hand beneath her shirt, and his palm slid up her stomach before he cupped her breast over the bra. Her whimper almost ended him there and then.

When he found the tight bud of her nipple, he ran his thumb over it in a circle, rewarded with more of those glorious feminine moans.

His cock was so hard it felt like stone. He was hurting for her. He actually fucking *hurt*.

He tore his mouth from hers, tugged the shirt up, and lowered his head to take her nipple between his lips. Then he sucked, only the thin lace of the bra separating them.

Bonnie's fingers dug into his hair, her core grinding against him. "Oh God, Zane."

He wasn't sure what it was. The way she said his name, her voice cutting through the quiet, or something else…but those three words suddenly tugged him back to reality.

The one where he had an enemy. One who somehow had a reach outside the four walls of his prison cell.

He lifted his head. "Shit, Bonnie."

He didn't rise immediately, instead touching his forehead to hers.

"Zane." She cupped his cheek with her warm hand. "Are you okay?"

No. He was far from okay. He wanted things. He wanted *her*. But damn, Monty was fucking with him. "We shouldn't have done that."

Her body tensed beneath him. "Why not?"

Slowly, he forced himself up. He didn't look into her eyes as he pulled her top down and gripped her upper arms to help her up. "It's complicated."

He stepped away from her, finally looking at her, seeing the confusion in her eyes.

"What's complicated?" she whispered.

"I've already told you, we both have stuff going on." He scrubbed a hand over his face.

"What stuff do you have going on?"

There was no way in hell he was telling her about Monty. Not while she was dealing with so much. "Even your brother warned me not to do anything that would ruin everything."

Bonnie frowned. "My brother? When did you talk to him?"

"He was waiting for me this morning. He wanted to make sure I was a good guy. That I wasn't going to screw this up." And here he was, doing exactly that.

* * *

BONNIE'S JAW DROPPED. Or maybe it completely hit the floor, she wasn't sure. Because last she checked, she was a thirty-one-year-old woman who *did not* need her protective older brother vetting the guys she was dating…or wanting to date.

She shook her head. "I don't know what to say."

"Let me walk you out."

"Actually, I do know what to say. He had no right to talk to you about me. But I'll deal with him later." She jumped off the desk and jabbed him in the chest with her finger. "*You*, on the other hand, should know that what you and I do is none of his business."

Something passed over his face. Something that told her Zane didn't actually care what her brother said.

"But you already know that, don't you?" she continued. "What are you not telling me?"

His lips sealed shut. He was never going to tell her.

"I'm going to walk you out now, Bonnie."

That was it. He'd made a decision, and she just got no say in it. "You know what? Don't. I'm an adult. I have pepper spray in my bag. I don't need you doing me any favors."

Zane glanced over his shoulder to the hall at the back of the gym.

Great. He wasn't even listening to what she was saying anymore.

"I'll see you later." She turned away from him, but he grabbed her arm. "Hey, I—"

His hand came over her mouth, his body suddenly pressed to her back. Then his whispered voice was in her ear. "Shh. There's someone in the gym."

Her heart stopped, fear wrapping around her chest like clingwrap.

The lights suddenly flicked off—and then she couldn't breathe. Someone was here. And that someone had plunged the gym into darkness.

Oh, God.

Zane's mouth lowered to her ear again. "Stay behind me."

His hand shifted from her mouth to her wrist, and he tugged her toward his bag. She expected him to pull out his phone, maybe use the flashlight function. It had gotten pretty dark outside, which made it even darker in here.

He didn't take out either of those things.

It took her a second to realize he held a gun.

"Come on," he whispered.

Hand still in his, they moved toward the back of the gym. When they stepped into the hall, the darkness surrounded them, making it hard to see. She inched closer, the heat of Zane's back radiating onto her.

Safe. She was safe with Zane. She just needed to keep reminding herself of that.

They passed a few closed doors. At the end of the hall by a

back door, Zane stopped at the circuit breaker. He cursed before flicking a switch.

Light flooded the gym, making her blink.

"Someone turned it off?" she asked.

"Yes."

Her breathing shortened, and she almost didn't want to ask the next question. "How…how did they get in?"

Without a word, Zane opened the back door, just a crack. It opened easily. So not locked.

Before stepping out, Zane crouched in front of the lock and studied it. "They broke the lock."

"Why turn the lights off? Do you think they're still here?"

"I don't know." Zane lifted the gun again before stepping outside.

Her limbs trembled as she followed him, scared of what they might find. But no way in hell was she remaining inside without him.

The cool evening air slipped over her skin, making goose bumps rise over her arms. Was someone out here? Carlos? Jane? Maybe even some of Dean's old high school friends?

The small parking lot was empty other than Zane's truck.

"No one's here," Bonnie whispered.

Zane turned toward her and opened his mouth like he was going to say something. But he stopped, his gaze landing on something behind her. She turned.

The chill of her skin slipped into her blood at the spray-painted words on the building.

"You have blood on your hands," she read, her words almost a whisper. "Now it's your turn to bleed."

Her stomach rolled. What the hell?

"But is it for you or me?"

Her eyes widened and swung to Zane at his question. He'd asked so quietly, she'd almost missed it. Like maybe it had only been meant for him. "Zane—"

"I'll call Jesse." Before she could say anything else, he tugged his phone from his pocket and dialed the sheriff's station.

As Zane spoke on the phone, Bonnie looked back at the writing.

They were about Dean…weren't they?

But is it for you or me?

She looked back at Zane, his words repeating in her head. Did he have blood on his hands?

CHAPTER 13

*B*onnie's fingers wrapped tightly around the wheel. So tightly that her knuckles were white.

She was nervous. She probably didn't need to be nervous. This was her family. But not just one or two members—her entire family. Well, except Aunt Pam. Bars weren't really her aunt's thing. But she was about to see everyone else. Her siblings. Her cousins. Everyone's partners. She'd seen so many of them already, she shouldn't be nervous.

But this was different. This was everyone all at once.

Maybe she was also a bit nervous because she had so much going on. Heck, a week ago, someone had spray-painted a threatening message on the back door of The Pit.

They'd left no evidence of who'd done it. It was a mystery. Just like the person who'd assaulted her outside her apartment.

Noah was angry. So was Jesse. They were trained soldiers, and right now, someone was slipping beneath their radar.

To make everything worse, the only time she'd seen Zane in the last week was during the shelter's self-defense lesson. And dammit, she missed him. She missed the feeling of safety he instilled in her. She missed his touch. His voice.

But he didn't want to be with her. He clearly had a secret, and that secret felt like an immoveable mountain between them.

She turned right, CJ's coming into view up ahead. Even from here, she could see how busy the bar was. Cars packed the road. People were coming and going from the entrance.

It felt strange coming to the bar as an adult. She'd lived her entire childhood in Amber Ridge. She's walked past CJ's so many times but never gone inside.

When she pulled into the parking lot, she didn't get straight out. She didn't even take off her seat belt. She just sat there, a million thoughts playing over in her head.

Sometimes she wondered what would have happened if she'd never left. Would the pain of her parents dying have eased faster? Would she and Indie have grown closer rather than apart? And would the White family eventually have stopped blaming her for their son's death?

Maybe some of that stuff might have happened. Or maybe she would have drowned. Maybe as a young eighteen-year-old who felt responsible for the deaths of those closest to her, the water would have lapped over her head, and she would have sunk to the bottom of the ocean.

A knock on the window made her jump and turn to see Noah on the other side of the glass.

Time was up.

She unclipped her seat belt, grabbed her cell and keys, and climbed out.

But it wasn't just Noah outside her car. A woman with blond hair stood beside him.

Noah tugged Bonnie into his arms. "Hey, Bon."

She dug her head into Noah's chest. It was strange how so much time could pass, and they could both change into completely different people, yet a hug from her big brother still felt exactly the same every time.

When she finally pulled back, Noah turned to the woman beside him. "Bonnie, this is Addie. Addie, Bonnie."

Addie's blue eyes scrunched as she smiled. "Bonnie, I've heard so much about you." She stepped forward and embraced her.

Bonnie hugged her back. "I've heard a lot about you too. It's good to finally meet you."

When Addie pulled away, she was still smiling. And Bonnie could see everything that had drawn her brother to the woman. There was a warmth in her. And when she smiled, it was with her entire face, including her eyes.

Noah studied Bonnie's temple. "The bruise okay?"

"There's barely a mark anymore." It was true. How much time had passed? Two weeks? Enough for the bruise to almost disappear.

"And nothing else has happened since The Pit?" Noah asked.

"You know I would have told you if it had."

He looked at her like he wasn't sure if that was true. "Come on."

They headed toward the entrance, and the closer they got to the door, the harder her heart beat against her ribs.

Why was she so nervous? This was her family.

But that wasn't all it was. It was the history that they shared and she'd missed. Her family and the new lives they'd created were a reminder of everything she'd left behind.

They stepped inside the bar and surprisingly, the place wasn't too full. Sure, it was busy. But compared to the bars in San Francisco, it was manageable.

Noah held Addie's hand, but with his other, he touched the small of Bonnie's back and led her toward two standing tables that had been pushed together.

She sucked in a sharp breath at the sight of everyone. Indie, Jesse, Becket, Clara. And all their partners.

Becket threw up his hands. "Bon-Bon! It's been so damn long. Missed your favorite cousin?" He grinned and pulled her against his broad chest, and it was exactly what she needed to break the ice.

When Becket pulled back, he introduced her to Sky. Then Bonnie went around and greeted everyone before settling beside Indie with a can of Sun Cruiser.

"How are you settling back into Amber Ridge?" Clara asked from the other side of Indie.

"It's different. There was no Tea House when I left, and I'd never stepped foot inside this bar, so I'm definitely feeling my age."

Aspen, Jesse's partner, sighed. "Thank God for Mrs. Gerald and her coffee. Half of us might have moved over to Bozeman otherwise."

"What?" Jesse turned to his partner, shock on his face. "You would have left me for good coffee?"

She shrugged. "I would have called from Bozeman."

Everyone laughed.

Over the next hour, Bonnie smiled more than she had in a long time. People talked and joked. She heard stories about the adventure park. About Sky's doggy daycare and Aspen's career as a writer.

It was good. No one mentioned her leaving thirteen years ago or her continued absence since. It just felt...normal.

"So," Clara said, when people broke off into smaller conversations. "Glad to be home?"

"I am. There have been a few...challenges." Challenges? Being assaulted and blatantly hated on felt like more than a *challenge*. "I should have come home sooner."

"Why didn't you?" Indie asked softly.

Bonnie looked at her sister, playing the question over in her head a few times before answering. "I guess I was scared. I'd hurt so many people by leaving. And the idea of coming back and facing it all just felt...hard. Too hard to even consider tackling. It was only when Noah reached out and talked to me like I wasn't the worst person in the world that I thought…maybe I could do it."

There was a moment of silence while both women just looked at her, empathy on their faces.

Then Indie touched her back. "I'm glad Noah reached out and made the move easier."

"Me too. And good timing with my little niece or nephew on the way."

Indie grinned and rubbed her belly. "*Perfect* timing. I'm gonna need someone to hand bubs off to when the smelly diaper changes are needed."

They all laughed.

As the two women started talking baby names, Bonnie sipped her Cruiser, her gaze moving around the bar.

That's when she spotted them…broad shoulders that almost made her choke on her drink.

Zane. Even from behind, she knew it was him. He sat at the bar beside a man whose shoulders looked just as wide.

She swallowed the liquid, memories of their last kiss flicking through her mind. Of his mouth on her body. The way he'd pinned her to the desk.

She flushed and dragged her gaze away, only for it to land smack dab on her brother beside her. And he was watching her closely.

"What?" she asked innocently.

"Are you dating him?"

"No. And by the way, he told me you paid him a visit."

"You slept at his apartment. I was just looking out for you."

Her brother didn't look guilty at all. "You don't need to do that. I am fully capable of looking after myself."

"I know you are. I just want you to be happy."

"I am." Kind of. "And we're not dating anyway, so it doesn't matter."

"Why not?"

"Why aren't we dating?" She swung her focus to Zane for a second time. "Timing, I guess."

It sounded as weak out loud as it did in her head. Timing was never perfect. Zane was the reason. Zane and his secret.

The second Noah turned away from her, her gaze returned to Zane.

What secrets are you hiding?

The question had flitted through her head so many times in the last week. It had to be big for him to continually pull away from her the way he was.

And if that message had been for him, it meant the secret was a dangerous one.

* * *

"There's no way it was him."

Zane's fingers tightened around his beer, the music in the bar loud in his ear. "Are you sure?"

Ethan leaned closer. "He hasn't left Montana State Prison."

"He could have paid someone to do it."

"It's more likely that it was about her. You said the town doesn't like her."

"Yeah, there are a lot of assholes around here who've been making her life hell." Understatement of the century.

"Why?"

"Her boyfriend got behind the wheel drunk. Crashed and killed himself thirteen years ago."

"How's that her fault?"

"It's not. But according to locals, she was supposed to drive him home that night."

"Small towns." Ethan's phone lit up, and he lifted it from the bar before cursing.

Zane frowned. "What's wrong?"

"They've officially ended the search for the woman who went missing in the mountains."

"That didn't take long."

"No. But it was longer than Ward wanted."

Ward was the town sheriff of Deep River. He'd been useless twenty years ago, when Zane was a teenager, and apparently nothing had changed. "You already searched with the team?"

Ethan scoffed. "Our search and rescue team is made up of retired locals who have no idea what they're doing. I'm the only one with a scrap of training." He scrubbed a hand over his face. "If my team was there, we'd be scouring those mountains until we found her."

Well, that was because there was a big damn difference between former Navy SEALs and retired librarians and shop-keepers.

"How's your team doing?" Zane asked.

"No one really likes their jobs since getting out. And we miss each other. It's hard to go from living in each other's pockets to never seeing each other. It feels like I'm missing my left arm."

"Shame you didn't all move to the same town."

Ethan laughed. "Yeah. Would have been nice."

Someone stepped beside him at the bar. He knew who it was before he turned his head. From her scent. The warmth of her body.

"Bonnie."

A small smile curved her lips. "Hey. I saw you across the bar and thought I'd come say hi."

How the hell hadn't he seen her? "Are you here alone?"

"I'm with my family." Her smile softened as she glanced over her shoulder. "It feels good saying that."

He followed her gaze to a couple of tables that were pushed together. Now that he was looking, it was hard to miss them.

Ethan reached out a hand across Zane. "I'm Ethan."

Bonnie smiled and shook his hand, forcing Zane to lean back. "Bonnie. Are you local?"

"No, I'm from Deep River, two hours south of here."

"That's quite a drive."

"Zane's a childhood friend. He's worth it…most of the time."

"I grew up in Deep River," Zane added. "Lived there with my grandmother for most of my life." Why the hell had he gone and added that? Because he wanted her to know more about him?

"I didn't know you were raised by your grandmother," she said softly.

"It's why he's such a gentleman," Ethan added with a laugh.

Zane shoved his shoulder.

Bonnie grinned. "What's it like in Deep River?"

Zane lifted a shoulder. "Similar to here, but also different."

"We're near Yellowstone National Park and known for the large river that cuts through our town," Ethan said.

"They also have a hard time moving into the twenty-first century," Zane added.

Ethan dipped his head. "It's true. Our town has one bar, which hasn't changed since the eighties. Still has its old-school TV and karaoke. We have a town square, where all the older women congregate and gossip. And a community center with bingo and dances."

"That sounds—" Someone bumped her hard from behind.

All three of them turned to see a woman standing behind her.

Bonnie frowned. "Maisie?"

The woman's eyes were glazed. "Bonnie! M'sorry, I didn't see you there. But I'm glad I do now!" Her words slurred, and she threw her arms around Bonnie, but she didn't return the hug.

"Are you drunk?" Bonnie asked

She held up two pinched fingers. "A teeny-tiny bit." She cocked her head. "You know, I've been meanin' to tell you it's really cool of you to not tell anyone what happened that night. People could've turned on *me* like they turned on you."

"You should go home." There wasn't a hint of a smile on Bonnie's face. "Sleep off the alcohol."

"Wait! I need to tell you something first. Something I've been hangin' on to for a long time." The woman's chest rose as she sucked in a deep breath. "It wasn't the first time I fucked him. We'd been having sex for a while. Two years kinda while. God, it's good to get that out."

Bonnie's lips thinned. "I have to go, Maisie."

She stepped around the woman, only for a guy to walk straight up to her—and tip the entire contents of his beer onto her face and shirt.

The fuck?

Bonnie gasped while the guy laughed. "Whoops."

Zane was in front of her in a second, grabbing the piece of shit by his shirt collar and shoving him against the bar. "What the hell is wrong with you?"

"Get off me!"

Zane lowered his face. "Apologize to her."

"The fuck I will! Dean was my friend."

Zane spun him to face the bar and pulled his arm behind his back so high his shoulder twisted.

"Ow! *Fuck.* Get off!"

Zane lowered his head to the man's ear. "You have three seconds to apologize before I dislocate your shoulder."

A beat of silence passed before he growled, "Fine. I'm sorry."

"Not loud enough." Zane pulled him up and turned him to face Bonnie. "Again."

Bonnie was soaking wet, but she now had people around her. Her family. Indie on one side, and another woman on her other.

Another loud pause. "I'm sorry," he repeated through gritted teeth.

"Do it again and you will be." Zane released the asshole.

The guy looked at Jesse. "You gonna do anything?"

Jesse turned to Bonnie. "You want to press charges for assault?"

The asshole's jaw dropped.

Bonnie shook her head. "Not this time. But if it happens again, I will."

The guy's jaw remained open like a fucking gaping fish maw.

The women shuffled her out, but rage still burned through Zane's blood. He wanted to follow the guy into the crowd. *Really* teach him a lesson.

And maybe he would have. But Ethan rose and set a hand on Zane's shoulder. "Leave it, brother."

He forced air through his lungs. For now, he would. But he was getting tired of this town's poor treatment of Bonnie. So damn tired that soon, walking away wouldn't be an option.

CHAPTER 14

Bonnie's fingers trembled as she stepped out of the shower and reached for her towel. She'd thought getting clean would help. That some time alone would wash away the embarrassment and frustration and maybe even a bit of the ache pulsing through her belly.

The shower hadn't helped. Being back in her own space hadn't helped. It shouldn't surprise her. Time didn't seem to help anything these days. It certainly hadn't helped people in this town see her as human. And it hadn't helped her get used to their treatment of her.

She wiped the condensation off the mirror to see eyes she barely recognized. Sad eyes with dark shadows beneath them.

Her gaze caught on the tiny bit of bruising remaining on her temple.

She'd known coming back here would be hard, but this? Being assaulted and threatened and so openly hated...it was so much worse than she'd ever thought. Mending things with her family should have been the hardest part. It wasn't. They'd welcomed her back. It was everyone else.

They hated her. This town hated her so much that they wanted her to *hurt*.

She closed her eyes, a tear slipping down her cheek.

She kept telling herself it would get better. Easier. But when? Or would it *never* stop? Would this town keep pushing and pushing until she finally tipped over the edge?

In the bedroom, she dropped the towel and pulled on panties and an oversized sweatshirt. The shaking in her fingers continued, and no matter how often she blinked them away, fresh tears continued to gather.

She'd made bad choices in her life. Dating Dean. Going out the night her parents told her not to. And then running from this town and staying away for so long. But leaving Dean at the party that night after finding him in bed with Maisie?

No. That wasn't on her. That was on him. *Them.* Yet Bonnie was forever paying the price.

A knock on her door had her head shooting up.

Who was that? Noah? Indie? Her sister and Colt had dropped her off at home an hour ago. Indie had wanted to stay, but Bonnie had refused to let her, needing some time alone.

Quickly, Bonnie swiped her face dry before moving to the door and looking through the peephole.

Zane. He wore the same clothes he'd had on at the bar, and the look on his face was something between anger and disgust and worry.

She squeezed her eyes closed, a part of her wanting to open the door. To fall into his arms and let him hold her together.

But he wasn't her boyfriend. He wasn't her anything.

"Now's not a good time, Zane." She leaned her head against the door, the chill from the wood seeping into her skin.

"I need you to open up, Bonnie. I need to see that you're okay."

The softness of his tone made new tears spring to her eyes. She told herself not to open it. To send him away.

But she didn't want to do that. Everything in her hurt, and all she wanted was one bit of comfort.

"I'm not," she whispered, when she opened the door. "I'm not okay."

More tears. She couldn't stop them from falling. Maybe she should be stronger than this. It was just a drink in her face.

But it wasn't. It was the accumulation of everything.

Zane cursed before stepping inside her apartment and closing the door. His strong arms slipped behind her knees and back, and he lifted her.

She didn't fight him. She didn't even gasp in surprise. She just leaned her head against his chest and breathed him in. Because for whatever reason, he took the edge off all the ugly emotions.

He lowered her to the couch, then crouched in front of her. "Where do you keep your alcohol?"

"Second cabinet to the right."

She watched as he found the whiskey in the kitchen and two shot glasses. When they were filled, he returned to her and handed her one. She didn't blink, just threw the shot back, letting the liquid burn the back of her throat and warm her belly.

It felt good. Or maybe that was Zane's closeness.

He sat beside her and tossed his own back before placing the empty glasses on the end table. "They're assholes. Everyone who has touched you. Hurt you. Done anything to make you feel like you're not exactly where you are meant to be are the scum of the earth. And everything they do says nothing about you and *everything* about them. Do you understand?"

"I know. But it doesn't make it hurt any less."

"No one can make you feel inferior without your consent."

One side of her mouth lifted. "Quoting Eleanor Roosevelt. Impressive."

"I thought the moment called for it."

Her small smile slipped. "When will it stop? It's relentless. And everyone is so brazen and obvious with their hate, like they're *proud* of it. Even tonight, when I'm standing beside you, with my family a few feet away, they're *still* not afraid to hurt me."

"I don't know when it will stop. But you're not alone, Bonnie. You have your family. And you have me."

She paused to study him. "Do I? Have you?"

Something flickered over his face. Something hot and dark that she wanted to touch. "Yeah. You do." He leaned forward and cupped her cheek, and God, she leaned into that touch like it was the only thing keeping her breathing. Then she closed her eyes and turned her head to press a kiss to his wrist.

There was a small intake of air from Zane, and when she looked back at him, he was staring at her like she silenced his inner turmoil as much as he silenced hers.

And maybe she did. Maybe his secret was as big and painful as hers, and she was the refuge he never saw coming.

There was this loud voice in her head telling her that she should maintain a bit of distance between them. He was keeping his problems to himself, with, as far as she could tell, no inclination to share.

But there was also this quieter voice, whispering to her that it was okay to take what she wanted. To be brave and embrace whatever goodness she could find.

She listened to the whisper.

Without taking her gaze off him, she climbed onto his lap. She didn't lower her head right away. Instead, she pressed her palms to his cheeks, feeling his warmth. The stubble of his day-old beard.

"I don't like needing other people," she whispered, her lips barely an inch from his mouth. "But I like needing you."

"You have me."

She lowered her head and kissed him. And the second her lips touched his, it was like the weight that had been sitting on her shoulders, pressing her to the floor for the past hour, suddenly lifted.

She swiped her mouth across his. His lips were soft. In a man who was all hard edges, this felt like the only soft part on him.

His hands slid up her bare thighs to grip her hips, and the second she parted her lips, he slipped his tongue inside.

And Jesus Christ, he tasted good. Like whiskey but also something so infinitely Zane.

She swirled her tongue around his, slipping her fingers into his hair and tugging at the strands. But it wasn't enough. She wanted to feel more of him. She wanted to know this man as well as she knew herself.

She reached for the hem of his shirt and tugged it up. Their mouths only separated for a second before they found each other again and his tongue dove straight inside.

The feel of his hands slipping up her body made her skin burn. She wanted more touches. She wanted this man to feel every inch of her. It was only when he pulled his mouth from hers that she felt the cool air over her breasts. With her shirt bunched up high, he took a naked nipple between his lips.

The cry that fell from her throat was loud and anguished. He ran his tongue over her hard bud, tormenting her. And it felt like he was everywhere.

Her chest heaved and she grabbed his shoulders like that could somehow steady her. He swirled her nipple with his tongue then sucked, making her lower belly ripple in pleasure.

Need. It was all she felt. It consumed her body and soul. Need for this man and his body and everything he had to give.

When he switched to her other breast it was the same torture. The same swirling of his tongue on her hard nipple. The same sucking that drove her wild.

She dug her fingers into his shoulders, sure she was close to breaking skin. Her hips started moving of their own volition. Grinding against him. Trying to dull the pulse between her thighs.

He went to stand up, but she shook her head. "No. Here."

His brows flickered.

"I want you," she whispered. "Now."

She pulled her sweatshirt over her head.

His eyes flared and darkened to a rich blue, like the color of the ocean when it was too deep to see to the bottom.

She reached for the button then the zipper of his jeans. And the second she pulled him out, her entire body shuddered.

He was big. And tonight, he was hers.

She wrapped her fingers around him, feeling the muscles strain in Zane's thighs. Then she slipped her palm up to his tip.

He growled, his fingers digging into her hips, his head touching her chest. "Bonnie…" Her name almost sounded like a warning.

When he looked up again, she took his lips, and he plunged inside her mouth, kissing her. Devouring her.

She continued to touch and explore until his growl cut through the room, and he rolled her back to the couch.

She grabbed him to steady herself, but he was moving again, kissing his way down her body before slipping her panties down her thighs. When he widened her legs, her breath hitched. Then he lowered his head and swiped her clit with his tongue.

She cried out, her back arching and legs trying to snap closed. He didn't let them. He kept her thighs open with his broad shoulders and tasted her again and again, until she couldn't breathe, his tongue swirling around her clit, making her ache and burn and throb for him.

"Zane…" She breathed his name. "Now. God, please, now!"

She tugged at his arms, and he kissed up her body, finding her nipple and sucking one last time before meeting her lips again.

She wrapped her thighs around his waist, her heart stopping at the feel of his tip at her entrance.

He tensed and cursed. "I'm not wearing anything."

"I'm on the pill." She nipped his bottom lip before tugging him a little bit deeper. "I'm safe."

Another deep growl, then he slid inside her, filling her. Making every pain, everything that was wrong with her world, slip away.

* * *

Fuck, Bonnie was tight. Her walls clenched his cock in an iron grip, and he was drowning in her. In the feel of her. In her scent. She took him somewhere he'd never fucking been before, and not a single part of him wanted to leave.

Her soft breath whispered against his lips before she nipped his bottom lip again. He kissed her. Once. Twice. Then slipped his tongue inside her mouth, tasting her as he began to move. To lift his hips and lower back inside her in an even, rhythmic motion.

Her sighs danced through the room like music. So damn pretty, he wanted to bottle them up.

He tried not to think about what this woman was starting to mean to him. Or the fact that he'd begun to crave her. Need her on an almost desperate level.

He reached for her breast and cupped her. Massaging. Finding her hard nipple and rolling it with his thumb.

Her moans were sweet and drove him crazy.

He sped up his thrusts, sinking deeper, driving hard.

Still, he needed more. He wanted to drink her in. To know and taste all of her.

He slid an arm around her waist and raised her up so he was sitting and she was on his lap once again. The position sank him deeper, making her groan against him.

"Ride me," he whispered, as he reached up and played with her nipples, rolling and gently pinching them.

Her breathing stuttered. Then she lifted her hips and lowered back onto him. Shit. Just the rise and fall of her breasts in his palms almost tipped him over the edge.

As she continued to move, he dropped his head, taking her nipple between his lips once again. They were so fucking pretty. And they were almost sweet, making him crave the taste of her.

At the same time, he lowered his hand to touch her clit with his fingers.

Her groan was deep and rumbled into him. He ran his thumb in a circle over her core, his teeth grazing her nipple.

Her breathing became choppy. "Oh God, Zane." She gripped his shoulders.

When he drew his head back, he took a moment to just watch her. The bounce of her full breasts. The *O* of her gorgeous lips.

Fuck, she was beautiful. Like something forbidden he shouldn't be allowed to touch.

He gripped her hips and started lifting her. Thrusting higher, deeper.

He was fucking close, but he needed her to get there first.

She lowered her head and kissed him again, slipping her tongue inside his mouth and curving it around his.

Then he felt it—her walls tightened around his cock, her breath halted, and she broke. Screamed as she fell over the edge, her head tipped back, body pulsing around his cock.

He didn't stop. He kept thrusting, prolonging her orgasm, losing himself in the fucking sight of her. Until he couldn't hold off any longer and fell along with her. Plunging so deep into everything that was Bonnie that he had no fucking idea who he was…just that he was hers.

When he finally stilled, he dropped his forehead to her chest and breathed. He felt her temple touch the top of his head, and they both remained exactly as they were for what felt like endless moments.

When he finally gathered the strength to look up, it was to see her looking dazed, almost in shock.

Yeah, he felt it too. The shifting of things between them. Like they hadn't realized it would be so powerful.

Carefully, he pulled out of her. But he didn't release her. He stood, holding her in his arms, her legs tight around him, and moved into the bathroom to turn on the shower. He carried her under the stream of water and was about to set her down when she lowered her head to his shoulder and closed her eyes.

And he just...couldn't. Couldn't put her down. Couldn't release her. So he held her. Let the softness that was Bonnie smooth over his hard edges.

When she finally lifted her head, her eyes were wide and solely focused on him.

He slipped a piece of hair from her cheek. "You okay?"

"I think you just ruined me." A soft smile curved her mouth before she covered his. But this kiss was soft. A graze of lips against lips before she lowered her head to his chest again, and he held her, wondering what the hell he'd just gotten himself into.

CHAPTER 15

*B*onnie's skin tingled where Zane's heavy arm lay over her belly. But it wasn't just her stomach that felt like it was on fire. It was her entire back, where his muscled abdomen pressed against her. The backs of her legs, which nestled with his.

She closed her eyes, a slow smile curving her lips. She'd had sex with Zane Merrick last night. Then the shower after…

Oh, Lordy Lord. It was all so good. There had been nothing slow or hesitant or awkward about anything they'd done—it had just felt right.

It was interesting that her family had wanted to stay with her last night, but all she'd wanted was to be alone. Then Zane had shown up, and suddenly, alone was the last thing she'd wanted.

She nibbled her bottom lip, nervous to know what he thought about the past few hours.

That could wait, right? If she slipped out quietly enough, she might just be able to sneak in a shower, maybe even some coffee before she faced him. That was, if she could pull off the great escape…which was questionable.

Carefully, she tried to ease out from under him. His fingers twitched.

She froze, nose wrinkling.

But he didn't wake.

Maybe legs first.

She shifted her legs forward so that her body lay in an unnatural *L* shape.

Legs were free. Good.

But how the heck did she get out from beneath his arm? An arm that seemed to weigh a ton.

Slowly, she lifted her arm, which also lifted his *arm*. And yep, it was ridiculously heavy.

Once there was a small space between his arm and her upper body, she rolled away, leading with her hips, before slowly setting his arm back on the bed.

And she was out. She'd done it. She'd actually rolled out from a freaking Army Ranger's embrace. Huh. Maybe she should join some stealthy military group.

With soft, measured steps, she crossed to the dresser. The scraping sound when she opened the drawer made her freeze. She glanced over her shoulder. Still asleep. Good.

She rummaged around her drawer for an oversized shirt and pulled it over her body. What she really needed was a full set of clothes to take into the bathroom, but she had zero faith in her ability to pull that off, creeping all around the room without waking him.

She lifted her phone from the dresser, and yep, she had half a dozen messages and two missed calls. And it was only eight in the morning.

Both missed calls were from her brother.

Quietly she moved to the kitchen and had just set the pod in the machine when she opened his texts first.

She froze.

Noah: Did you see the article in The Amber Ridge Chronicle?

Noah: Read this and call me.

There was a link.

She wasn't sure why, but her heart started to pound, like she was about to read something that would change everything.

She clicked the link.

Zane Merrick: Military Hero Turned UFC Fighter? Or Criminal Who Got Away with Murder?

Air caught in her lungs, making it hard to breathe.

And suddenly, she didn't want to read it. But she also did. She couldn't not.

Her gaze shifted over the article.

To many here in Amber Ridge, Zane Merrick is a hero turned small-town gym owner. But according to locals in Billings, he has a past. One he's tried to bury.

Less than a year ago, Zane Merrick was found standing over the dead body of twenty-two-year-old Amber Levado, the murder weapon in his grip.

Bonnie gasped, the phone almost dropping from her fingers as all the blood drained from her head.

No.

He had a secret, she knew that. But *this*?

Her gaze started to blur, but she forced herself to focus, words like "party" and "drugs" and "blood" standing out like they'd been bolded.

She skimmed down to the next part.

According to neighbors, while Merrick was out on bail, police went to his home to find a thirty-three-year-old man dead in his living room.

The phone dropped from her fingers.

Two? There were *two* bodies? One in his home, and the other at a party where he'd been holding the murder weapon?

"Bonnie?"

She screamed and reflexively grabbed a knife from the board, then swung around to him.

He only wore briefs. His brows were drawn together, his gaze going to the knife then back to her. "What's going on, Bonnie?"

"Who are you?" There was a shake in her voice, and she hated that. She wanted to be strong and brave and firm.

He gave her nothing. She couldn't read his features at all. "You know who I am."

"Did you kill two people in Billings?"

His frown deepened, and when he stepped toward her, her fingers tightened on the knife. Somehow, he looked bigger. His shoulders broader. Taller and more…dangerous.

"Bonnie, put down the weapon."

"Answer my question first. Did you kill two people in Billings?"

"No."

Air rushed from her chest. Because she believed him. He wouldn't—

"I killed one person. A man. In my home."

She flinched. "You…you killed someone? In your house?"

"It was self-defense. And if you put the knife down, I'll tell you everything." He took another step toward her.

She stepped around the island, her hip hitting the counter. "What about the woman? It said you were holding the murder weapon. Is that part true?"

"What said that?"

"Is it true, Zane?"

A muscle clicked in his jaw. "Yes."

Oh, Jesus.

"I'm not a cold-blooded murderer, Bonnie."

"Then why didn't you tell me any of this? Why keep it all a secret? We had *sex* last night, and now all of this stuff comes out? I feel like I don't know you at all!"

Pain cut across his features. "I should have told you. I was trying to protect you. I'm sorry."

Tears pressed at her eyes. She lowered the knife, but she didn't move toward him. "I need you to go."

"Bonnie—"

"I know there's more to the story, but right now I'm hurt and angry and I need some space."

For a second, he just stood there, and she was sure he wasn't going to leave. But then he gave a small nod. "Okay. I'll go. But before I do, I need you to know one thing."

"What?" Her voice was almost a whisper.

"I'm not the bad guy here. You don't have to be afraid of me."

Then he stepped out of the kitchen, and she heard him pull on his clothes before leaving her apartment.

Air rushed from her chest, and for a moment, she didn't move. All she could do was breathe.

Twenty minutes ago, she'd been on top of the world. Now? Now she had no idea who she'd slept with. Or who she'd fallen for.

* * *

THAT FUCKING REPORTER.

Zane pressed his foot to the floor of the car, far exceeding the speed limit but not giving a single fuck. All he could think about, all that consumed him, was finding the asshole and murdering him.

Bonnie knew. Only she didn't. Because the reporter hadn't printed the entire story. He'd only printed enough to make Zane look like a cold-blooded murderer. And he was going to pay for that.

It wasn't just Bonnie who knew, though. The whole of Amber Ridge would have read the article. And if they hadn't, someone would tell them. Nothing stayed secret in small towns for long.

He'd come here to get away from the stories and the gossip and the stares. He'd come here for a scrap of anonymity. The reporter had stolen that from him.

He pulled up outside the apartment block and climbed from the car. Just as he reached the building, an older woman stepped outside. Zane took the opportunity and stepped in before the door closed behind her.

He knew exactly what floor the jerk was on. And unlike last time, he wasn't waiting around for him to come outside.

When he reached the second floor, he stormed down the hall and was just approaching the apartment when the door opened and Abe stepped out, suitcase in hand.

Abe met his gaze. The weasel gasped before rushing back into the apartment. But it was too late. Zane grabbed him before he could close the door, pushing him inside and slamming the door closed after them.

Then he shoved the guy into the wall. "I told you to drop the story."

Real fear widened Abe's eyes. "I-I did! Or I tried to. But my boss had a copy and printed it anyway. It was a slow news week."

Zane pulled him off the wall and thumped him against it again. "I should *kill* you for what you've done."

Abe lifted his arms and tried for a nervous laugh. "Come on, I was just doing my job."

"The entire town thinks I'm a murderer!"

"Well…I mean…aren't you?"

Zane threw him to the floor and took one step before the door flew open and someone grabbed his arms. "Zane. Stop."

Ethan. Of course his friend had learned the news and come.

"I'm going to tear him apart with my bare hands," Zane growled.

Suddenly, Ethan was in front of him. "No. You touch him, and you'll just make it worse."

"So what? He just gets away with it?"

"Hell no." Ethan turned to the reporter. "You're going to print a retraction. Write the *real* story."

The guy frowned. "I don't know if my boss—"

"You figure it out." Ethan said the words slowly, like the idiot wouldn't understand otherwise.

Abe's mouth opened and closed. "And if I don't?"

Ethan took a half step closer. "You don't want to know."

Zane's jaw clenched. He didn't want to leave. The rage was crawling through his gut like poison, and he needed to get it out. But Ethan was right. This wouldn't achieve anything. And it sure as hell wouldn't make anything better.

"You print the retraction, and you do it fast." They were Zane's last words before he stepped back out of the apartment and stormed down the stairs.

When they got outside, Ethan grabbed his arm again. "Zane, wait. Are you okay?"

"How did you know?" Zane asked, turning.

"The second you told me about the guy, I signed up for the *Chronicle*. Drove straight up this morning."

Fuck, Ethan was a good friend.

Zane ran his fingers through his hair. He wanted to hit something. To drown out the frustration with some kind of physical pain.

Ethan stepped closer. "Hey. The town will care for a second, the retraction will be printed, and everyone will move on to the next small-town gossip."

"I don't care about the damn town."

"Then what—"

"Bonnie. You should have seen the way she looked at me this morning. Like I was a murderer. Like I was a stranger. A *mistake*."

Mistake…the word tasted like acid on his tongue.

Ethan's brows flickered. "You slept with her?"

"Yeah, I slept with her. I slept with her without telling her about anything I'd been through. And now I look like the asshole."

There was a small pause. "Okay. So she read the article. Had an immediate reaction. That's all it was—a reaction. She'll come around."

Zane shook his head. "I should have told her. She told me her shit. I should have told her mine. I didn't. I fucked up." And now he was paying the price. "I need to go."

"Zane—"

"Thanks for driving down, Ethan." He dropped into his car and slammed the door.

He almost expected to find a group of people at his gym. Maybe some more spray paint on the building. There was none of that. It was quiet.

He stepped inside and moved straight to a bag.

He needed to hit something like he needed to breathe. It took him seconds to drop his bag, pull off his shirt and shoes, and wrap his hands. Then he started hitting leather. Pounding the shit out of it like it was the only fucking thing allowing him to breathe.

The reporter, Monty…it was like a fucking shitstorm he couldn't escape.

He'd been at the bag for a good thirty minutes when the door opened. He turned to see Stetson step into the gym, phone in hand.

Stetson frowned at him. "Hey. I, uh, read the article."

"And?"

"Is it true?"

"Part of it."

Stetson's frown deepened, and for a moment he seemed to think about it. Finally, he nodded. "Okay. I'm gonna put my bag in the changing room."

"Stet."

He turned back to him. "Yeah, boss?"

"You're okay?"

"Yeah." That was it. That was all he said.

When Stetson left, Zane turned back to the bag. But before

throwing another hit, he pulled out his phone. He should give her time. He knew he should.

He couldn't.

Zane: Please. Just give me a chance to explain.

He dropped his phone. The ball was in her court now.

Bonnie frowned at the text message from Zane. It was the third in the last three days. And she hadn't responded to any of them.

She swallowed as she glanced up at the exterior of her aunt Pam's house.

It wasn't that she thought Zane was a cold-blooded murderer. She didn't. Sure, when she'd first read the article, her gut reaction had been shock and fear. But when that wore off, she'd remembered that this was Zane. The man who'd defended her time and again. Who'd let her climb into his bed when she was scared. Who'd held her when she hadn't been able to sleep.

He wasn't a murderer.

But he'd also omitted a huge part of his life from her after she'd shared so much of hers. And maybe it all hurt more because she'd slept with him. Not just slept with him...started falling in love with him.

A knock on the car window had her jumping. She glanced outside to see Becket, Sky and...was that a dog in Becket's arms?

First of all, her cousin hated dogs. That had been a well-known fact since they were kids. Secondly, was it even a dog? It looked like a big rat.

She climbed out. "Um, who's that?"

Becket smiled at the animal he held. "This is Bella."

Bella? Was that name really fitting? "Is she a—"

"Chinese Crested," Sky said affectionately, rubbing the dog's head. "We adopted her."

Her cousin had adopted a dog. Interesting.

She smiled as she locked her car and walked up to the door. "So, Becket's a dog dad now?"

"It's a long story," Sky laughed. "But yes. He loves her as much as he loves me."

"Most of the time," Becket muttered.

He opened the door, and the second Bonnie stepped inside the house, her breath caught and she felt like she was thrown back in time.

Everything looked the same. The gray couch with the pink throw cushions. The wooden coffee table with the crack from when Becket had pushed Jesse and he fell onto the thing, when he was twelve. Even the old family photo of everyone together still hung on the wall.

And suddenly, she realized exactly why she'd avoided this for so long. Because the last time she'd stepped foot inside this house had been for her parents' wake.

She swallowed hard, trying to blink back the tears.

Becket's hand on her arm made her jump.

"Hey." His gaze was gentle as he looked at her. "You okay?"

"Yeah." She blinked madly. She was not going to cry. "I just… it's been a while."

He nodded, the usual humor in his eyes absent. "Come on. Let's get out there. I think we're the last to arrive."

Sky offered an empathetic smile before they stepped out the back. And yep, they were the last ones. The entire family was scattered around the backyard. Some waved. Some smiled. But it was Pam who stopped what she was doing by a table and crossed over to them.

Emotion welled in Bonnie's chest for the second time.

Becket squeezed her arm before taking Sky's hand and heading toward the closest group.

"Oh, Bonnie." Pam pulled her into the biggest, warmest hug she'd felt in a long time. "You've been so deeply missed, my darling."

Bonnie wrapped her arms around her aunt. Even her smell was familiar, thrusting her right back to her childhood. She dug her head into her aunt's shoulder, and neither of them moved for long seconds.

When they finally separated, a tear must have fallen, because Pam wiped it away with her thumb. "You realize now that you're home, you're not allowed to leave again, right? None of us will allow it."

"You're not angry at me for leaving?" Not just for leaving. For everything that had come before that. For going out the night her parents had died. For being the reason they'd been on the road.

Pam slipped a piece of hair behind her ear. "Honey, there is enough anger in this world without me adding to it. I'm just glad you're back."

She'd been so worried for so long about returning to her family. Worried about the anger and resentment they'd hold toward her. Her aunt was the last family member she'd still avoided seeing since coming home. And knowing that there was nothing but love from the woman felt like a gray cloud finally lifting. One that had sat over her head for thirteen years.

"Thank you."

Pam's lips stretched into a smile. "Come on. You've got a lot to catch me up on."

Over the next hour, Bonnie laughed and smiled so much that her cheeks hurt. There was always a drink in her hand, and everyone made her feel like she'd never left. Like she'd missed nothing and was still a part of the fold.

After she went back into the house to use the bathroom, she was just passing the library when she stopped. The door was ajar, and the voices hushed, but she could still make out the words.

"I'm just worried about her."

Noah?

"Why?" Jesse asked.

"We didn't know Zane had this past. They're getting into a relationship, and her track record for making good decisions isn't great."

Bonnie flinched like she'd been slapped. And she must have gasped, because the voices suddenly stopped, then the door flew open.

Noah cursed. "Bonnie—"

"I'm going back outside."

She got just a few steps away before Noah grabbed her arm. "It's not how it sounded."

"There wasn't much up for interpretation, Noah."

He cringed. "I'm sorry. With all this stuff getting out about Zane, I'm just worried about you."

And you don't trust me. The words were a whisper in her head.

"It's fine." It wasn't. "I'm going to get back out there."

She moved toward the back, an impossibly heavy weight on her chest. But Noah's words were fair, because the Bonnie he knew, the eighteen-year-old who'd left Amber Ridge, *had* made bad decisions.

So it wasn't really his fault that he still saw her like that, was it?

Maybe a part of her had been hoping that she'd proven herself to be someone else by now. Someone with more maturity. Who made better choices.

Obviously not.

When she stepped outside again, she felt different. Her smile felt a bit more forced and an old, familiar heaviness returned to her chest.

Because even though everyone was welcoming her, there was now a voice inside her head questioning whether it was all for show. Was there something else hidden behind their expressions? A perennial distrust? A questioning of her character because of past mistakes?

* * *

ZANE KICKED the bag hard and watched it fly back. Every muscle in his body ached. It was late. So late that it was dark outside and the gym was empty, bar him.

Good. He didn't feel like dealing with people right now.

Three days. Three entire fucking days of no Bonnie, and it was killing him. He hadn't heard her voice. He didn't know if she was safe.

All because of the past that followed him, stalked him, wouldn't leave him the hell alone.

Punch, punch, left hook.

Business had also been down. Locals were treating him differently. Crossing the road so they didn't share a sidewalk with him. Looking away so they didn't make eye contact.

Cross punch, kick.

It was the reason he'd left Billings. And it was happening again. Only this time, he only cared about the loss of Bonnie.

He'd texted her every day. And not a single response.

A part of him wanted to be angry that she wouldn't hear him out. But he couldn't be. He was the one who'd fucked up. He should have told her everything before sleeping with her. He should have shared his story before their relationship had gotten to that point.

Punch, punch, hook.

The click of the door opening sounded. He turned, chest heaving.

Zane frowned. "What are you doing here, Noah?"

Noah dropped a bag against the wall and tugged his sweatshirt over his head. "Not long ago, you told me you'd spar with me anytime."

"You want a round in the ring?"

"You don't?"

Fuck yes, he did. "Straps or gloves?"

Noah's gaze lowered to Zane's hands. "Straps."

Zane pulled some from the equipment box and threw them Noah's way. He caught them and toed off his shoes before stepping into the octagonal ring and strapping his hands.

"You want a warm-up?" Zane asked, as he joined Noah.

"I'm warm."

Fine with Zane. He lifted his hands to his face, protecting his chin and temples, and bent his knees.

The second Noah finished with his straps, he threw the first punch. Zane dodged it easily.

Noah's jaw clenched. "I love my sister."

Another punch from Noah. Another dodge from Zane.

"And I thought I trusted her," he continued as they bounced around each other. "But then that article about you came out and, fuck, I just…I realized that maybe I don't. Maybe I'm scared that shitty things are going to happen to her again, and she'll run a second time."

Shitty things being him.

Noah threw a punch, then a hook.

Zane avoided both.

"Thirteen years she was gone," Noah said quietly. "She wouldn't even take our calls. I don't want that happening again."

"Unless she's said it's a possibility, maybe you should trust that she's here to stay," Zane replied.

"I should."

This time, Noah's punch swiped the side of Zane's chin. It was more of a graze, and Zane countered with his first hit—a hook that landed in Noah's side.

He barely reacted, just bounced back.

"I don't know if she's mentioned it, but she's not talking to me," Zane growled, a bite of frustration behind each word. "So I don't think you have anything to worry about right now."

"Do you know how many times she looked at her phone today? So many I lost count." Noah jabbed, then side-kicked.

Both hit their marks. But Zane remained on his feet, absorbing the blows.

"It was because of you," Noah continued. "She was checking for a text or a call from *you*."

"And that's a bad thing?"

"It is if you aren't the person I thought you were." Another missed hit from Noah. "Who are you, Zane?"

"I'm a guy who trusted the wrong person. I trusted family. But not everyone has family like yours." Zane threw an uppercut, but Noah dodged. "I didn't see what I should have, and it almost cost me my life."

Noah's brows drew together, and he studied Zane like he was trying to figure out if he was telling the truth.

"I'll also tell you who I'm not," Zane continued. "I'm not a guy who would hurt her. I'm not a guy who'd put her in danger, from me or anyone else. And if the worst-case scenario happened, and either she or I needed to leave...I'd go." But fuck, he hoped it didn't come to that.

"So she can trust you?" Noah asked.

"You both can."

Another flicker of Noah's brows before he quickly shuffled forward and threw a jab and an uppercut.

The two of them continued in the ring for a while. And fuck, it felt good

This is why he'd gotten into the UFC. Not for money or notoriety. Because being in the ring made the noise in his head quiet. And now, just for a moment, he forgot about the ache in his chest, the one that had been there since leaving Bonnie's apartment.

When they finally stopped, both their chests heaved. Noah was good in the ring. Especially for a soldier who hadn't done the specific training Zane had.

They both began to unstrap their hands. "Did I pass?" Zane asked, knowing this entire thing had been a test.

Noah's gaze shot up. "Maybe." He tossed the wraps to Zane. "But you hurt her, and I'll kill you myself."

"I hurt her, and I hope you do."

CHAPTER 17

$\mathcal{B}$onnie pulled into her apartment complex. But she didn't get straight out of the car. She leaned her head back and closed her eyes, blowing out a long breath.

What a long, horrible day. She hadn't been able to take the women to the self-defense session at The Pit because Shelley had dumped three other time-sensitive jobs on her. Then she'd blasted Bonnie for doing two of those jobs incorrectly—or more accurately, not how Shelley would have done them.

Two new women had also arrived at the shelter, and both had come from awful circumstances. Bonnie had almost cried when she'd read their files.

And now, she had a blazing headache.

With a long sigh, she undid her seat belt and climbed out of the car, immediately pulling her cell phone from her pocket and ordering a pizza.

Tonight was definitely a pizza kind of night. The question was, had Burt's Pizza improved over the last thirteen years? Because back in high school, the stuff was terrible. Barely edible kind of terrible.

She ordered a ham and pineapple with extra cheese. She

wasn't sure how much she'd eat, because of her headache, but she had to eat something before she died in her bed.

She hung up and crossed the remaining distance to her apartment building, her hand close to the pepper spray in her bag the entire time. Since the attack, she hadn't been able to step into the building without feeling an uncomfortable tightness in her chest. Without her heart beating at a million miles a minute.

The one good thing about this last week was that no one had threatened her. No one had so much as looked at her the wrong way.

Maybe everything going on with Zane had taken the attention off her. Not exactly a good thing though.

Inside, she climbed the stairs two at a time. When she reached her floor, she'd just stepped into the hall when she stopped. Her throat dried.

Zane.

He sat in front of her apartment door, head tilted back against the wall, eyes closed.

For a moment she didn't move. Just stood there, a million questions in her head. The top one—how long had he been there?

His eyes opened and he turned his head, his gaze meeting hers. She felt his gaze like a gut punch. *That's* what he did to her.

Slowly, he rose, and the second he was upright, he took up all the space in the hallway.

She forced herself to move, one foot in front of the other.

"Hey, Bon. I missed you today."

She stopped in front of him, really having to work hard to get words out. "I had to stay back at work. I wasn't avoiding you."

One side of his mouth lifted like he didn't quite believe her. If she were him, she probably wouldn't believe her either.

"What are you doing here?" Even though she asked, she knew.

He shoved his hands into his pockets, eyes gentle. "I've tried to give you space. But I need to talk to you. I need you to hear my side of the story."

She swallowed hard, but it did nothing to wet her dry throat.

She wanted to hear his side too. But her day had been so long and terrible and her head was pounding.

"Can you give me an hour to shower and change and try to feel human? Then I'll text you if I'm up to it."

His brows flickered, as if he didn't want to let her go without a guarantee she'd go to him. "Okay. Shower. Rest. If you're not up to it tonight, we can try another night. But if you need me, I'm just down the hall." Then he kissed her forehead. And she couldn't stop herself. She leaned into that kiss. Closed her eyes and let his warmth weave itself around her.

God, there was something about this man when he got close to her…he just became the center of everything.

When he lifted his head, it was too soon.

But she forced herself to turn. To unlock her door and step inside before closing it after her. When the lock clicked, she touched her head to the wood.

She missed him. Jesus, she missed him so much.

Slowly, she slipped off her shoes and moved into her bedroom. When she got into the shower, she wanted to just stay there and wash the terrible day away.

Shelley's treatment of her was almost starting to feel personal. The way she overloaded Bonnie with work that wasn't hers. Reprimanded her for things that weren't her fault. Today, she'd scolded Bonnie for not telling her about next week's activities even though Bonnie *had* told her about them in an email. And when Shelley had asked why Bonnie hadn't responded to her eleven p.m. text last night, and she'd told her it was because she was sleeping, Shelley had looked at her like that was crazy.

It wasn't. Shelley's expectations were. And every day, Bonnie stood up for herself a little more.

Was it because of Dean? Shelley hadn't grown up here, but maybe she'd heard whispers around town.

Who the heck knew?

When she stepped out of the shower, she wanted to throw on her oversized shirt and slide into bed, but she also wanted to see Zane. Maybe she'd down an aspirin, eat a slice of pizza, and go to his apartment.

After pulling on some yoga pants and a sweatshirt, she moved to the kitchen, where she swallowed the aspirin with some water. As she waited for her pizza, she lifted her phone, hesitating before typing out the text.

She should ask him in person. But she was impatient and texting took less courage.

Bonnie: Why didn't you tell me?

The second she hit send, she scrunched her eyes. They popped right back open when the text came through.

Zane: Because my past is heavy and complicated, and I didn't want to pile that on you. You have enough going on. It was a mistake. I should have realized you can handle it.

She was about to respond when a knock came at the door. She frowned. Was that the pizza? She'd expected to collect it downstairs. Had someone let them in?

She crossed to the door and looked through the peephole, but no one was there.

Strange.

She unlocked the door and tugged it open. A pizza sat in the hall.

Another frown. Had she even given her apartment number? She didn't think so.

Her hands turned clammy, heart racing just a bit faster.

With shaking fingers, she lifted the box and closed the door. She set it on her dining room table.

But the second it was down, she noticed red on her palms.

What the hell?

She studied her hand and fingertips…it was everywhere.

Her chest started to heave as she looked back at the box, now noticing red liquid on the sides. It was paint, right? It had to be paint.

A voice in her head told her not to open the box. Hell, it screamed it.

But she had to. She had to know what was inside.

Slowly, she lifted the lid.

Nausea hit her so hard, she leaned over and was almost sick.

She stumbled back before looking at the box again. Still there. She hadn't made it up.

There was a dead mouse on top of the pizza. Only it wasn't the entire mouse...the creature was missing its head, and there was blood everywhere.

She couldn't breathe. Out. She needed to get out!

Her knees shook as she stumbled toward the door and out into the hall, only stopping when she reached his door.

She needed Zane.

* * *

"He's being transferred."

Zane stopped in his kitchen, fingers tightening around his cell. "What do you mean, Monty's being transferred. Why?"

"Overcrowding." There was a pause from Ethan. "They're sending him and a handful of other prisoners to Dawson County Corrections. The transfer's happening in a month."

He shouldn't care. This should be a non-fucking issue. But that transfer would move him closer to Amber Ridge. And Zane didn't want that scumbag anywhere near him or his town. "Can you get all the details? Time. Names of other prisoners. Even the guards."

"I'll see what I can find."

He poured himself a shot of scotch, hoping like hell he was worrying about nothing.

"Abernathy Koch's correction article is also supposed to come out in a few days," Ethan added.

Zane tipped back the scotch, the liquid burning his throat. "The damage is already done."

"The gym doing okay?"

"Business has been picking up these last few days. Being the only gym in Amber Ridge doesn't leave locals a lot of options."

"I'm glad not everyone's bought into the bullshit."

"How's Deep River? Any new information on the missing person?"

Ethan sighed. "None. As far as Ward's concerned, she's a missing person who won't be found."

"Shit, he's annoying."

"That's putting it lightly."

"Anything I can do to help?"

"No. My trips to Amber Ridge are helping by giving me a much-needed break from the guy. He seems to be everywhere. I can't walk down the street without seeing him."

"I'm always happy to have you here."

"Thanks. I, uh…also went on a date."

Zane's lips twitched. "A good date?"

"Pretty good."

Zane frowned. That wasn't convincing. "You gonna go on another?"

"I haven't decided. I should. She's nice."

Nice? That one word told Zane everything. It wasn't going anywhere. "You should give her a chance." Ethan rarely dated.

"I should." He sighed. "I should go."

"Thanks for keeping an eye on everything."

"I'm on your side, always."

Zane hung up and scrubbed a hand over his mouth. Monty was being transferred. It would be fine. Prisoners were transferred all the time. This was just a small change.

He'd just put the glass in the sink when banging sounded on the door.

Was that Bonnie? He shot a glance at the time. It had only been half an hour.

He moved to the door and looked through the peephole. A string of curses fell from his mouth at the fear on her face. He yanked it open. "What's wrong?"

Her chest heaved and her face was so pale there was barely a scrap of color in it. She glanced down the hall to her apartment, then back to him. "There was…I…I can't…"

"Hey." He stepped into the hall and placed a hand on the small of her back. "It's okay. Come inside."

She moved inside his apartment, but before following, he glanced down the hall.

Empty.

Once the door was locked, he turned back to her. "Bonnie, what—" He stopped, eyes narrowing on the red staining her hands. The fuck? "Are you hurt?" He gripped her wrists and lifted her hands, searching for injuries.

She shook her head, fingers shaking. "No. It's…it's not my blood."

"Whose is it?"

"I ordered a pizza from Burt's and it was left at my door, but there was…"

"You're safe, Bon. Deep breaths."

Her chest rose and fell before she looked at him again. "There was a decapitated mouse in the box. And there was blood everywhere."

The son of a bitch. Zane was going to tear the fucker apart with his bare hands. But first, he needed to take care of Bonnie.

Gently, he gripped her hips and led her down the hall. In the bathroom, he stood behind her at the basin and turned on the water, making it warm. Then, gently, he guided her hands under the stream.

As the water turned crimson, he felt that thing again. Not anger. This was darker. This clawed at his insides, almost making him shake with the need to hurt the person who'd hurt Bonnie.

With soap on his fingers, he ran his hands over her palms, making sure every inch of her skin was clean.

Her entire body shook, and it sharpened every instinct in him with this unbearable need to fix this. Protect her. Guard her.

Once the water ran clear, he grabbed a towel and dried her hands before leading her into his bedroom. She sat at the foot of the bed while he grabbed one of his sweatshirts. There was a smear of blood on hers, and he couldn't fucking look at it without feeling like he was going to explode.

He crouched in front of her. "Lift for me, honey."

She lifted her arms. He tugged the sweatshirt over her head, barely looking at the soft skin pressing at her lacy bra. This wasn't about sex. All he cared about was making sure Bonnie was okay.

Once his sweatshirt was over her head, he gripped her thighs. "I'm going to your apartment."

Her eyes flared. "You don't want to see it."

"I've seen worse." He slipped a piece of hair behind her ear. "Will you be all right while I'm gone?"

"Yeah. I might, um, lie down if that's okay. I've got the worst headache."

He cupped her cheek, studying her eyes, wishing there was more color to her skin. "I'll get you some Tylenol."

"I've already taken aspirin. But I think the two are okay to take together."

"As a one-off, it's actually a more effective painkiller combination."

He pulled back the covers at the head of the bed before going into the kitchen and grabbing a glass of water and two pills. When he returned, Bonnie was still exactly where he'd left her.

She took the pills and water.

"Do you want me to call your brother or sister?" he asked.

She shook her head before he'd finished speaking. "I'm tired. I'll call them tomorrow."

"Okay. I'm going to call Jesse though. He needs to know what happened."

Her brow creased. "I'm not up to talking to him tonight."

"I know."

She nibbled her bottom lip before looking at him again. "Thank you."

"I'm so fucking angry for you. But you coming to me…that's the only part I'm grateful for."

She leaned forward, her temple touching his chest.

For a moment, he didn't move. He couldn't. She trusted him to protect her. To look after her. To hold her. And fuck, that was everything.

It wasn't until she sat back that he forced himself up and out of the room.

When he reached the hall, he locked his apartment door before crossing to hers. The door was still open, and he saw the mess the second he stepped inside. It sat on the dining table, lid open, a headless mouse on top of the pizza.

Dead. This person who was messing with her was going to breathe his last damn breath pretty fucking soon.

It took every ounce of self-restraint he possessed to remain inside the apartment. To turn around and search the place for Bonnie's cell. It was on the dresser in her room. He lifted it and searched for the number he was looking for.

Jesse answered immediately. "Bonnie, is everything okay?"

"This is Zane Merrick."

There was a small pause. "Why are you calling from Bonnie's cell?"

"Someone decapitated a mouse and left it on top of a pizza by her front door."

Jesse cursed viciously. "I'll be there in ten."

"Bonnie isn't up to talking to anyone tonight. But I'll send you my number and a photo of the pizza box. Text me when you arrive and I'll let you into her apartment."

"Is she okay?"

"No. Not even a little bit."

Jesse's voice was harder now. "I'll be there soon."

Zane took Bonnie's phone and keys with him before heading back to his apartment. He thought she might still be sitting where he'd left her. She wasn't. She was lying in the bed, eyes closed, chest rising and falling rhythmically.

Asleep.

He tugged the sheet and comforter higher, making a vow that he would find the asshole messing with her, and he'd make this stop. All of it.

CHAPTER 18

*onnie checked her watch, the music bouncing off the walls
and blasting in her ears.*

*Ten? How was it only ten? She felt like she'd been at this party for
hours.*

A guy bumped into her, his beer spilling on her shirt.

He muttered a sorry before stumbling away.

That was it. She was done.

*She weaved through the throng of people. Everyone from her grade
danced and drank and laughed. It was wild that she could be
surrounded by a roomful of people, people she'd gone through her entire
school life with, and still feel completely alone. Maybe more alone than
if she was actually by herself.*

*Where was Dean? She wanted to go, and if he wanted a lift home, he
needed to go too.*

*She slipped through the crowd, searching. Her phone vibrated with a
text. She pulled it out.*

Mom: What time will you be home?

*She pushed her cell back into her pocket. She loved her parents, but
they didn't understand her. No one in her family did. They were too
different. Happy and driven, and her siblings knew exactly what they*

were doing with their lives. While she didn't even know what she was doing in the next couple weeks.

She had no drive to do...anything. Sometimes she wondered if something was wrong with her.

But when she said any of that to her parents, they told her she was perfect. That she'd figure things out. That she just needed to throw herself into stuff.

She bumped into a big body.

Theodore turned, eyes glazed as a lazy smile curved his lips. "Bonnie...baby! Wanna dance?"

He slipped an arm around her waist and started to sway.

She shoved at his chest. "Stop. I'm looking for Dean."

The frown on his face was almost comical. "You still want Dean when you have a masterpiece like me right in front of you?"

Another shove at his chest. "Do you know where he is?"

He huffed and stepped back. "Weren't you two fighting earlier?"

They always fought. Today, it was about her possibly going to college in Santa Fe. Yesterday, it was about not wanting to have sex. Fighting seemed to be all they were good at lately. "Do you know where he is or not?"

His gaze flicked to the stairs, then back to her. "No. I haven't seen him."

She frowned. "Why did you look to the stairs?"

"Uh...because I like stairs."

Her frown deepened—and she turned toward the stairs.

"Bonnie...give him time to cool off."

She ignored Theodore. Dean's best friend was a tool ninety percent of the time.

She jogged up the steps and knocked on the bathroom door. When no one answered, she cracked it open.

Empty.

She opened the next door—a spare bedroom. Again, it was empty.

Maybe no one was up here. She knocked and opened the third door, not waiting for a response.

Curses sounded, and the rustle of sheets. Then she saw them.

Her jaw dropped—because there, in the bed, were Dean and Maisie.

Maisie tugged the sheet over her body while Dean gaped, mouth so far open it was almost comical. "Bonnie."

Interesting. She didn't feel upset or disappointed. She didn't even want to cry.

Anger, though? Yeah, she definitely felt that.

Dean grabbed his briefs and pulled them on before stepping toward her. "I can explain."

"Don't. I'm leaving. Maisie, I'm sure you can give him a ride home." She closed the door and jogged down the stairs. Every step made the rage inside her ripple and burn.

Her boyfriend and her best friend.

Her freaking boyfriend and best damn friend!

She'd trusted them. Both of them. There were so few people in the world she trusted, but them? She'd told them everything. About her lack of ambition. Her feelings of not fitting into her family.

Dean called to her from the top of the stairs, but she ignored him and stormed outside. A few people stood on the grass. One drinking, a couple smoking, another person throwing up in the bushes.

All she wanted was to get away. To go where, she wasn't sure.

She was halfway across the lawn when rough fingers wrapped around her arm and swung her around. "Bonnie. Stop! I didn't mean to."

Her brows shot up. "Really? You didn't mean to put your dick in my best friend? What did you mean to do?"

"Jesus, keep your voice down!"

"Why? Because you don't want everyone knowing you're a cheating piece of shit?"

Maisie stepped outside, cell to her ear.

Dean tugged Bonnie closer and growled between gritted teeth, "I said, keep your damn voice down."

"No." She shoved his chest hard and walked away.

"You're a fucking mouse, you know that? Weak. Passive. Worthless. What did you expect me to do? Put up with your shit forever?"

She kept walking, angry tears falling down her cheeks.

"Bonnie."

Her arm was grabbed again, this time softer.

"Bonnie. Wake up."

Her eyes swung open and she shot up, chest heaving.

Darkness. It surrounded her.

She looked down at the hand on her arm, then at the shirtless man beside her. "Zane."

Zane's eyes flashed open. Not at any sound. At the movement beside him. The dipping of the mattress. The rustle of the sheets.

He turned his head to see Bonnie's head moving, brows tugged together in a deep frown.

He sat up. "Bonnie."

She continued to throw her head from side to side.

He grabbed her arm gently but firmly. "Bonnie, wake up."

Her eyes flashed open and she shot up in bed. Her breathing was ragged, and her gaze darted around the dark room before they zeroed in on his hand. When she looked at him, she frowned. "Zane."

"Hey, Bon." He kept his voice soft. "Everything okay?"

Her gaze shifted between his eyes. "He called me a mouse."

"Who?"

"Dean. When we fought, that last night, he called me a mouse. He told me I was weak and passive and worthless." A shudder ran down her spine. "It was the last thing he ever said to me."

The pieces clicked together. The headless mouse delivered to her doorstep hadn't just been to scare her...it was a threat. *She was the mouse.*

Motherfucker.

"Who knows?" Zane asked quietly.

She blinked. "What?"

"Who knows that he called you that?"

"Well…Maisie, because she was outside. And there were a handful of other people too. But I also told the police, so it's probably in a police report, which I'm sure his parents got a copy of."

"We'll tell Jesse in the morning."

She glanced up at him. "Did he go to my apartment?"

"Yeah. He wanted to see you, but I told him you were sleeping. He's going to drop by in the morning."

"I bet he told Noah."

He absolutely told Noah. Exactly why Zane had gotten a text from her brother, asking if she was okay. That's all it had said. He'd replied yes, expecting follow-up questions. They hadn't come.

"Tell me about it," he said softly.

"My dream?"

"Yeah."

She pulled her legs up to her chest and wrapped her arms around them. "It was our graduation party. I found Dean in bed with Maisie. I was so angry. I ran outside, and he followed. We fought and I left without him. It was the last time I saw him alive."

"Did Maisie talk to you after?"

She shook her head. "No. We were both at his funeral but didn't speak to each other. I didn't even know she'd married Dean's brother until I came back."

"Could it be her?"

Bonnie's brows flickered. "I want to say no. The person who pushed me against the wall was definitely a male. But a few months ago, I wouldn't have thought anyone would cut the head off a mouse and leave it at my doorstep, so…anything's possible." A visible shudder rolled down her spine.

He set a hand on the small of her back. "What can I do?"

She leaned a cheek on her knee and looked at him. "Tell me about Billings."

It was three in the morning. Hardly the time to rehash his past. But sitting in bed with Bonnie, watching the sadness in her eyes, he would have done anything she asked. "I have a cousin. His name is Monty Cruz. He was part of the UFC while I was an Army Ranger. I wanted a change, and he got in my ear about how good the UFC lifestyle was. How good it felt to be in the ring. So when my contract ended, I got out and started training. I got good. Spent most of my time in Billings with him but also traveled a lot."

"You were close."

"Really close. My grandmother who raised me had passed. I had no siblings. He was my closest family. I thought I knew him."

"What happened?"

"He had a party. That whole scene wasn't really my thing, but I went because he was the host. When I was ready to leave, I went to find him. He was upstairs in his bedroom, standing over the body of a woman who'd been shot."

Bonnie sucked in a shaky breath. "The woman in the article."

"He'd already dropped the pistol. And when I told him I was calling 9-1-1, he flipped out. We fought. I got to the gun before him."

She gasped.

"He didn't want me to tell anyone. He wanted to use his money to make it disappear."

"What did you do?"

"Someone else walked in. Saw us. Called the police. He told them a different story than what happened. Tried to pin the murder on me. We went to trial. During the trial, we were both out on bail when he sent someone to kill me."

Her skin chilled. "Who?"

"A paid hit man."

"And you killed him in self-defense." Her frown deepened. "How did they prove Monty was guilty if you were holding the murder weapon?"

"Monty had cameras in the halls in his home. He tried to have the footage erased but police recovered it. It was the audio that saved me. It caught everything he said. They also traced the money that the hit man was paid back to Monty."

He traced a circle on her thigh with his finger.

"The story divided a lot of people in Billings though," he continued. "Not everyone believed I was innocent. Some thought I was an accomplice. It made living there hard."

"So you moved."

"So I moved."

"I'm sorry."

"Like you, I know that trusting the wrong person can hurt you."

Bonnie shook her head. "But he was your cousin. He was family. I can't imagine how that would have felt."

"Not everyone has a great family."

For a moment she just watched him, a new softness in her eyes. A tinge of sadness. Then she crawled into his lap, her legs and arms wrapping around him as she hugged him. "I'm sorry. I'm sorry that happened. I'm sorry I didn't hear you out sooner. I'm sorry that the reporter published part of your story—the parts that made you look like the bad guy."

He wrapped his arms around her. And for some reason, holding her, feeling the softness that was Bonnie, took the edge off the pain of his past.

onnie cracked one eye open. Darkness. Well, close to darkness. There was a small slip of light sneaking in from behind the curtains. She could just make out Zane's navy bedsheets beneath her. His dark oak drawers against the wall.

The previous night kicked at her belly. The blood. The dead animal and running to Zane's apartment. Then the dream that had followed.

She scrunched her eyes, but all she saw was the decapitated mouse.

Nausea rolled in her belly.

Argh.

She sat up. Where was Zane? Had he left early just like last time?

Her gaze caught on clothes neatly stacked on top of the dresser. Her clothes. Jeans. A T-shirt. There was even a pair of neatly folded panties on top.

Her cheeks heated. Zane had gone through her underwear drawer. Why did that feel like ten million degrees of embarrassment?

She set her feet on the floor, and that's when she saw the folded piece of paper beside her phone on the bedside table.

She lifted it, her gaze running over the masculine, slanted writing.

Morning, Bon. Stetson's sick so I've had to run into work. Take your time getting ready. The apartment's locked up. I've left a spare key for you on the kitchen counter. Your brother said he'd be over at nine.

She tapped the screen of her phone.

Eight forty-five! Shit. And her brother was never late.

She shot to her feet, knowing she shouldn't care if Noah found her in Zane's room. Actually, she didn't. She was a grown-ass woman who could date whoever she wanted.

Okay, she cared a little bit. He'd apologized for what he'd said about her at her aunt's house, but a part of her couldn't help but wonder what else he thought about her and wasn't sharing.

She was just reaching for her clothes, when she froze.

Was that the front door opening? No. It couldn't be. Zane was at work and if Stetson was sick, he'd be there all day.

But it had definitely sounded like the door.

Her heart started to pound, fear propelling the blood in her veins to move faster.

A weapon. She needed a weapon. But where did Zane keep one? Did he even have a weapon in the bedroom?

Her gaze landed on the antiperspirant spray on top of his wooden dresser.

That could work.

Silently, she padded toward the drawers. There was a small shake to her fingers as she lifted the can. She cringed at the small click when she pulled off the cap.

Spray and run. The words whispered in her head. She ignored everything else. The fear. The panic.

Three more steps and she reached the closed bedroom door. She wrinkled her nose, setting a hand on the knob. Opening it slowly, she listened.

Silence…from her and the hall. Maybe she was wrong. Maybe the noise had been in her head.

The door opened and the first thing she saw was a big, broad chest. She screamed and lifted the can to spray, aiming for the intruder's eyes.

He moved so quickly, she didn't have time to react, throwing his head to the side so the antiperspirant missed and grabbing her wrist before tugging it down.

His fingers weren't punishing though. In fact, they were oddly gentle, but still firm.

When she finally focused on him, she frowned. "I know you. Well, I don't know you, but…Ethan, right?"

"It's good to see you again, Bonnie." His deep, gravelly voice was clearly amused. He didn't seem annoyed at all that she'd almost blinded him. Was there a ghost of a smile on his face?

"What are you doing here?" she gasped.

"I came to see Zane. I knocked but no one answered." He lifted his other hand. "I have a key."

He'd knocked. And she'd slept through it. "He had to run into work."

Ethan released her arm. "I think Zane might kill me for scaring you. And for seeing you dressed in that."

She glanced down. And yep, her braless nipples were pushing through the thin material of Zane's sweatshirt.

She crossed her arms, as if that would do anything. "I, um, should get changed."

"Good idea."

Suddenly, there was a knock at the front door.

Shit.

"Expecting company?" Ethan asked, glancing over his shoulder.

"My brother. Maybe my cousin too."

He looked back at her, completely unfazed. "Shower. Change. I'll let them in."

"I don't know if you want to do that. They're kind of intense."

"I can handle them." He winked at her before heading down the hall.

Dammit.

She slammed the door a bit too hard and ran into the connecting bathroom, where she had the quickest shower of her life before pulling on her clothes. Thank God Zane had left her something to wear.

When she stepped into the living room, she didn't see Ethan. Noah, Jesse, and a female deputy were there instead, her brother and cousin looking big and intense and angry.

Noah rose from the couch. "Are you okay?" He stepped right up to her and gripped her arms.

"Yeah. Last night was…a shock." Understatement of the century. "But I'm feeling better this morning."

Noah's frown deepened, then he tugged her into his chest. And God, a hug from him felt good. The last bit of tension eased from her body as she leaned into her brother.

When they separated, she looked over at Jesse and the deputy before searching the room again. "Where's—"

"Ethan left," Jesse said. "We'd really like to hear what happened last night from your perspective."

Her gaze caught on the to-go cup from The Tea House.

"Dirty chai with almond milk," Noah said, pushing it in front of a seat at Zane's small dining table.

"Thank God." She dropped into the seat.

Jesse nodded to the other woman. "Bonnie, this is Deputy Claudia Russell. She'll take notes. Can you start at the beginning?"

Bonnie wrapped her fingers around the to-go cup, the warmth slipping up her arms to her shoulders. "There's not much to tell. I ordered a pizza from Burt. Half an hour later, there was a knock on the door. I opened it and the pizza was sitting in the hall. I realized after I picked it up that there was blood on my hand. When I opened it, I saw…the dead, headless mouse."

Suddenly, the cup wasn't warm enough. Her fingers, her skin…everything was cold.

"There was no message left with it?" Jesse asked.

"No. But…" She swallowed. "The night Dean White died, he and I had a fight. We were standing outside the party, and he called me a mouse. I'm guessing that's why the decapitated mouse was left on my doorstep."

Tension suddenly thickened the air in the room. Noah's muscles visibly tightened, and Jesse's jaw clenched.

"Did his dad know that he called you that?" Noah asked.

"I'm not sure. A few people were around at the time, and it went into a police report." She nibbled her lip before looking at Jesse. "Have you spoken to Burt? Surely his delivery driver would have a description of the person who took the pizza."

Jesse leaned forward, suddenly looking more intense than ever. "I spoke to Pete, Burt's nephew and delivery driver, this morning. He said less than a minute after you placed your order, he received a second call. This one from a man who claimed to be your partner. He knew your address. Your order. And he asked that Pete leave the pizza outside the apartment building door for contactless delivery. He went so far as to request he not buzz the apartment."

Oh God, that meant—

"Someone was there," she whispered. "Someone was in the parking lot when I made the call. They heard. They changed the delivery details."

The room fell silent. But no one needed to speak. It was true. Someone had been watching her last night. And that someone had been *very* close.

ZANE CIRCULATED THROUGH THE GYM. He'd hated leaving Bonnie early that morning, but if he hadn't come in, the place wouldn't have opened. Today was one of their early openings. Before the sun came up. And they always did good business before work hours.

Half a dozen people filled the space. Some warming up with jump ropes. Two in the ring. A few at bags. One of them was Damien White, Dean White's brother. Zane only knew that because of the intake form he'd filled out.

At first, he'd felt like throwing the guy's ass out like he had his father. But unlike Carlos, Damien hadn't done anything to Bonnie. As far as he knew, at least.

So he'd let him stay—for now.

Zane stopped beside the guy and Damien dropped his hands, shooting a nervous glance Zane's way.

"Everything okay?" Damien asked, pulling an AirPod out of his ear.

"Just checking in. How are you doing?"

"Yeah. Okay."

It was clear he hadn't hit a bag much before. His technique was sloppy and inexperienced. He didn't utilize the power in his body, and he was heaving for air after a dozen hits.

"Remember to hit with your whole body, not just your arms," Zane said. "Rotate your hips. Push off your back foot."

The guy nodded quickly. "I will. Thanks."

"I haven't seen your dad around town lately."

There was a small flicker of unease in the other man's eyes. "He, um, probably got scared by all the questioning after Bonnie was assaulted outside her apartment. I think he's laying low."

"And you don't know who would have done that to Bonnie, do you?"

"No." The answer came quickly. "I hate what happened to my brother. I hate that Bonnie left him at that party. But none of us would actually hurt her because of it."

Zane studied the other man. Something he'd learned early in his life was that silence often broke a person faster than words. And right now, Damien was squirming.

The man cleared his throat. "Well, I should, uh, get back to my workout."

Zane dipped his head before moving back. But only two steps before he continued to watch Damien hit the bag. He still wasn't using his whole body. But maybe that was because he was nervous. Nervous at Zane watching? Or nervous because he had something to hide? Something that involved Bonnie?

The door to the gym opened, and Zane turned to see Ethan step around the partition.

Zane frowned before crossing the space between them. "What are you doing here?"

"I had to get out of Deep River. There was a town meeting last night and Ward was spewing shit about there being nothing further he could do to find the hiker. He pisses me off."

"Well, it's good to see you here."

Ethan cleared his throat. "I have to tell you something. You're not gonna be happy."

The muscles in his forearms tightened. "About Monty?"

"No. About this morning."

"What?"

"I, uh, used my key to get into your apartment."

For a moment, Zane was quiet. "You walked into my apartment while Bonnie was there?"

"Yeah. And she tried to spray me with your antiperspirant. I dodged it. But I definitely scared her."

"Fuck, Ethan."

"I know. I'm sorry. I'm not used to you dating someone. You *are* dating, right?"

"I don't know. Someone decapitated a fucking mouse and left it on her doorstep last night. She came to me."

"Jesus Christ. What kind of sick asshole does that?"

"The kind who wants to scare Bonnie." And it was working. Zane looked back at Damien. Jesus, his form was terrible. "You working out?"

"Yeah. Might even give you a round in the ring."

"Feel like getting your ass beat?"

Ethan scoffed. "You wish."

As Ethan went back to the changing room, Zane stepped into his office to check his emails. He wasn't even there for five minutes, but when he stepped out, there was a new person in the gym.

Maisie.

She stood beside her husband, and they were talking in hushed tones. What the hell was she doing here? He didn't even know the woman and he still didn't like her. Yeah, she'd only been eighteen when she'd slept with Bonnie's boyfriend, but she wasn't eighteen anymore, and by the sound of it, she'd taken no accountability for what she'd done.

He crossed over to her. "What are you doing here?"

She turned, eyes widening. "Oh, sorry, I just came to pick up my husband. Is that not okay?"

"If you're not working out, you can't be in this section of the gym."

"Um, okay. Is it okay if I use your bathroom? Then I'll wait outside."

"Be quick." He was being an ass. He didn't care.

She straightened the bag on her shoulder before crossing the gym.

Zane circled the gym again, talking to a couple of people, giving advice when he could. By the time Ethan returned from changing, Maisie still hadn't returned.

What the hell was she doing back there?

He crossed to the back hallway. He couldn't walk into the women's bathroom, so he leaned against the wall.

But when Maisie stepped out, it wasn't from the women's room.

She gasped and clutched her bag. "Zane."

He shot his gaze behind her before returning his attention to her face. "What were you doing in the storage room?"

"I, um, dropped my lipstick as I was coming out of the bathroom." She lifted a lipstick from her purse. "The door was ajar and it rolled in there. I'm sorry."

She passed him quickly.

He glanced at her over his shoulder before stepping into the storage room. Everything looked exactly as it was supposed to. Nothing was moved or out of place.

So had she really dropped her lipstick? And if not...what the hell had she been doing in there?

CHAPTER 20

*B*onnie watched Zane demonstrate how to get out of a
hold.

She should be happy. She'd woken in Zane's bed. The last
week had been quiet, but even if it hadn't, the combination of
him and her family had her feeling safe and protected.

So why wasn't she smiling?

Because this morning she'd actually stood up for herself when
Shelley had tried to dump work on her that wasn't hers to do.
She'd done it politely and respectfully, and what had Shelley
done? She'd threatened her job. Told her that if she couldn't
handle the work, then she could leave. Reminded her that they
had a review coming up and this wouldn't look good.

Her fingers dug into her palms.

And on top of that, Zane had been acting strangely since
yesterday. Was strange even the right word for it? She'd called
him at lunch, and he hadn't answered. A first for Zane. He'd sent
her a quick text instead, saying he couldn't talk because he was
busy. He'd proceeded to get home late last night and barely spoke
to her. Now he seemed almost distracted.

What wasn't he telling her? And *why* wasn't he telling her?

She'd thought they were past this keeping-secrets thing. Heck, just last Sunday, he'd gone with her to Aunt Pam's house for their family lunch and everything had felt so right.

She nibbled her bottom lip, feet itching to approach him so they could talk. And she would. As soon as there was a break in the lesson.

Sarah rose and walked toward the bathroom.

Bonnie watched her with a frown. The woman had been pale all morning, and when Bonnie asked if she was okay, she'd given a quiet, "I'm fine," even though she'd looked the furthest from it.

Chett stopped coloring to stare down the hall at his mother's disappearing form.

Quietly, Bonnie crouched beside the boy. "What are you doing?"

He looked back to his book. "Coloring Spider-Man."

"Wow. He looks so good I almost thought he was going to jump out at me."

Chett laughed, and she grinned before rising and moving to the hall. In the bathroom, she saw one stall door was closed, and there was heavy breathing coming from the other side of the door.

Sarah wasn't all right. Not even close.

Slowly, Bonnie crossed over and knocked on the wood. "Sarah? It's Bonnie. Are you okay?"

The heavy breathing continued, and Sarah took so long to respond that Bonnie almost thought she wasn't going to. Then there was a small, breathless "No."

Shit. Not good. "Can you open the door for me?"

"I-I can't breathe. I think I'm having a p-panic attack."

Double shit. Bonnie glanced into the next stall, but even if she stood on the toilet, she wasn't sure she'd make it over. She was going to have to go under.

A quick breath and she dropped to her belly and slithered under the door.

Gross, gross, gross.

But she forgot about it the second she saw Sarah. The other woman sat on the floor, thighs pulled to her chest and elbows on her knees with her head in her hands.

"Sarah." Bonnie kept her voice gentle as she crouched in front of her.

Sarah's chest moved so quickly that she obviously couldn't take in a full breath.

"Sarah, can you look at me?"

The other woman did, but her gaze was unfocused, her pupils large.

"I want you to breathe with me, okay? Deep breaths. In." Bonnie filled her chest with air. "And out."

At first, nothing changed. Bonnie continued, and eventually Sarah joined her, syncing their breaths. And slowly, focus started to seep back into Sarah's expression.

"There you go." Bonnie squeezed her thigh. "Can you tell me what's wrong?"

"I got a letter from Jeremiah. He shouldn't know where I am, but the letter arrived at the shelter! Shelley gave it to me this morning."

Bonnie frowned. Why would she give it to her? Weren't all letters from prison marked? Unless he got someone outside the prison to send it?

"It didn't have any prison postmarks on it," Sarah said, reading Bonnie's thoughts. "But it was him. His handwriting. And signed by him."

How the hell had he pulled that off? She mentally shook her head. That wasn't important right now. "What did it say?"

Tears filled Sarah's eyes. "It said he wants his family back… and that he has a surprise for me."

That son of a bitch.

Bonnie had so many questions, but first, she needed to make sure Sarah was okay. "Chett's father is in prison, Sarah. We can even ask our town sheriff to confirm that and find out how that letter got to you. And you're right, he shouldn't know where you are."

"Shelley's looking into a new shelter for me and Chett. I don't feel safe."

"Good. You'll be out of his reach again."

"But what if he finds me a second time? What if he gets out and—"

"Look at me."

Sarah did.

"He's not getting out. He has a life sentence. And even if he did, the shelter is secure. Okay?"

Sarah didn't nod or agree, she just looked at Bonnie like she was too scared to believe her.

"What do you need?" Bonnie asked.

"Um…maybe just a few minutes to collect myself. I don't want Chett to see me like this."

"Okay. Let me know if there's anything I can do to help."

This time Sarah did nod. And even though Bonnie hated doing it, she slipped back under the door and let Sarah have a few more minutes alone.

How had this happened? How had her ex found her? He shouldn't have that kind of reach. But then, all he really needed was a friend or family member to visit him. They could have gotten the letter to Sarah.

And maybe he'd hired someone to find her?

Argh. She hated this.

She'd just stepped into the hall when a text beeped from her phone. She pulled out her cell, and her neck prickled at the name in the first line of the text. A name she hadn't seen on her cell for years.

Unknown number: This is Jane White. I wasn't sure if I should write this, but honestly, I can't keep it inside any longer. I need you to leave. You can spin the story however you like to your family, but you are the reason my son is dead. You left him that night when he needed you, and he got behind the wheel and never came home. And now, like nothing happened, you're back. Smiling. Dating.

Her breathing grew labored, a mixture of anger and sadness and...something else. Something that hurt more, tangling in her belly.

She wasn't sure if replying was the best thing to do, but she was sick of letting these things go without saying anything.

Bonnie: You have no right to message me like this. I'm blocking your number.

But before she could block it, the next text came through.

Unknown number: If you're staying because you think you have a future with that boy from the gym, you don't. There is no future for you in this town. You ruin families. You can't be truly loved because you don't know how to love back. For the love of God, leave.

Air cut off in Bonnie's throat, the words hitting her like a kick to the gut, almost making her keel over.

For a moment she couldn't move, just reading and re-rereading the words designed to hurt. She shouldn't let them sink so deeply inside her. And maybe on a better day, she wouldn't. But today already felt so heavy, with Shelley, then Sarah...and of course, Zane distancing himself from her.

You can't be truly loved.

Why did that line hurt the most? Because she'd gone without love for so long? Years. She'd spent years never really allowing herself to get close to anyone.

"Bonnie."

She jumped at her name and looked up to see Zane heading toward her. "Is everything okay?"

"I was going to ask you the same question."

"Um...yeah, I was just helping one of the women." She pushed her cell into her pocket.

He studied her like he didn't quite believe her. "You sure?"

She nodded, not wanting to mention the text right now,

because he was finally talking to her and they were alone. She stepped closer and touched his arm. "Is everything okay with *you*?"

Something flashed in his eyes. It came and went so quickly, she almost missed it. "Yes. Why?"

"You just seem a bit…off."

"Everything's fine, Bonnie." He kissed her forehead before heading back down the hall.

No. Something was definitely on his mind. The question was, did it have something to do with his past? Or her? And why wasn't he telling her? Hiding things from her had already caused damage once. Why would he risk it again?

Could it be that he was having second thoughts about them?

The idea made her heart do a painful squeeze in her chest. Because even though they hadn't been dating long, she'd started falling in love with him.

Everyone was back in the van, and they were halfway to the shelter when Chett started crying.

She looked at him through the rearview mirror. "What's going on?"

Sarah glanced up. "He left his coloring book at the gym."

"Well, that's an easy fix." She turned the van around. After parking in front of the gym, she raced inside, spotting the book near the back where Chett had been sitting in front of the office.

She frowned when she didn't see Zane and Stetson.

She jogged over to the book and grabbed it. She was just straightening when Zane's voice came from inside the office.

The door was ajar. She was moments from sticking her head in to say a quick hi, when his next words landed.

"There are no relationships in my life. My grandmother's dead and she was the last woman I'll ever love. So whatever you're getting at, leave it the fuck alone. And don't call me again."

She flinched as if she'd been hit. For a moment, she was frozen, not sure if she'd heard the words correctly.

But she had. There'd been no mistaking them.

You can't be truly loved.

Jane's words played over in her head again…and suddenly, all she wanted to do was run.

* * *

THE SECOND THE WOMEN LEFT, the gym felt too quiet. But then, whenever Bonnie left any space, it felt too quiet to Zane, even if the place was filled with people.

Over the last week, a need had grown inside him. A need to be close to her at all times. To touch her and hear her voice.

Until yesterday. Until he'd seen the missed call on his phone.

"You really like her, don't you?"

Zane shifted his gaze to Stetson. "Yeah, I do." So why the fuck hadn't he told her about the missed call? History had proven that secrets did more harm than good.

But fuck, what was he supposed to say? That Monty was planning something? That he'd called from prison? What the hell would any of that achieve other than scaring her?

"You two make a good couple," Stetson said. "I was only a kid when she dated my cousin, but I still remember thinking that he didn't treat her well. Then the way my family turned on her after Dean died…I never liked it."

"I know you're not like them."

"Good. I mean, Damien's not too bad. Maybe a bit of an over-achieving prick, but that's probably because he grew up with money. I like her, by the way."

"Most people who get to know her do." He checked his watch. "You can go if you want."

"Really? I still have half an hour on my shift."

"Go. Have an early one."

"This is why you're my favorite boss."

His lips twitched. "I'm your only boss."

170

Once Stetson was gone, Zane picked up the last of the gloves from the floor and chucked them into the equipment box. He'd just stepped into his office when his phone rang, that unknown number on his cell again.

Something dark curled in his stomach. It was the same number as yesterday. And he knew exactly who it was.

He gritted his teeth before answering. "Hello?"

"You're receiving a call from Monty Cruz, an inmate at Montana State Prison. This call is subject to monitoring and recording. To accept, press three. To decline, hang up."

And there it was…the confirmation he hadn't wanted.

He closed his eyes, ice slipping into his veins. For a moment, he considered hanging up. But there was a reason Monty was trying to reach him. And fuck, he needed to know what it was.

He hit three, his fingers tight around the cell as he pressed it back to his ear.

There was a small pause before Monty spoke. "Hey, cousin."

The full-body reaction was immediate. The tensing of his muscles. The roaring of blood between his ears. "What the fuck do you want?"

"Aw, I miss you too."

"Monty." There was warning in his voice.

"I'm just checking in. How are you doing? You know, with all that freedom you have? All that money you made from the UFC? The money you wouldn't have made without *me*? You enjoying your life in Amber Ridge?"

It shouldn't surprise Zane that Monty knew where he was. The guy had his own money. Resources. Exactly why Zane had been watching his back. Yet it still felt like a kick in the gut. "It's money *I* earned in *my* fights. And freedom I'm entitled to—unlike you. Now what do you really want?"

"Yeah, you're right. You've earned everything you have. And everything still to come. I'm glad you're happy in your new town…developing new friendships. New *relationships*."

A cold weight dropped into his stomach. Did he know about Bonnie? If he knew about Amber Ridge, it wasn't that big of a stretch.

Every part of him—every fucking fiber—rebelled against the idea. And he needed Monty to think she wasn't his. That she was nothing to him. "There are no relationships in my life. My grandmother's dead and she was the last woman I'll ever love. So whatever you're getting at, leave it the fuck alone. And don't call me again."

He hung up and threw the cell into the wall across the room.
Fuck!

The asshole had already sent a hit man to his house. Zane couldn't have him targeting Bonnie next.

He turned and slammed his fist into the wall. But it did nothing. The pain didn't even take the edge off the frustration that trembled and clawed inside him.

He should have killed him. Zane should have picked up the damn gun the night of the party and shot him.

He shut his eyes, the memory hitting him hard.

Where the fuck was he?

Zane moved through the crowd of people, searching for Monty. The house was fucking huge. No one needed a house this big. Yet Monty had still managed to fill it with a million people he didn't know.

That was his cousin though. He liked to have extravagant things and flaunt the shit out of them.

Monty hadn't always been like that. There'd been a time when his cousin had been down to earth. Easy to talk to. But the fame and money had gone to his head. That seemed to be the UFC world though. If he'd known a few years ago, he might never have gotten involved. But then, being in the ring felt so damn good that maybe he would have.

He passed a group of fighters, the smell of alcohol and drugs so thick he couldn't avoid it. There probably wasn't a single person in this house who wasn't drunk or stoned apart from him.

Why the hell had he even come tonight?

But he already knew the answer to that—it was Monty's birthday. His cousin had claimed he needed Zane here, that they were the only family either of them had left.

Yeah, well…now Zane was ready to get the hell out of there.

He could probably just go and send his cousin a text on the way out. But Monty could be a child sometimes.

A woman stopped in front of him, her hands sliding down his chest. "Hey, Zane. I've been looking for you."

He'd never seen the woman before in his life. Random strangers knowing his name was something he'd never get used to.

"Excuse me." He took the blonde's hands off his shirt before stepping around her, ignoring her pout.

He'd give the second floor one search, and if he didn't find his cousin, he was leaving. He took the stairs two at a time and went straight to Monty's bedroom. The door was closed, which probably meant he was with his girlfriend, Sasha. The two of them were fucking toxic. She was with him for money and notoriety, and he was with her because he liked the way she looked. They did nothing but fight.

That was none of his damn business though.

He knocked on the door.

Silence.

"Monty, you there?" He knocked again. "I'm leaving, man. I just wanted to say goodbye."

"Zane?"

He frowned. Why was Monty's voice so strained?

Fuck it. He pushed inside. "Hey, are you—"

He stopped, his stomach dropping at the scene in front of him.

Sasha lay on the floor in the center of the room, only wearing panties, a bullet wound in the center of her chest. And her eyes…they were open and so fucking blank there was no mistaking what he was looking at.

Dead. She was dead.

And the pistol, likely the murder weapon, sat right beside her. Like Monty had shot her, dropped the gun, and stepped back.

Zane looked at Monty, his words almost quiet. "What have you done?"

His cousin's mouth opened and closed. "I didn't mean to. She was just being so fucking annoying! You know how she gets. She wouldn't stop. I just wanted her to shut up!"

"You killed her." It wasn't a question.

"It's okay. I know people who can take care of this." Monty's words were rushed now...desperate.

"The fuck are you talking about? We're calling the police."

Monty's eyes widened. "No. They'll send me away for life, Merrick."

"You killed her, Monty. You fucking shot her!"

"And I told you why. But I can make this go away." He pulled out his phone.

"We're calling the police."

Monty paused. "Zane..." His voice was different now. The panic was still there, but so was an edge of warning. "You don't want to do that."

Now Zane pulled out his phone.

"No," Monty growled, his gaze shooting to the gun beside the body.

Then he lunged.

Zane was faster, grabbing the pistol and aiming it right at Monty's chest.

A gasp sounded behind him as someone stepped into the doorway of the room.

Zane blinked, forcing himself back to the present. But he may as well still be back in that room. Because a year had passed, and the asshole was still fucking with him.

CHAPTER 21

Zane paced his living room, his skin feeling tight, like he couldn't contain the rage inside him.

"He was messing with you," Ethan said over the phone. "He's trying to get in your head."

"Or he was sending me a message. That he's keeping tabs on me like I'm keeping tabs on him. He wants me to know that he still has reach from inside the prison."

"Zane. You know he can't touch you."

"He sent a fucking hit man after me in Billings, Ethan," Zane shouted. "He has money and that buys him access to people he shouldn't have. It doesn't matter that he's locked up."

Ethan sighed. "So, what do you want to do?"

"I want Bonnie protected. And I don't know if that means she should be close to me or far fucking away."

"If he *is* having you watched, he already knows about her, so you should be sticking close."

Ethan was right. Of course he was right.

He moved over to the window and pressed his palm to the glass, the dark night glaring back at him from outside.

"We're watching him, Zane. But to be safe, let the town sheriff and her brother know. Make sure everyone is aware that they need to watch their backs." There was a pause from Ethan. "Have you spoken to Bonnie?"

"No. I texted her an hour ago, but she hasn't texted back." He checked his watch. It was almost six. Usually, she was home from work by now. Where the hell was she?

A knock suddenly sounded at the door.

Ethan must have heard it. "Could that be her?"

"She has a key." He crossed the room and checked the peephole.

The fuck?

He opened it, and before he could utter a word, Noah asked, "Is she here?"

"No. Should she be?"

"Her workplace said she left an hour ago, calls keep going to voicemail, and she's not in her apartment."

A cold weight dropped in his stomach. "Where is she then?"

Ethan, who could obviously hear everything, suddenly spoke over the line. "Has anyone checked with that Dean guy's parents?"

Zane looked at Noah. "Have you tried Carlos?"

"I have his home number." Noah lifted his phone and called. A second later, he shook his head. "No answer."

That's where he'd start.

"I'll call you later," Zane said quickly to Ethan before hanging up. Then he grabbed his keys and left his apartment, not even caring that he hadn't locked up and left Noah behind.

In the car, he sped to the house. He knew where Carlos and Jane White lived because he'd asked Ethan for the information weeks ago, knowing that one day he might need it.

Two minutes later, he pulled up in front of a huge house with dark timber beams and slate-gray stone walls. Two cars pulled up behind his—Noah's and a patrol car.

Zane didn't stop or pause. He stormed to the door and banged on the wood. But it wasn't Carlos or Jane who opened it.

Damien frowned. "Zane. Is everything okay?"

"Where is she?"

Footsteps sounded behind him.

Carlos sneered. "What the hell do you want?"

Behind him, Maisie and Jane also appeared.

"I want to know where the hell you've been this afternoon," Zane growled.

The older man scowled. "That's none of your fucking business."

"It is if it has something to do with Bonnie."

"Something happened to Bonnie?" Maisie asked.

A hand touched his shoulder, then Jesse spoke. "Zane. Step back."

"Yeah, and while you're at it, get the hell off my porch," Carlos shouted.

"I'll get off when I'm good and ready," Zane retorted.

"The hell you will." Carlos tried to lunge forward, but Damien grabbed his father by the shoulders and forced him back.

Jesse pulled Zane away. "I need you to wait at your car."

He ground his teeth together. He didn't want to move. He wanted to find out right fucking now if these people knew where Bonnie was.

But he also knew Jesse had more chance of getting that information than he did.

He forced himself to step back. To turn and return to his car, hands fisted the entire time. When he reached his car, he tried her number.

No answer. He tried again. Same thing.

Goddammit.

Noah joined him. They didn't speak, just watched Jesse talk to the family from the street. Carlos looked calmer. When Jesse stepped inside, Zane frowned. Was the White family letting him check the place?

Five minutes later, Jesse returned. "They've been together all afternoon. None of them have seen Bonnie today."

"Then where is she?" Zane shouted.

Noah's phone rang, and he pulled it out before pressing it to her ear. "Indie, have you—" He stopped before sighing. "Thank God." He looked up at them. "Indie's with her. Where are you?" He frowned. "What do you mean, you're not telling me?" His jaw clicked before he hung up. "Indie's with her. Says she's safe. Colt's with them. But she wouldn't tell me where."

This time Zane frowned. "Why not?"

"I don't know."

What the hell was going on? He wanted eyes on Bonnie, and he wanted eyes on her *now*.

* * *

BONNIE TRACED the stars in the sky with her eyes. There was something so grounding about looking up at night. A gentle reminder of how small she and her problems were.

My grandmother's dead and she was the last woman I'll ever love.

Zane's words played over in her head. They shouldn't make her so upset. She and Zane hadn't been dating for long enough to say I love you. Hell, they hadn't even labeled what they were doing as dating.

But it hurt. Because she was falling, and she was falling hard.

She'd spent so many years alone. Sure, she'd had friends and short flings in San Francisco. But the friends were the superficial kind, and she'd never dated anyone she saw herself with long term.

Zane felt different.

The engine of a car sounded from the parking lot to her right, causing the fine hairs on her arms to stand on end. No one ever came to this lookout. The park beside it was overgrown, and people in this town had long forgotten it existed.

She was about to rise when the passenger door of the car opened, and her sister climbed out.

How had she known where to find her?

Indie walked straight over to her and lowered to the ground with a groan. "I'm gonna need your help getting back up. This belly feels like a bowling ball."

"What are you doing here?" she asked, sitting up beside her.

"Well, I got a call from Noah, telling me you weren't in your apartment or Zane's apartment, and you weren't at work. So, of course I looked in the place you used to run to when you were a teenager. How many times did I find you here after fights with Mom and Dad?"

"Every time. And you always used to try to drag my ass back."

"But you were stubborn. Plus, things always blew over. I was just impatient." Indie turned to look at her. "What's going on, Bon?"

"I just had a really shitty day."

"Tell me about it."

She ran her finger over a tear in her jeans. "Shelley, my boss, has been awful. Zane's been standoffish. And then…"

"And then what?"

"It's stupid."

"I love hearing stupid things."

"I got a text from Jane White."

"Dean's mother?"

"Mm-hmm." She opened the text and handed the cell to Indie. Her gaze ran over the screen. "That bitch."

"Yeah. I was overthinking it, letting it bother me. Then, like clockwork, I overheard Zane say something that I wasn't supposed to hear."

"What did he say?"

She nibbled her bottom lip. "That he'd never love me."

Indie's frown deepened. "And that hurt because…"

"I'm falling in love with him. I probably already *am* in love."

Indie was quiet for a moment. "Do you want to know what I think?"

Did she? She wasn't sure. Running and hiding out in the mountains felt safer than receiving advice she might not like.

"Tough luck, you're getting it," Indie said when Bonnie took too long to answer. "There is no way that man could *not* love you."

She laughed. "I don't know if that's true. Besides, you have to say that, you're my sister."

"Not true. If I didn't believe it, I would give you some fluffy 'there are more fish in the sea' crap." Indie tilted her head. "You should talk to him. He's worried. So is Noah."

"My phone died." It was a weak excuse, and she knew it. There was a charging cable in the car. But when the world got loud, quiet became her solitude.

"Is that all?" Indie asked quietly.

She wished that was all. "Living in this town just feels…like a lot right now. Some days I think I can handle it. Other days, not so much."

"There's only a couple of people who are jerks. The rest of them love you."

"Love might be a stretch." But Indie was right. The hate and abuse was mostly coming from the same few people. But God, it felt like more. "I need you to know something."

Emotion flickered in Indie's eyes. "Okay."

"I didn't want to leave you. I just…I wanted to exist without hurting, and I couldn't here. Everywhere I looked, I was reminded of who I'd lost. Dean. Mom. Dad."

"I know." Indie slipped a piece of hair behind Bonnie's ear. "I just thought you'd come back sooner."

"I wanted to. I should have."

"Why didn't you take my calls?"

"Because I was eighteen and scared, and I thought it had to be all or nothing." Tears pressed at her eyes. "And the guilt...God, it felt like chains around my neck. Mom and Dad died going to pick me up that night."

"Bonnie, look at me." She forced her gaze back to her sister. "That doesn't make it your fault."

"It felt like it did. It all felt like my fault."

Indie swiped a tear from Bonnie's face before cupping her cheek. "None of those deaths were your fault. Do you understand? Not Mom's. Not Dad's. And not Dean's."

Bonnie nodded.

"Come here." Indie pressed a hand to her head, and Bonnie laid her cheek on her sister's shoulder.

"Thank you." It wasn't just for Indie's words. She was thanking her for welcoming her back into her life after Bonnie had done everything possible to escape it. She was thanking her for loving her regardless of what she'd done.

Indie kissed her temple. "You're my sister. I'll always love you."

The words sank deep inside her, filling a gap that had been empty for so long. "I love you too. And I should call Noah."

"I already have. I think he was with Zane."

She cringed. "I need to talk to Zane about what I heard too."

"Only when you're ready. And Bonnie...you don't need to run anymore."

Bonnie's heart squeezed. Because Indie was right. She was good at running. It was her default. But it was time to stop.

CHAPTER 22

Zane paced the hall. He wasn't sure how long he'd been doing it, but he couldn't stay still. Not until he saw Bonnie with his own two eyes and knew she was safe.

Every call was still going to voicemail. Every text went unanswered. It was killing him. All of it. Especially after Monty's call.

He shoved his fingers through his hair, pulling at the damn strands. It was only when he heard footsteps on the stairs and distant voices that his hands stilled.

Then Bonnie stepped into the hall, Indie and Colt beside her, and his heart fucking stopped.

Safe. She was safe and unharmed, and damn, that almost dropped him to his knees.

She stopped when she saw him, brows flickering. She turned to the couple and said something quietly. Indie shot him a glance before pulling Bonnie into a hug. Zane received a chin lift from Colt before he put a hand on Indie's back, then he and his wife headed back down the stairs.

"How long have you been out here?" Bonnie asked when she reached him.

"Not long." A damn lie. He'd been here for over an hour. "Can I come in?"

She looked at the closed door. For a second he was sure she'd say no. Then she unlocked it and stepped inside her apartment, leaving the door open behind her.

He followed her in, closing and locking the door after him.

"My phone died," she said quietly. "But I'm sorry I disappeared on you."

"I was worried." A fucking understatement.

"Do you want a coffee?" She walked to the kitchen and put a pod into the machine.

He crossed the room and the second he stood behind her, he gently gripped her hips, needing to touch her. She froze, the smallest gasp slipping into the air. "Bonnie...what happened today?"

The only sound in the room was her breathing. Deep. Even. "I got a text from Jane White. It threw me. I was still feeling shaky when I heard you."

"Heard me what?"

"Chett left his coloring book at the gym. I went back in, and I heard you say you would never love another person again."

Shit.

She turned in his arms, a glint of tears in her eyes as she stared at his chest. "I know we haven't been dating for long. It just...it hurt and I ran." She lifted a shoulder. "I've lived all of my adult life without having any meaningful relationships. And I guess I was hoping that this was different."

She hadn't met his gaze. Not once the entire time she was speaking.

"Bonnie." He touched her chin to lift her head. It took a second, but she finally looked at him. "I said that to protect you."

Confusion shadowed her eyes. "I don't understand."

He fucking hated talking about Monty. But if he wanted Bonnie in his life, he had to be honest with her. She needed all the information, not just the bits he was willing to part with. "Monty called today."

Her eyes widened. "From prison?"

"Yeah. He gave me some bullshit reason. Said he was checking that I was good. He made sure to mention Amber Ridge and *relationships*. So I told him I didn't have any relationships."

"Do you think he knows about us?"

There was that damn squeeze of his chest again. "He was pretty clear in his wording. He obviously knows I'm dating someone. I was thinking…"

"What?"

Fuck, he wasn't even sure what he was thinking. "Maybe we should lay low for a while…just to be safe."

"Lay low." Her gaze shifted between his eyes, brows tugged together. "What does that mean?"

He slipped a thumb beneath her shirt and grazed her skin. "It means, for the moment, our relationship is here. Away from watchful eyes."

She nodded, her expression completely unreadable.

He tightened his hold on her. "What are you thinking?"

"Maybe tonight we should sleep in our own apartments. It's been a long day, and we both have a lot going on."

Panic started to crawl up his chest. Panic that she could be considering ending things. Panic that he could lose the best damn thing in his life. "Is that what you want?"

She nodded, but there was uncertainty in her eyes that was in conflict with her words. "We can see how we feel tomorrow. When the world gets loud, I need time to think."

He didn't want to leave her. But if she needed space, he didn't want to take that from her.

"Okay." He lowered his head and pressed a kiss to her temple. "Lock your doors after me, Bon. And if you need me…I'll be here in a second."

She nodded, her eyes holding him hostage for a moment.

Instead of pulling her closer like he wanted, he released her. Forced himself to step back. And the second he was out of her apartment, he felt it. The suffocating quiet that only came when he wasn't with Bonnie.

* * *

BONNIE GASPED, her eyes shooting open as she sat up, nausea swirling in her belly.

A dream. It was just a dream.

But it had felt so real.

She dropped her head into her hands, but she couldn't get the nightmare out of her head. She'd opened her apartment door and Dean was standing there, pale and bleeding…and in his hands, the mouse's head.

Oh, God. She really might be sick.

She swallowed the bile trying to crawl up her throat. It wasn't real. Dean was gone. It was just a dream.

She glanced beside her to the empty bed, suddenly wanting —craving—Zane's presence. But he wasn't there, because of her. Because she'd suggested they sleep in their own apartments.

Why? Because he'd asked to keep their relationship private? Because when he'd suggested Monty might know about her, she'd become scared that she might be used against Zane? And she couldn't handle something else, another tragedy, being her fault.

Indie had told her to stop running. And here she was, doing it again. Running from this perfect man just down the hall. Allowing herself to suffer alone when she didn't have to.

God, what was wrong with her? Zane was safety and comfort and strength, and she needed all of that. At eighteen years old, she had an excuse for making bad decisions. She'd been young and hurting.

But now, thirteen years later, she was *still* doing it—running from the good in her life.

She could. She would.

She threw off the sheets and climbed out of bed. The creak of the floorboard was loud in the quiet room, and the darkness made a shudder course down her spine.

She grabbed her phone and left her bedroom. She only wore an oversized shirt, but she didn't bother to pull on sweats or shoes. She lifted both the keys to her apartment and Zane's from the hall table.

The only moment she questioned her decision was when she stepped into the empty hall. It was late. Or early, depending on which way you looked at it. Two-in-the-morning kind of early.

Quickly, she locked her apartment and jogged to Zane's door. It wasn't until she'd stepped inside and locked the door after her that she breathed a sigh of relief and felt that this was the right decision. It slipped through her entire body and felt warm and safe.

Then, she padded down the hall.

She wasn't sure why she'd expected to find him asleep. He was a former Army Ranger. Of course he'd woken the second she'd opened the door.

He lowered the gun back to the drawer. "Bonnie. What's wrong?"

Without a word, she crossed the room, set her phone and the keys on his bedside table, and pulled back the sheets. But she didn't slip into bed beside him. She climbed right on top of him, her entire body covering his. Then she laid her cheek on his chest, his heart thumping loudly beneath her ear. "It was a bad idea."

"What was?"

"Sleeping separately. I want to be here with you."

There was a moment of pause, when he didn't move. And she almost wondered if she was alone in this realization.

But then he grabbed the sheets and pulled them over both of them. His strong arms wrapped around her, making her feel immediately safe. "I want you here too."

That last bit of tightness eased from her chest and she breathed him in, his earthy scent filling her. It was crazy how one person's scent could become so familiar so quickly.

"I'm sorry I ran earlier today," she whispered, the frustration bleeding out of her. Frustration in herself. In the decisions she'd made in her life. "It's my crutch. It's what I do when things get hard."

"You run, I follow, Bon. Always."

She looked up at him. "Really?"

His blue eyes seared into her, so intense. "You think there's anywhere else I'd rather be?"

Her heart gave one of those giant thumps. The kind you felt from your head down to your toes.

Just like in her apartment, he lifted his mouth and kissed her forehead. "Sleep," he whispered. "I've got you."

She lowered her head back to his chest and closed her eyes, letting the strong beats of his heart lull her to sleep.

CHAPTER 23

Monty Cruz leaned his head back against the wall of the van, the low rumble of the engine vibrating beneath him. Two prisoners sat to his left and one to his right. There were more on the other side of the partition.

Nine in total. Everyone knew what was about to go down. There were others involved. The DOC Correctional Transport Officer. A couple more paid on the outside. The prison warden had been the hardest to get onboard. But even that was easier than it should have been.

He bit back a laugh. People were so fucking easy. Flash a few dollars in front of them and they fell at his fucking feet.

The best part though? Zane wouldn't see this coming. It would hit him square in the fucking face—and Monty would enjoy every second of it. He'd waited long enough to get his revenge after what that asshole had taken from him. Too damn long.

Monty had given him *everything*. A new life in the UFC that came with money and freedom and the opportunity to fuck any bitch he wanted. And the one time Monty needed him, he hadn't been there. No, instead of helping him cover up Sasha's death,

Zane had done everything he could to make sure he was locked away.

A familiar rage clawed at his insides, climbing up his throat like bile.

Well, cousin, your time is coming, and it's coming soon.

Jeremiah tapped his foot beside Monty. The guy was just as excited. Maybe more. But then, he had a kid and a woman at the shelter in Amber Ridge. He'd probably kill her. Monty didn't give a fuck *what* the guy did. As long as he fulfilled his end of things today.

He couldn't see outside, but he knew the exact moment the van hit the dirt road. The ride changed from quiet and smooth to loud and bumpy.

They were close.

Jeremiah's breathing quickened, like he was so fucking excited he couldn't hold it together. The guy would probably get himself caught or killed within the first day. Again, not Monty's problem. His plan was too perfectly laid out to care. Although, he might use a couple of them later on.

The bang of a gun being fired sounded from the front of the van.

The energy in the van changed, the guys sitting a bit straighter. The air felt thicker.

Monty didn't so much as smile. He wouldn't smile until he was out.

The van stopped. A few seconds later, the back doors opened and the transport officer stood on the other side. He didn't look nervous. He looked excited. Apparently, offering him a million dollars to pull this off made a guy excited about shooting a colleague and freeing felons.

He pulled Jeremiah from the van, then Monty. Monty was uncuffed first. The moment Jeremiah was free—the first fucking second—he grabbed the pistol from the officer's belt.

The officer's eyes widened. "Hey, what are you—"

Jeremiah shot the officer in the forehead.

And that was why Monty needed the guy. Well…that, and to free everyone else while he got the hell out of there and make sure every one of them headed to Amber Ridge.

They should anyway. Because they knew that if they didn't, every person they loved on the outside was at risk.

Jeremiah grabbed keys from the dead CTO. As he started uncuffing everyone, Monty jogged toward the mountains, the cool air slipping over his skin.

Fuck, this air tasted better than the stale shit he'd breathed in prison.

It didn't take long to find the go car. The one the CTO had arranged for himself.

The key was affixed behind the back tire. Monty grabbed it and opened the trunk to find spare clothes. Quickly, he changed and tossed the orange jumpsuit behind a tree.

It was only when he climbed behind a wheel that he let the first smile curve his lips.

He'd done it. He was free. The officers were dead. There would be nine felons free, causing chaos in the small town of Amber Ridge. Murderers. Thieves. They'd be one huge fucking distraction while he did what he had to do.

Thank fuck for money. It bought allies. Freedom. And eventually, it would buy him revenge.

* * *

ZANE STEPPED out of The Pit, sunlight hitting his eyes as he walked down the street.

It had only been a week since that mess after the call from Monty, but the second he'd made things right with Bonnie, he'd decided he wasn't letting that asshole get into his head. It was what Monty wanted. Exactly why Zane wasn't giving it to him.

He lifted his phone and texted her.

Zane: How's your day been, Bon?

It was midafternoon, which meant they were both almost done. Bonnie was meeting him at the gym after work, and fuck, he was excited to see her. He was always excited to see her. Being with her, he actually felt normal and good and alive for the first time in over a year.

Bonnie: It's been okay.

Zane: Uh-oh. What's wrong?

Bonnie: I don't know. I've just had this bad feeling all day, like something's going to happen. And there's been this strange heaviness around the shelter.

He stopped outside The Tea House.

Zane: You think it has something to do with Carlos?

Jesse hadn't been able to find anything linking Carlos to the dead fucking mouse incident. Nothing. Just like the night Bonnie had been shoved against the building, he had an alibi, but this time he'd been with his wife. The same wife who'd sent that god-awful text to Bonnie.

Shit, he hated that family.

Bonnie: No. This feels different. I'm probably being silly. There are a lot of big emotions in the shelter today. You still want me to come to The Pit after work?

Zane: Come anytime.

Bonnie: I've only got a couple of hours to go. I'll see you soon.

Nothing felt soon enough. He wanted eyes on her all the time, and he didn't care if that was normal or not.

He stepped inside The Tea House, spotting Jesse at a table to the side of the room. He sat with his brother, Becket, and best friend, Holden. When the guys saw him, they waved. Zane dipped his head before stepping up to the counter.

Mrs. Gerald hung up the phone and faced him, brows tugged together. "Hi, Zane."

"Is everything okay?"

"Um. I'm not sure. That was one of my girls. She was

supposed to come in for the last couple hours of the day to do the close, but on her way here, she found a man on the side of the road. He was unconscious and naked."

The fuck? "Like, someone beat him up and took his clothes?"

"That's what it sounded like."

"Jesse's over there if you want to talk to him."

"She's called the sheriff's station, but yes, I might mention it to Jesse too." Another worker called the shop owner over. "Sorry. I'll be back in a moment."

Who the hell would beat someone up and take their clothes? Especially in this town.

He looked over at Jesse to see the three guys already heading his way.

"Hey. Everything okay?" Jesse asked.

"Mrs. Gerald just got a report that some guy was beaten up and his clothes were taken."

Jesse's head reared back. "Just now?"

"Apparently."

"Here in Amber Ridge?" Becket asked.

"Yeah."

Jesse pulled his cell from his pocket just as it started ringing. "It's the station. Maybe that's what they're calling about." He put the phone to his ear. "Sheriff Hayes speaking." His eyes flared. *"What?"* There was a small pause. "How many?" Another pause, then Jesse cursed. "We need to call in everyone currently off duty, then I want everyone out on patrol in pairs, keeping an eye out for escapees."

Zane's pulse sped up. "Escapees?"

"There was a prisoner transfer from Montana State Prison. Contact was lost with the transport officers, and the van was just found in the mountains, here in Amber Ridge." Jesse met his gaze. "Both transport officers are dead and the van's empty."

Zane flinched like someone had hit him.

"How many inmates?" Becket asked through gritted teeth.

"Nine."

"Do you know any of the inmates' names?" Zane asked quietly.

Jesse shook his head. "No. I've got to get to the station."

"I'm coming with you," Becket said.

"Me too," Holden agreed, following them out.

Zane's cell rang, Ethan's name on the screen.

And he knew. He fucking knew exactly what was about to be said. He almost didn't want to answer because that would make it real. "Ethan—"

"They transferred them early." Air blew over the line. "He's out, Zane. Monty's in Amber Ridge."

There it was. The confirmation he hadn't wanted. And the start of his nightmare.

Ethan kept talking. About the other prisoners who were in the van. About driving to Amber Ridge to help find and contain them.

Zane was barely listening. He could only think about—only had the *capacity* for—one thing.

Bonnie.

"I have to go, Ethan." He hung up and rushed out of The Tea House, hitting Bonnie's name on his cell.

The call rang out.

Fuck.

He called again. And again, no answer.

No. This couldn't be happening.

He started running, sprinting down the street. He didn't even stop at The Pit to get his car. Running was faster. And he needed to get to her as quickly as possible. Because if Monty got to her first, Zane could lose the only good thing in his life.

CHAPTER 24

*B*onnie's fingers flew over the keyboard. She'd already responded to a million emails today. A lot of them about donations, but not just the monetary kind. They needed things like hygiene kits and clothing and bedding. There was also a baby here, which meant they needed diapers and formula and baby clothes. The list was extensive.

Other emails, like the one she was writing now, were about activities she was planning. She typed out the message to the women's law center, which would be giving them a Zoom presentation to talk about protective orders and safety planning.

She *loved* this stuff. Organizing meaningful, helpful activities for women and children in need. It made her feel like she was doing something important and making a small difference.

The smell of food from the Crock-Pot in the kitchen filled the air, and the TV's background noise filtered down the hall. Even from her office she knew exactly what was on—*Bluey*, Chett's favorite.

This morning, she'd arrived to him waiting with a picture he'd drawn, of her and him sitting on Bluey's porch steps.

She smiled as she glanced at her bag on the floor, the corner of the picture poking from the opening.

Would she have a kid as cute as Chett one day?

A boy with laser-blue eyes flashed in her mind.

She blinked. Where had that come from? It was far too soon to be thinking about kids with Zane. Sure, the last week had been good—no, *great*. But they were still fairly new.

She'd just hit send on the email when the piercing scream of a child cut through the house, followed by the sound of breaking glass.

Bonnie shot out of her seat and raced down the hall. All the women in the living room were on their feet and staring into the kitchen, where Sarah was crouched in front of Chett, who looked terrified.

Bonnie ran over to them.

"Chett, it's okay, darling," Sarah said.

"No! I-I saw…" The little boy's chest heaved, his face completely devoid of color.

She cupped his cheek. "Baby. Breathe. Tell me what you saw."

Bonnie glanced out the window, but all she saw was the backyard.

"I saw D-dad," Chett whispered, the words so quiet that Bonnie almost missed them.

Sarah flinched, and for a moment was completely still. Then she shook her head. "No. That's not possible. He's in prison."

"I *saw* him!"

As Sarah spoke to her son, Bonnie inched around them, taking slow steps toward the kitchen window. She scanned the yard. The bushes. The trees. The fence that bordered the property.

He couldn't have seen his father. Even if the guy had somehow gotten out of prison, the gate was coded. He couldn't get in here.

She was about to turn away when she saw it—a flash of orange from behind a tree.

She stumbled back.

"Get upstairs." Her words were quiet.

Sarah heard them. She rose, face paling. "What?"

"Get upstairs," she repeated, louder now, almost yelling as she glanced at the women. "Everyone. *Now.*"

The last bit of color drained from Sarah's face. "He…he's really here?"

Bonnie gripped Sarah's shoulders. "I'm not sure. Maybe. I need you to take Chett upstairs, and all of you, lock yourselves in the bedrooms. As quickly as you can."

Another woman stepped forward. "What about you?"

"I'm going to make sure no one gets inside this house. Go. *Now.*"

Sarah gave her one more scared look before lifting Chett and following the women upstairs.

Bonnie's heart thundered as she raced to the shelter phone. Shelley had left early today, which meant, for the first time since starting here, it was just her. She was the only staff member in the house.

Her fingers shook as she typed in her cousin's number.

Jesse took so long to answer, she thought he wasn't going to. Fear bled into her body, making her knees tremble.

She was about to hang up when—

"Bonnie, now's not a good time."

"I need you to get to the shelter as soon as you can." She raced to the back door and checked the handle. Locked. Good. She put on the safety chain.

"Why?" Jesse's voice shifted to one of urgency. "What's wrong?"

"Sarah Parlor, one of the women here, has an ex who's in jail for murder. Her son thinks he saw him, and I just saw someone wearing orange in the yard."

She sprinted to the front door and checked the handle. Also locked. Again, she pulled the safety chain across just for that extra bit of protection.

Jesse cursed. "I'm coming now, Bonnie. Lock the doors. Stay safe."

"I will."

She hung up and ran to the living room window, where she pulled the blackout curtains across.

Stay calm, Bonnie. You're trained for this. You'll be okay.

But how did he even get here? The guy was supposed to be in prison, for God's sake!

He was wearing an orange jumpsuit. That meant he'd escaped, right?

She raced to the first bedroom off the hall, checked the window, then pulled the curtains across. Then the next. She'd just reached her office when the sight of a tall man in a jumpsuit on the other side of the glass made her screech and fall back. He had dark hair and a scar on the left side of his face.

She opened her mouth to scream just as he lifted a gun and fired.

She covered her head and dropped to the floor, glass shattering around her.

A ringing sounded in her ears.

Get up, Bonnie. You need to get up.

She forced herself to move. To crawl out of the office and into the hall before stumbling to her feet. But she didn't run up the stairs. She couldn't lead him to the women. But she also couldn't leave the house and desert them.

She sprinted to the kitchen and dove behind the island. She didn't have a weapon. But all the knives were in drawers, and he'd have heard her rummaging around for them.

Her heart hammered in her throat. It was also a terrible hiding spot. But hiding long term wasn't her goal. If she heard him head upstairs, she'd have to follow. Or make noise to lure him back. She had to protect Sarah and Chett and everyone else, at all costs.

She closed her eyes, listening for footsteps. And they came. They were loud and heavy, hitting the floorboards in the living room hard.

He was coming. He'd followed her.

Fear wrapped its fingers around her chest, squeezing, making it hard to breathe. But she had to be strong, at least until Jesse arrived.

The footsteps grew closer. Quieter now, but in the silent room, they were still loud. She shifted, only slightly so that she was on her butt and ready to kick.

She saw his foot first and immediately shot her foot into his shin.

He fired, and she cried out as the bullet grazed her right arm. She kicked him again, this time in the knee, sending him to the tiled floor. His head hit the counter on his way down, and the gun flew from his fingers.

She lunged for it, but the man dove on top of her, his body heavy, pressing her to the floor as he reached over her head for the weapon.

* * *

ZANE SPRINTED DOWN THE STREET, pushing his body to move as fast as it could, when the shelter finally came into view.

He didn't have a weapon. He didn't have the time to stop and get one from The Pit. Those few minutes could cost Bonnie her life.

He didn't need one. He was a former fucking Army Ranger. A former UFC fighter. He'd brought down a hundred men with just his hands, and anyone who touched a hair on Bonnie's head was as good as dead.

When he reached the house, the gate was already open but the curtains were drawn, so he couldn't see inside. He remained low, scanning the grounds.

No one was there.

He tried the front door handle. Locked.

Was that good or bad? Did it mean she was safe inside?

No. The gate shouldn't be open.

He jogged around the house and tried the back door. Again, it was locked.

Slowly, he crept around the house, checking every window. They were all locked, curtains closed. Until he reached the last one.

His stomach twisted. Glass. It was shattered from the outside.

He leapt inside, glass crunching beneath his feet. As he passed the desk, he grabbed a letter opener. It was sharp and the closest thing he had to a weapon.

He moved slowly down the hall, scanning every room he passed. He was almost done with the hall when a gunshot shattered the quiet.

Zane sprinted through the living room and into the kitchen.

His heart fucking stopped at the sight of the asshole on top of Bonnie.

He lunged, grabbing the fucker by the back of his jumpsuit seconds before he could grab the gun on the floor. Zane threw him into the wall and held the letter opener to his throat.

He froze. It wasn't Monty. But it *was* one of the escaped prisoners.

Had Monty sent him after Bonnie?

The guy threw a punch, not seeming to care about the sharp edge against his throat. Zane dodged the hit easily and threw him to the floor.

The guy grunted and rolled, attempting to stand, but Zane dropped to his back and pressed an elbow to his neck. "Move and you'll never walk again."

He tried to shove up anyway, and Zane delivered one hard blow to his skull, rendering him unconscious.

Idiot.

The second the guy was out, Zane rushed over to Bonnie, who was now standing by the kitchen counter, chest heaving, pistol in her shaky hands.

Gently, he took the grip of the gun from her fingers and set the weapon on the counter before lightly grabbing her hips. "Are you—" He stopped at the sight of the blood on her arm. "You're hurt!"

Shit.

He lifted her arm, feet twitching to turn around and kill the guy.

"The bullet grazed me," she said quietly, eyes only on him. "Are you okay?"

He grabbed a hanging tea towel and wrapped it around her arm. "I'm fine. But we need to get you to a hospital."

"I have to make sure everyone upstairs is okay."

Zane cupped her cheek, still studying her, looking for more injuries. If he'd been any later, she might not be here right now. And that fucking killed him. "Do you know who he is?"

"The ex of one of the women here. He's also the father of her child."

This attack hadn't been targeted toward Bonnie. "I thought…"

"You thought what?" She frowned.

Before he could respond, a shuffling noise sounded behind him. He spun just as the prisoner lunged from the floor.

Then a loud bang, and he went down again—a bullet wound in his back and a knife Zane hadn't noticed dropping from his hold.

Zane's head whipped to the side. A woman was at the base of the stairs, a pistol in her hands.

"Sarah!" Bonnie gasped.

"He…he was going to stab him," she whispered.

Bonnie raced over to the woman and took the weapon from her. "Where'd you get this?"

"It…it's mine."

Zane leaned down and touched his pulse. Dead.

Banging sounded on the door and Zane hurried toward it, looking through the peephole before opening it to Jesse, Becket, Holden and a deputy.

They all entered, guns raised, only to stop at the sight of the dead felon.

"What happened?" Jesse asked, gun lowering.

Over the next hour, everyone at the shelter spoke to Jesse and the deputy, giving their version of events. Zane stuck to Bonnie's side the entire time. He needed to talk to Jesse about Monty, but he also needed to get Bonnie to the hospital to have her arm looked at.

Jesse crossed over to him. "How did you know to come here? Did Bonnie call you?"

"I couldn't get through to Bonnie," he said quietly. "I was worried. I came here straight from The Tea House."

"Bonnie?" A woman ran into the house, going straight to Bonnie. "I got your message. Is everyone okay?"

Zane eyed the new woman, wondering if she was Bonnie's boss. If so…where the hell had she been?

Right now, he didn't really care. Because if she was here, that meant he could finally take Bonnie to the hospital.

Jesse was called over by one of his deputies, and Zane slipped an arm around Bonnie. "We're leaving."

She shook her head. "No, I need to help Shelley find new accommodations for everyone. I need—"

"Bonnie." He gripped her hips. "You were shot."

"The bullet barely touched me."

"We're going to the hospital."

"But—"

"We're going to the hospital. This isn't up for discussion."

She rubbed a hand over her pale face before finally nodding. "Okay."

Thank God. With her tucked close to his side, he grabbed her bag and headed toward her car.

He scanned the area, so fucking aware that even though this time it hadn't been Monty, the next time, it might be.

$\mathcal{B}$onnie felt sick. Not because a nurse was putting stitches in her arm. Or because she'd just had to fight for her life at the shelter. She felt sick for Zane. Because the man who'd tried to destroy his life a year ago was out of prison. Not just out...he was almost certainly here, in Amber Ridge.

She shifted her gaze from the nurse to him. He stood less than a foot from the bed, but he didn't need to be any closer for her to feel the tornado of emotions inside him. At the top of those emotions was fear. And in all the time she'd known Zane, she'd rarely seen fear on him. It looked strange and out of place.

Then there was the way his muscles were tense, his eyes trained on the door, like he was waiting for someone to crash into the room. Like he was ready to go to war to protect them.

"All done." The nurse stepped back. "You'll need to come back in a week to get the stitches removed. If you get any redness or swelling before then, please come see us."

Bonnie nodded. "I will. Thank you."

The nurse stepped out and the room felt too quiet. But the tension... God, it was so thick she could almost feel it.

"Zane—"

The door opened and Noah stepped in, his gaze going right to Bonnie. He was across the room in a second, his hands on her sides. "Are you okay?"

"I'm fine. The bullet grazed my arm."

Her brother growled before tugging her against his chest.

"How's it looking out there?" Zane asked, when Noah stepped back.

"It's a mess." Noah's jaw clenched. "People are scared. Jesse and his deputies are trying to get the word out that only absolutely necessary outings should be taken. There's a curfew. The state police are just arriving, and so is the Department of Corrections. You'd think they'd have gotten the hell out of town, but crimes have already been committed. Businesses and homes have been broken into. Assaults and thefts are actively happening."

Jesus. This was really bad.

Zane scrubbed a hand through his hair, like he was internally blaming himself. "There's something you need to know."

Bonnie's stomach cramped.

"What?" Noah asked with a frown.

"Monty Cruz is one of the guys who escaped. I was the reason he was put away, and I'm pretty sure he's the cause of all this."

For a moment Noah was quiet, like he couldn't quite wrap his head around what Zane had just said. "So this is about you? Some asshole wants revenge?"

"Yeah, I think so." The muscles in Zane's arms visibly flexed. "He has a shitload of money from his career in the UFC. He has the means to pull this off. And the motive."

"We need to tell Jesse," Noah said quickly.

Zane nodded. "I plan to do that."

There was a pause before Noah shifted his gaze to her. "And you can't stay with him."

She straightened. "I *am* staying with him."

"Bonnie, this asshole pulled off an entire damn prison escape to get to Zane. He's dangerous, and Zane's his target."

Her stomach twisted. Because there was no way she was leaving Zane alone to deal with this. It wasn't just about the physical danger. It was about the mental toll this was taking on him. He shouldn't be alone. "No. We're not separating."

Noah cursed under his breath before looking at Zane.

Then *she* looked at Zane. At the frown on his face…the uncertainty…and it made new fear flutter in her belly.

Back me up, she whispered in her head. *Tell my brother that we're in this together.*

But he didn't. He just stood there, looking at her like he was actually considering it.

No.

She stood. "Zane. Tell him I'm not going anywhere."

"Noah's right. I'm a target for a dangerous man. You have a brother who can protect you just as well as I can. It would be safer for you to go with him."

"I don't care about me. I care about *you*. You shouldn't be alone."

"I can protect myself."

She shook her head. "No. I'm not talking about that. I want to be with you." She pressed a palm to his chest.

"Bonnie—" Noah started.

"I need a few minutes with Zane," she said, without looking at her brother.

For a second there was silence. Then Noah sighed. "I'll wait in the hall."

The second he stepped out, Bonnie inched closer to Zane. "Let me stay with you."

"You'll have Noah and your cousins to protect you. It's the smart decision."

"You shouldn't be by yourself."

"Bonnie—"

"We're *not* separating." She turned and moved toward her bag, only to stop at the strong fingers on her arm.

"I don't want you out of my sight either," he whispered in her ear. "But if anything happened to you because of me, I'd never forgive myself."

Tears of frustration built in her eyes. And anger. Because Zane had been through enough. They'd *both* been through enough.

He lowered his head to the crook of her neck. "I'm going to find him. And I'm going to end him. I promise."

"No." Hell no. "You leave that to Jesse and his deputies."

"Bonnie—"

"He's dangerous, Zane."

"So am I."

Fear crept beneath her skin. "I can't lose you."

"You won't."

It didn't feel that way. It felt like he was sand slipping between her fingers.

Unexpected tears gathered in her eyes. "Things just keep pulling us apart."

He lowered his forehead to hers. "It won't be forever."

A tear trailed down her cheek. He lowered his head and kissed it away. Then his lips found hers. The kiss was long and slow. It was emotional and hungry and filled with underlying yearning. A yearning to be together. To love each other without interruption or fear.

But that wasn't going to happen…not until Monty was gone.

* * *

It took a lot to walk away from Bonnie. So much willpower that he wasn't even sure how he managed.

And the second he was in the hall, all he wanted to do was

turn around and go back to her. There was a fucking prisoner outbreak, for Christ's sake. The need to be close to her, to protect her, ran so deep it was in his bones.

He pulled the door shut, looking at her brother. Noah was right. He had a target on his back. Even if Monty already knew about her, being away from her would be an extra layer of protection. She had people who could protect her, and putting her in the line of fire just to keep her by his side would be too fucking selfish. He couldn't afford to be selfish. He had too much to lose.

"You protect her with your life," Zane said, the words damn hard to get out. "You hear me?"

"Of course I will."

He turned and stormed down the hall, anger almost choking him. Pounding at his ribs like a fist.

He'd expected Monty to retaliate, but this? This was so much worse than he could have ever anticipated. It was smart of him to release a van full of convicts. It meant they took the attention off him.

And the difference between Monty a year ago and now was that he had nothing to lose. He was already a man with a life sentence against his name, which meant he wasn't bound by consequences. It made him more dangerous than anyone else.

He shoved outside, scanning the parking lot. There were already state police outside the hospital doors. Men in uniforms, also with their hands by their weapons, waiting for trouble.

This would be the new normal...for the moment, at least.

Zane didn't have his car but he wasn't going back to his apartment. The station wasn't far. Walking distance.

He'd just reached it when a patrol car pulled up out front. Jesse and a deputy climbed out. They pulled a shirtless guy in jeans from the back seat. His wrists were cuffed, and he had splatters of blood on his chest.

The guy growled as he was yanked forward. "Get the fuck off

me! I'm not doing more time for this. That asshole threatened my family if I left Amber Ridge. He—" He fell silent when he saw Zane, his brows tugging together. "*You.*"

Jesse frowned. "You know him?"

"You live here?" the guy asked, ignoring Jesse—then throwing back his head and laughing. "*That's* why he did it. You're a dead man. You know that, right?"

"Shut up." Jesse pulled him inside, and Zane followed. When another deputy came out of a hallway, Jesse handed the guy over. Then he moved to the door of an office before turning to Zane. "In."

Zane stepped inside but didn't sit. He couldn't. He needed to pace. To move. To breathe without feeling caged.

The door clicked shut behind Jesse. "I'm gonna be honest, Zane. I've had a bad fucking day. My town is under threat. My family is out there doing a job that's not theirs to do. One dead and two arrested means if all those convicts came our way, I still have another six on the loose." He stepped around his desk looking pissed. "So I need you to tell me what the hell that guy was talking about—and do it fast."

"Monty Cruz is one of the felons. He's that guy who tried to get away with murder in Billings. He's my cousin. And I'm the reason he was found guilty."

"This is about you?" Jesse asked, disbelief in his tone.

"Yeah. I didn't need confirmation from that guy to know that. These other convicts are just distractions. A means to keep you and your deputies busy."

Jesse laughed but there was no humor behind the sound. "They're doing that."

"Cruz has money, and he uses that money to buy the help he needs. I'm sure that's how the guy breached the shelter today and knew his wife and kid were there."

"I've got all the bios and mug shots, so knowing that this Cruz guy is the ringleader will help."

"I need to know the second you have information on him." Zane stepped closer. "And I'm going to scour this town until I find him. I'm not leaving a stone unturned. I need you to keep me in the loop. I need this to be over."

"You and me both." Jesse's jaw clenched. "I'll keep you in the loop. But you need to do the same for me. Keeping this town safe is my responsibility and my priority."

"I know. We'll get things back to how it's supposed to be."

"Of course we will."

Zane nodded and turned toward the door.

"Zane."

He stopped, hand on the knob, before looking over his shoulder at Jesse. "Yeah?"

"Watch your back."

"You too. Monty's smart. And he doesn't fight fair."

In the parking lot, Zane headed straight toward Ethan, who was leaning against his truck.

"Ready?"

"Let's go." Zane slid into the passenger seat.

Ethan pulled out of the parking lot. "I've booked a cabin under another name. We'll head there. Make a list of places he could be staying."

"He could be anywhere."

"Yeah, but we're better than him. He can't hide from us for long."

They *were* better. But Monty had time on his side. He'd no doubt been planning this since the judge passed down his sentence.

Ethan shot him a look. "Bonnie's with her brother?"

Her name, the sheer fucking sound of it, made his lungs restrict. "Yes."

"You know he probably already knows about her."

"Yeah, but I'm hoping I'm at the top of his hit list and she's safe with her family."

Ethan nodded. "We're gonna find him, Zane. And when we do—"

"We end him."

CHAPTER 26

*B*onnie's fingers hovered over her phone.

She wanted to text him. No, what she really wanted to do was call him and hear his voice. But the last few times she'd done that, he hadn't answered. And she wasn't sure her heart could take another unanswered phone call.

She knew why. He was scared. Scared of having contact with her in case that connected them. Scared of everything that was coming.

And maybe she was being selfish in wanting to hear his voice. But it had been three whole days of not seeing him while the town, while *he,* was going through this terrible crisis. She wanted to know he was okay.

Quickly, she typed out four words.

Bonnie: I'm thinking of you.

Send. Done.

Her phone suddenly rang, but it wasn't Zane's name on the screen, it was Jesse's.

Nerves tickled her spine. "Jesse? Is everything okay?"

"I just wanted to call and update you on the shelter."

By the sound of Jesse's voice, it wasn't good. "Okay."

"Shelley cracked and told me that she received payment to share both Sarah's location and the code to the gate."

Bonnie's jaw dropped. "Are you serious?"

"I'm afraid so. We found the money trail in her account."

Jesus. So the woman wasn't just a terrible boss, she was also a terrible person. "I'm guessing she's been arrested?"

"Yes."

"Okay. Um, thanks for letting me know."

"Are you doing okay?"

"I'm not sure. I'm surprised." Understatement of the century. "Noah's taking great care of me."

"Good. Call if you need anything."

"I will." She hung up, nibbling her bottom lip. Shelley had given out information about Sarah and Chett. She'd taken money from a *criminal*. Put innocent women and children in danger.

She was awful. Worse than awful.

Bonnie shook her head. She needed a distraction.

She dropped her phone to the bed. If she took it out of the bedroom with her, all she'd do was stare at the screen and wait for a call from Zane.

She was halfway down the hall when she stopped and closed her eyes.

She couldn't do it.

Quickly, she raced back and grabbed it again.

Pathetic. She was pathetic.

"Give me that."

Bonnie frowned at Indie's angry tone.

"No way. The last time you had this spoon, you hit me with it," Noah said.

"Because you licked it!"

"You mean like this?"

There was a gasp. "Ew!"

Bonnie walked into the living room in time to see Indie punch their brother on the shoulder.

"Ow," Noah groaned.

"Don't be a baby." Indie turned away from Noah and spotted her. "Bonnie. Hey."

She stopped at the kitchen island, taking in the ingredients spread across the counter and the bowl in front of Indie. "Baking something?"

"Sure are." Noah grinned. "Chocolate chip cookies, but swapping the chocolate chips for M&M's."

Bonnie chuckled. "I think I'm twelve again."

Indie lifted a shoulder. "Nothing wrong with that."

Noah pushed the bag of M&M's across the counter. "Here. I get whacked every time I eat one, but I bet Indie will let you have some."

Bonnie grinned as she took a few. "Are you still eating all the ingredients?"

"All of them," Indie groaned. "And the dough. Luckily, I doubled the recipe."

"I see we haven't gotten better at keeping the flour inside the bowl." Bonnie ran her finger over the floured counter.

"Remember how mad Mom and Dad used to get at the mess?" Indie asked softly.

"What I remember is you both blaming *me*," Bonnie scoffed.

Noah's grin widened. "You were the youngest—least chance of getting yelled at."

"Hey, they preferred us baking than some of our other activities. Remember the rope swing?" Indie laughed.

Noah scrubbed a hand over his face. "Don't remind me. It wasn't my finest moment."

"Flooding the backyard and sending me flying across on your newest invention wasn't your finest moment?" Bonnie asked, feigning innocence.

Indie cringed. "I can still hear your screams when you hit the fence."

"That's how I lost my third tooth," Bonnie said, almost

proudly.

"Jesus Christ." Noah almost looked embarrassed. Probably because his job now was all about safety.

Bonnie eyed the bowl. "Can I mix?"

"Sure." Indie pushed the bowl toward her.

Immediately, Bonnie lifted the spoon and ate a huge mouthful of dough.

"Hey!" Indie crossed her arms. "With you two here, we'll be lucky to get one cookie out of the mixture."

Bonnie lifted a shoulder. "I always preferred the dough."

Noah laughed with her and, after a moment, Indie joined in.

Over the next hour, they baked cookies and ate ridiculous amounts of raw dough and M&M's. Technically, the town was in lockdown, but house-to-house visits were still happening so that everyone could check in on each other and stay sane.

It was nice. Throughout the years, Bonnie had convinced herself that she'd never gotten along with her siblings. But now, standing here, she wasn't sure that was true. Before they'd hit their teenage years, they *had* gotten along. And the three of them had done everything together. Noah was the oldest, so he was usually the leader. Indie was the pragmatic one and the most safety conscious. While Bonnie, as the youngest, was up for anything and just happy to be included.

How had she forgotten?

Or maybe she *hadn't* forgotten. Maybe it was just too hard to think about while there was so much separation between them.

Indie checked her phone. "Colt will be here to pick me up in a few minutes. I'm just going to pee for the fiftieth time today, because baby likes doing gymnastics on my bladder."

When Indie left, Bonnie turned back to Noah. "Where's Addie?"

"She's with Jules. I'm going to pick her up later. She's under strict instructions to keep the house locked and remain inside until I get there."

The light feeling of a few moments ago faded, and she was thrown back into reality.

She pulled an M&M off the cookie in her hand. "Any more progress finding and detaining those felons?"

"Actually, yeah. Someone held up the grocery store today. Holden was there. He took the guy down. Apparently, it was quite the heroic act."

"The grocery store." Bonnie swallowed. "Some of them aren't even trying to hide."

"Well, when they've been threatened to stay in town, they already know they're going to get caught."

It was unbelievable that Monty had done that. But it also wasn't. Zane had told her the lengths Monty would go to hurt him. He wasn't wrong.

She glanced down at her cell. Still no response from Zane.

She lowered the cookie to her plate, appetite suddenly nonexistent. "So that leaves…five, right? There were nine—three have been arrested and one dead."

"Yeah. Five to go."

Her phone suddenly vibrated, and a rush of air slipped from her lungs when she saw who it was.

Zane: I've done nothing but think of you, Bonnie. Are you safe?

Zane's words made butterflies flutter in her belly.

Bonnie: I am. Are you?

Zane: Yeah. No sign of Monty, which is both a relief and annoying as hell. How's your arm?

Bonnie: I barely feel the wound.

"That Zane?"

She glanced at her brother. "Yeah. I hate being away from him."

"It's not forever."

"That's what he said." And yet, it didn't make it any easier.

Noah cleared his throat. "I'm glad you have him."

"Really?"

"Yeah." He leaned his hip against the counter. "After all that stuff came out about him, I wasn't sure. But now…"

"Now what?"

"He's a good guy and he really cares about you. I trust him."

A small smile curved her lips. She wasn't sure why, but she liked that her brother approved.

Her phone vibrated, and she looked down again, expecting to see another text from Zane.

It wasn't.

Unknown number: Feeling safe?

Her heart stuttered, and she shot up so fast her stool hit the floor. "Noah."

"What is it?"

Another text came through.

Unknown number: You shouldn't be. No one Zane cares about is safe. He lost that privilege when he stabbed me in the back.

"He's messaging me," Bonnie whispered.

"Who?" Noah grabbed her cell, his gaze running over the words before he cursed. "I'm calling Jesse."

"What's going on?" Indie asked, as she stepped back into the room.

"He got my number." Bonnie turned to glance out at the street. "I'm closing the curtains."

It was probably overkill, but there was this pit in her stomach, and doing something felt better than nothing.

She moved to the window.

"What's that?" Indie asked.

Bonnie looked up. She'd just spotted the person crouching behind a car on the street when Indie screamed. Her sister dove on top of her as a bullet cut through the glass.

Bonnie gasped as they hit the floor, and a second later, Noah was dragging them both away from the window to the corner of the room. That's when Bonnie saw the blood.

Not *her* blood, though.

Her gaze shot up. "Indie…"

* * *

ZANE SLIPPED THROUGH THE TREES, the Airbnb house in view.

He couldn't see Ethan, but he knew his friend was on the other side somewhere. They'd already been to three other properties, all with booking dates that coincided with the prisoner break. Monty hadn't been at any of them.

Was he here? All the curtains were closed, and there were no vehicles out front. Didn't mean the house was empty though.

With the Glock held close to his body, he kept low and jogged forward, scanning his surroundings as he moved. When he reached the window, he lifted a rock and gently tossed it at the glass before dropping to the side of the house.

If there was someone inside, they'd hear it.

One minute passed. Then another. Nothing.

Quickly, he pulled out his pick and slipped it into the window. The lock clicked and he pushed the window open before climbing through and dropping inside with a quiet thud.

A twin bed centered the room, with bedside tables on either side, and an old freestanding armoire was positioned against the opposite wall. That was it. No bags. No people.

Weapon raised, he moved around the room, opening drawers and checking the closet. There was no sign of anyone staying here. None. In fact, there was a small film of dust on the drawers.

He entered the hall, Ethan stepping in from the other side. Their gazes met but only for a second.

From what he could hear, the house was silent. No footsteps or voices. So the most likely scenario was that the place was empty.

But why would someone book it, just to leave it vacant?

Ethan moved into the kitchen while Zane went to another room off the hall. He opened the door to find an empty bathroom and no sign that anyone had used it recently. There were no drops of water in the sink. No toothbrushes or tubes of toothpaste on the counter.

What the hell was going on?

He headed down the hall to the last unopened door and was just pulling it open when Ethan threw Zane to the floor as an explosion blasted out of the room.

Zane cursed and tucked his head, the floor beneath him shaking under the impact.

Another second passed and he rose and cursed again, flames already burning from the room into the hall.

Fuck.

"Come on." Ethan ran down the hall.

Zane followed back out the bedroom window. When his feet hit the ground, he sprinted into the trees. He wasn't taking a chance that something else had been rigged to blow.

Ethan was already on the phone to the fire department.

Zane waited until they reached his car before turning to his friend. "How did you know?"

Ethan handed him a piece of paper.

Boom! Did you make it? Did she?

Zane's heart fucking stopped. She…

Bonnie.

He pulled his cell from his pocket, hands trembling as he called her.

She didn't answer. She didn't fucking answer "I need to get to Noah's house."

He went to climb behind the wheel, but Ethan grabbed his arm. "I'm driving."

Zane didn't have time to argue. He sprinted around the car and dropped into the passenger seat. Ethan put his foot to the floor and sped out of the forest.

Zane tried Noah's number next. Again, nothing.

Shit.

He needed someone, anyone, to tell him she was safe. Someone to reassure him that she was alive.

He tried her number one more time, expecting it to go to voicemail again.

"Zane?"

"Bonnie." Relief hit him so hard, air whooshed from his chest. "Are you okay?"

"No." Her voice was quiet and pained.

"What happened? Where are you?"

"I'm at the Amber Ridge Hospital. I'm okay but…I need you."

"We need to get to the hospital," Zane growled to Ethan.

Ethan turned the car. "We're around the corner."

"I'm coming, honey."

"I'm in the waiting room. I have to go."

"Bonnie—"

She'd already hung up.

Dammit!

The second Ethan pulled into the parking lot, Zane was out and running. When he stepped into the waiting area, he saw her, sitting on a chair, eyes red, cheeks tear-stained. Noah sat beside her, and Addie beside him.

"Bonnie."

Her eyes lifted, and she stood before immediately falling into his arms.

"What happened? Are you hurt?"

She pulled back. "He tried to shoot me, but Indie threw herself onto me, and the bullet…it hit her, Zane."

Indie had been shot. Shot with a bullet intended for Bonnie.

"I don't know if she's okay," Bonnie whispered. "I don't know if her baby's okay!"

He cursed and pulled her back into his chest.

She tensed in his arms. "You smell like fire."

"Don't worry about that."

Noah's phone rang. He stood and answered it. "Colt?" There

was a short pause. "Thank God!" He hung up and turned to them. "Indie's out of surgery. Both her and the baby are okay."

Bonnie collapsed into his side, new tears building in her eyes. He tightened an arm around her, taking most of her weight.

"What's going on?" Ethan asked when he reached their little group.

"Indie was shot protecting Bonnie."

Ethan's eyes narrowed.

Bonnie frowned at Ethan, then him. "You both look like you were in a fire. Where have you been? And don't brush me off and say nowhere."

"We—"

The hospital doors opened, and Jesse and Holden stepped in.

"I came as fast as I could," Jesse said. "How is she?"

"Her and the baby are okay," Noah replied.

"Thank God. What happened?"

"There was a shooter on the street hiding behind a car." There was an edge of anger in Noah's voice. But also something else. Guilt, maybe? Because he'd been the one who was supposed to protect his sisters. "I didn't see him. He was to the side of the street and I…I wasn't looking. Fuck, I should have been looking."

Jesse gripped his shoulder. "It's not your fault."

"I got two texts," Bonnie said quietly.

Zane tensed. "Texts?"

She nodded and scrolled through her phone. Then she turned the cell so they could see.

Unknown number: Feeling safe?

Unknown number: You shouldn't be. No one Zane cares about is safe. He lost that privilege when he stabbed me in the back.

He'd gotten her number. Not just her number. Her location.

"Where's Becket?" Noah asked.

Jesse glanced at him. "He's at a house fire."

Bonnie turned to him and Ethan. "What the hell's going on?"

"Monty set up an explosion," Zane said through gritted teeth.

"He knew we'd search vacation rentals. He rigged the place and left a note."

"What did the note say?" Jesse asked.

Ethan handed it to the sheriff.

"He's a step ahead of us," Jesse growled, frustration threaded through his words.

"He knows me too well." They were family. But hell, for years they'd been more than that. They'd been best friends.

"So what does he think you'll do next?" Holden asked.

"I don't care." He really didn't. He only cared about one thing. "It doesn't matter, because I'm better than him. I'm going to find him. And I'm going to tear him apart."

"Zane—"

"Nothing and no one can change my mind," Zane pushed. He meant it. Absolutely nothing would get in his way. Especially after attempting to hurt Bonnie and getting her sister. All it had done was ignite a new fire inside him to murder the man.

"Fine," Jesse said. "But you're not alone. We're all with you."

"Hell yes, we are," Noah pushed. "He shot my sister and I'm going to make sure he pays for that."

"I'm staying with Zane," Bonnie said quickly.

Zane shook his head. "No, it's too—"

"Dangerous?" Bonnie lifted a brow. "He almost shot me today. He *did* shoot my pregnant sister. We've passed dangerous. I'm not endangering any more of my family. I'm either with you or by myself."

Zane didn't want to agree. Because every part of him knew that something big was coming for him.

But she was right. The danger had found her anyway, and at least with him, he'd be able to protect her himself. "Fine. You're coming with me."

*B*onnie shot up in bed, her heart racing.

Darkness surrounded her, the unfamiliar bedroom in the cabin making the fear settle deeper in her belly.

Just a dream. It was just a dream.

But it wasn't. It was a memory. Of Indie. Shoving her aside. Of the blood.

She dropped her head into her hands, fresh tears filling her eyes.

Indie had been hurt because of her...while *saving* her. She and her baby were okay, but it could have ended so much worse.

She turned to study the bed beside her. Empty.

Where was Zane?

After leaving the hospital, he'd brought her to this isolated cabin. It was big. So big that Ethan was in one of the bedrooms upstairs while she and Zane had the entire downstairs to themselves. They'd had dinner. Showered. And he'd held her until she'd fallen asleep.

But had *he* slept?

She pushed the covers back and touched her feet to the

wooden floorboards. Even though the cabin was old, it had clearly been updated with heating and top-notch security.

So why was she still so cold?

Without bothering with a sweatshirt or pants, she left the bedroom, only wearing one of Zane's shirts because they hadn't grabbed anything from her place yet. The shirt drowned her, and it also smelled exactly like him—a mix of eucalyptus and smoked vanilla. So uniquely Zane.

Her footsteps were quiet as she padded down the hall, the darkness keeping her pulse racing beneath her skin.

She searched the kitchen first, then the living room.

Nothing. Had he gone outside? Maybe he was doing a perimeter check.

She was about to shift the curtain aside to look through the window when something sounded. A dull thump, like a fist hitting leather.

Was there a bag in this house? Zane had given her a tour, but there hadn't been a workout room.

He'd only shown her the stairs to the basement though.

She turned and moved in that direction, then quietly opened the door and closed it behind her before descending. The thumps got louder, quickly accompanied by heavy breathing.

And that's where she found him.

Zane was shirtless, his back toward her, hands wrapped and wearing only shorts. Every time he hit the bag, a thousand muscles pulled and strained in his back.

She shuddered at the fury in his hits. Like every time a fist landed, he was trying to beat the rage out of his bones and silence something inside him.

For a moment, she didn't move. Just watched him throw hit after hit, her arms wrapped around her waist. She'd felt so much anger herself, about everything happening to him. The unfairness of it all.

But now, in this moment, all she could feel was a deep

sadness. Sadness that he'd been chasing peace for the last year but still couldn't reach it.

She stepped to the side of the bag. Two more hits and his eyes finally landed on her.

He took his earbuds out. "Bonnie."

She stepped toward him, gaze going to the straps on his hands. "How long have you been down here?"

"I'm not sure." He touched her chin and tilted her head up. The gentleness of his touch was in complete contrast to the aggression of his hits moments ago. "Are you okay?"

"I woke up and couldn't find you. I was worried."

"I couldn't sleep."

She nodded at his hands. "Can I take these off?"

His silence stretched so long she thought he'd say no. Then he nodded. Carefully, she started unwinding the material before switching to his other hand.

"I missed you." His quiet words whispered into the silence, almost knocking the breath from her chest.

She dropped the last bit of strapping. "It was only three days, but it felt like forever." She looked up, and the intensity in his eyes…it burned into her. Filling every cold crevice. Making all of her feel warm and claimed.

"I can't let him take you from me," he said, a fear she'd rarely heard slipping into his words.

She cupped his cheek. "I'm not going anywhere. Neither are you."

"Promise me." He touched his forehead to hers. "Promise me we have a future."

It wasn't a promise she should be making, and they both knew it. She didn't care. "Not just a future. We have forever, Zane."

Warm breath danced over her face. He ran his thumb over her bottom lip before touching his lips to hers. Once. Twice. The softest kisses she'd ever felt, while his hands slipped around her waist. On the third kiss, he stayed there, and the second she opened for him, he dove inside, his tongue curving around hers.

She groaned. "Love me, Zane."

The second the words slipped from her lips, he growled and lifted her so that her entire front pressed to his, her legs wrapping tightly around his waist. And she knew that *this*, being enveloped in the safety of his arms, was the only place in the world she wanted to be.

* * *

ZANE LOST himself in the kiss. As if the world had narrowed to the taste of her lips and the soft feel of her skin.

A second ago, he'd been drowning. Hitting the bag like it was his only refuge from a world that was crushing him. But it wasn't. *She* was his salvation. She was the one person who could pull him from the water when he was too deep to come up for air.

He threaded his fingers through her hair, his other arm secured around her, as if that could stop anything and anyone from taking her away.

She felt so fragile. Like she could slip from his grasp if his hold loosened. And she could. Today, he'd almost lost her. And it would have destroyed him. Pulled the foundation from beneath his feet and thrown him to his knees.

He turned and pressed her against the wall, her core surging into him, making blood roar between his ears. He tugged at the bottom of her top, pulling it over her head. Her creamy breasts bounced, so fucking beautiful that the need to touch them, taste them, throbbed like a pulse beneath his skin.

He lowered his head and took one pebbled nipple between his lips.

Bonnie's cry was fucking music to his ears. He could listen to it every day for the rest of his life and never tire of the sound.

He swirled his tongue around her bud, flicking it back and forth before sucking.

This time she was louder, her fingers latching onto his hair, pulling at the roots.

He switched to her other breast, cupping it as he tasted her.

Perfect. She was so fucking perfect. Made for him.

She arched, pushing her chest into his mouth as if she felt the suffocating need to be closer too.

He kissed back up her breasts then neck, stopping at a spot behind her ear and nibbling.

Another feminine groan slipped into the air, then her mouth was moving down *his* neck, onto his chest. Soft kisses that whispered over his skin. When she kissed a spot right over his heart, he swore the thing beat for her.

He cupped her cheek, and she turned her head and pressed her lips to his palm. But then she reached up and grabbed his hand to turn it over. And one by one, she kissed every scrape and bruise on his battered skin.

He felt her lips everywhere. They hollowed him out, making space for her. Only her.

At the lift of her gaze, she tugged his head but only so that her lips touched his ear as she whispered, "Feel this." She placed his hand on her chest right over her heart. "It's beating for you."

Time bent around her, so much so that nothing else mattered.

He held her with one hand and used the other to push down his shorts. After sliding her panties to the side, he positioned himself at her entrance. Before he could move, she tightened her legs, tugging his tip inside.

And fuck, he almost lost himself then and there.

"Bonnie." Her name was something between a whisper and a growl. His eyes shuttered, his temple touching hers.

He kissed her, slipping his tongue inside her mouth and curving it around hers. Then, slowly, he slipped the rest of the way inside her.

It was only then that he lifted his head, and the words finally slipped free.

"I love you, Bonnie."

Tears immediately filled her eyes, air stuttering from her chest. "I love you too, Zane. I think I've loved you for a long while."

He took a moment to breathe. To absorb her words and let them fill every part of him. Change him. Make her his.

He started to move, pulling out and sliding back in.

She whimpered, her hands now on his shoulders, fingers digging into his skin. "Zane."

"I've got you."

He kept moving. Thrusting in and out. Every time he returned to her, it was like coming home. Because somewhere along the line, this woman *had* become his home. The only damn home he wanted or needed.

He cupped her breast, rolling her nipple with his thumb as he moved.

Her breathing shortened and grew louder. Faster.

Beautiful. All of her. The sounds she made, the way her brow furrowed in that cute fucking pout he couldn't look away from.

He lowered his hand to her core and swiped her clit with his thumb.

Her cry shuddered through the room.

He did it again, this time rolling her clit in a circle.

She started to buck. She was close.

"Zane," she whispered.

He latched onto her throat, sucking. Then she screamed, her walls clenching his cock as she broke.

And fuck, she felt good around him. He wanted to keep going. To feel this, feel *her*, for longer, but he couldn't. Two more thrusts and he crashed and burned with her, his cock pulsing inside her body.

Long seconds of stillness passed where neither of them spoke or moved…they just breathed.

Until, finally, she touched her forehead to his chest. "God, I love you."

"You have no idea, honey." He kissed the top of her head.

And she really didn't. Because how could anyone understand this feeling inside him? *He* barely understood it. Only knew it was fierce and all-consuming and utterly unshakable.

*B*onnie tried hard to focus on Addie. She was telling a rock-climbing story. One that Bonnie absolutely should be listening to, just like the other women.

But it was hard to concentrate when the guys were huddled around the gym's front desk, talking about the remaining criminals who needed to be found and detained.

Not just talking about them. Studying profiles and photos. Talking about possible hiding places. Well, a hiding place for Monty... The rest had most likely hightailed it out of Amber Ridge.

The gym blinds were down, and pizza and drinks littered the tables, but none of that lightened her mood.

It had been five days since Indie was shot. Her sister was still in the hospital, mostly for observation because of the pregnancy. Indie had people with her. Colt. Holden. Clara. But their absence tonight felt big and heavy.

Bonnie wished she'd been able to visit her sister every day, but with Monty still out there, evasion was necessary. Plus, there was no way she wanted to bring danger to her sister's doorstep again. The only reason they were at the gym tonight was because

Zane needed to talk to the guys, and he didn't want to bring anyone to the cabin and risk the location.

When she couldn't hold off any longer, she glanced over at the men. They were still huddled over the desk, looking at mug shots. Of course, Bonnie could be over there if she wanted. All the women could.

She didn't want to. Plus, Zane would report back. And unlike the men, she didn't have a military background, so what would she do with the information anyway?

"Bonnie."

She looked back at Addie. The rest of the women were talking amongst themselves now, but Addie only had eyes for her.

The other woman's gaze was soft but also concerned. "Are you okay?"

"Just worried." Big truck-load levels of worried.

Addie glanced at the men, then back to her. "There are only three guys left and we don't know if they're all in Amber Ridge or some have left. That means it's possibly Monty against all of them."

Looking at the powerful men who, between them, had decades of tactical training and military experience, most would agree that the odds were in their favor. But Zane knew Monty best—and Zane was worried. That made Bonnie worried.

She nodded anyway. "How's Noah been?"

"It feels like we only just recovered from everything that happened at the park, and now we have this. Even though he won't admit it, it's been a lot for him. And he's worried about Indie, as we all are. But I just keep reassuring him that she'll be okay. And we'll get through this."

Bonnie touched Addie's arm. "I'm glad he has you."

"And I'm glad he has you back."

"I don't know about that. I got Indie shot." Shit. She hadn't meant to say that out loud.

"No, you didn't. You didn't ask someone to shoot at you. And it was Indie's choice to push you out of the way. I doubt she regrets saving you."

She wasn't sure she believed that. Saving Bonnie had probably been a reflex when Indie more than likely wished she'd protected her baby.

But the baby was safe and healthy. Bonnie just needed to keep reminding herself of that.

Footsteps sounded, then Noah was behind Addie, touching her back. "Hey. Ready to go?"

She rose. "Finished?"

"For tonight."

He sounded tired. But then, they all did. Even with the state police in town helping with this whole mess, it didn't feel like enough.

Noah glanced at her. "You okay, Bon?"

"Mm-hmm." She reached out and squeezed his hand.

As everyone said their goodbyes and filtered out of the gym, Bonnie moved over to Zane. His hand immediately slipped around her waist and tugged her closer, but he was still looking at the photos.

She frowned down at the three mug shots. A bald man with tattoos down his neck. A dark-haired guy with an eyebrow ring.

She frowned at the third picture. "That's Monty." She wasn't sure how she knew, but she did.

"Yeah. My dad and his mother were siblings. They've both passed now but they look similar, so we look similar."

That was it. He looked like Zane. But he also didn't. The difference was in the eyes. Monty's were flat and hollow, like they were completely devoid of warmth.

Zane was everything Monty wasn't. Good. Warm. Kind.

Instinctively, she wrapped her arms around his neck. "You know what I was thinking?"

"That we should get the hell out of this town and disappear?"

"No. That we've been dating all this time and we've never gone a round in the ring together."

A ghost of a smile curved his lips. "You want to get in the ring?"

"With you? Absolutely." She grinned before stepping out of his arms and crossing to the octagonal ring. Without a word, she slipped off her shoes, pulled off her sweatshirt, and held out her hands. "Glove me."

Humor danced in his eyes. But he grabbed two pairs of gloves from the equipment box. She barely held in the shudder as he strapped the gloves onto her hands. There was something so sexy about having a man—no, not a man, *Zane*—getting her ready to step into the ring.

When he had his gloves on, they both slipped into the ring.

"Ready?" he asked, the humor still there.

She lifted her gloved hands and softened her knees into a fighting stance. "Do you find something funny, Zane Merrick?"

"Of course not. I know better than to underestimate a beautiful woman wearing gloves."

"Damn straight." She danced forward and threw her first punch.

Zane dodged it with practiced ease. "That was good."

She lifted a brow. "Surprised?"

"By you? Always."

She grinned before throwing two more punches, followed by an uppercut.

Zane blocked all of them with his gloves but did look at least a bit impressed. "Who taught you this?"

She moved around him, staying light on her feet. "I told you. I did mixed martial arts when I left Amber Ridge. I had a lot of emotions to work through. I got kind of good."

"Are you telling me you could wrestle me to the floor right now?"

"Hot, right?"

He didn't even crack a smile, but the intensity in his eyes almost made her lose her breath.

"You haven't thrown a punch yet," she said, jabbing at his chest.

He absorbed the jab and threw a right hook, but it was more of a tap to her shoulder.

She lifted a brow. "You can do better than that."

He smiled, then threw an almost playful hook that grazed her chin.

God, she loved that smile. "You might not be treating me like a real threat, but don't think that means I'm gonna go easy on you." She threw two jabs, both dodged by him, followed by a hard and fast kick to his thigh.

He caught her leg and spun her so her back was pressed to his front, her leg still in his hold. Then his mouth touched her ear as he whispered, "That was good, Bon. But you give yourself away with your eyes."

"I do not!"

"You're too open." He kissed her ear. "Want a break?"

"No." Hell no. She threw a hard elbow to his gut. No reaction from him. No grunt or hunching. But still, he released her.

She lifted her hands to protect her face and danced around him.

He threw another playful punch, and as he did, she ducked and slipped under his arm, going to his back. She kicked at the back of his knee, but as if he had eyes in the back of his head, he moved. And the second she was thrown off balance, his strong arm wrapped around her waist and they fell to the floor, his back hitting it first before he rolled them and pinned her down.

"Gotcha." He grinned.

"I like it when you do that."

"Beat you?"

"Smile."

His smile softened, and he lowered his head and kissed her. A gentle kiss. Almost like he was scared to hurt her. His tongue slipped between her lips to taste her.

Too soon, he lifted his head and sighed. "We should go."

"We should." They needed to get back to the cabin. It was safe there. But right now, she didn't want to move a muscle.

Zane started to rise and, as he did, she swung a leg around and got him on his back and quickly straddled him.

Her smile widened. "I win." She lowered her head, hovering her mouth over his. "*Now*, we can go."

He chuckled, and the sound was exactly what she'd been hoping to achieve.

* * *

WHEN THEY STEPPED out of The Pit, the smile slipped from Zane's face as reality slammed back into him. He scanned the street, searching for danger. For any signs of Monty.

His hand hovered over the Glock in his concealed holster as Bonnie exited the gym after him. He locked the doors quickly. He didn't like being out of the safe house. But he'd needed to meet the guys and hadn't wanted to take anyone to the cabin. He trusted Bonnie's family, but the fewer people who knew about it, the better. And less chance for someone to follow a car there.

He slipped a hand to the small of Bonnie's back and led her to his car, the night looking quiet.

When they were both in the vehicle, he glanced over at Bonnie to see her smiling. It didn't quite reach her eyes though. She'd been doing that a lot this last week. Trying to be okay for him. Probably because he was doing a shit job at pretending nothing was wrong. It was. As long as Monty was on the loose, nothing was okay.

"Have you heard from Stetson since the gym closed?" Bonnie asked, as he pulled onto the street.

They'd had to close the gym since the inmate escape. Most

businesses had closed, actually. "A couple of texts here and there. I'm still paying him, so he's probably enjoying his days off."

She chuckled. "At least someone's happy."

He frowned into the rearview mirror before taking a right turn. "I don't like that all this stuff with Monty has made us stop looking for the person who assaulted and harassed you."

"Me neither. But maybe this has been a big enough distraction that they've dropped their vendetta against me."

That would be too easy. Anyone who went so far as to cut the head off a fucking mouse and send it to her in a pizza box wouldn't back off because of a distraction. The second this was over, Zane was shifting his attention back to finding the person.

He turned left, eyes narrowing on a car behind them. The same car that had been behind them since leaving The Pit.

He took another right.

A couple seconds later, the car appeared in his rearview mirror.

Bonnie frowned. "This isn't the way back."

"I need you to stay calm, okay?"

Immediately, she straightened. "Why?"

"We have a tail."

"*What?*"

She was about to turn to look behind her, but he grabbed her arm. "Don't. He's keeping his distance right now. We don't want that to change."

He hit a key on his wheel and used the car Bluetooth to make a call.

Jesse answered immediately. "Everything okay?"

"I'm heading to the sheriff's station. I have a tail."

Jesse cursed. "What are the details?"

"Gray Charger. Tinted windows. About three hundred feet behind us."

"Heading to the station now." He ended the call.

"Zane." Concern tinged Bonnie's voice. And he fucking hated it. "Do you think it's him?"

"More than likely. I need you to open the glove box for me."

She did.

"At the back there's a small pistol and a pocketknife. Put the pocketknife in your back pocket and just hold on to the pistol."

Bonnie grabbed both and did as he said. But he didn't miss the shake in her fingers. Fuck, he hated that she was with him.

Suddenly, the tail sped up.

Zane cursed, his own engine roaring as he pressed his foot to the floor.

He took a hard left. Bonnie gasped, and he grabbed her arm to keep her from hitting her side window.

"Hold on." He forced the car faster, surging forward.

Bonnie twisted to look behind them. This time he didn't stop her. "Shit. They're getting close, Zane."

He swerved to the other lane, overtaking a truck. Horns blared from oncoming traffic. Bonnie cried out, but he pulled back into their lane before a collision.

He took another right, but the tail stuck.

Fuck.

"If they box us in," Zane said, words loud and hard, "shoot first, ask questions later. Got it?"

He shot her a glance to see a jerky nod.

Tires squealed as he cut into a small alley.

He looked at her again. She was pale. Too fucking pale. "You okay?"

"I'm scared for us."

"We're almost at the station."

He pulled back onto the main street.

He checked the rearview mirror, then cursed before shouting, "Duck!"

"What—"

He shoved her head down as bullets peppered the glass at the back of the car.

Bonnie screamed.

He cursed again when the pop of a tire sounded.

Come on! Two more turns and he'd be there.

Bonnie sat up and twisted to look behind them. He'd just taken the first turn and pressed his foot back to the gas when they came out of nowhere—two cars, from streets on either side of them, perfectly timed.

Zane didn't have time to do anything but place a hand on her chest.

"Watch out!"

The cars hit them *hard*.

Metal shattered. Glass burst around them, and he hit the deployed airbag hard before he jerked sideways.

His head snapped back once, twice. There was a flash of pain behind his eyes. The last thing he saw was Bonnie's head crash against the side glass, then his world went black.

CHAPTER 29

*P*ain pulsed through Bonnie's head, making her eyes squeeze tight. But it wasn't just her head that hurt. It was her entire body. She felt bruised and battered, and a dull pulse throbbed at the base of her skull.

She was cold too. Not the kind that wrapped around her skin. This was deeper, like it was in her bones.

She tried to move—then froze. Were there ropes around her wrists?

Her breath caught, the furniture beneath her feeling impossibly hard.

She was tied to a wooden chair.

Panic hit her so quickly that she reacted on instinct, tugging at the ropes harder this time. The chair creaked, but there was no give.

"Bonnie."

Her head shot up, the flash of pain in her skull making her wince. At first, everything was a blur. A blur of shadows and stillness and dark shapes merging together.

She scrunched her eyes before opening them. Then she did it again.

Slowly, Zane came into focus.

He had a bruise on his left temple and a cut on his cheek and chin. But that wasn't the worst thing about this—he sat on a chair opposite her, arms behind his back.

He was bound too.

And suddenly, it all came back to her. The tail. The screeching tires. The deafening sound of metal hitting metal.

"Zane…" she whispered, a deep tremble in her voice, one that could only exist with fear.

"I'm here, Bon."

The deep gravel of his tone dragged her gaze back to his. "Are you okay?"

"As far as I can tell, I'm not injured."

But he wasn't okay. And neither was she. They were tied up. Stuck. Trapped.

"Where are we?" She studied the room. There were no windows, just concrete walls and a staircase to her right that led up.

"I assume a basement." There was an edge to his voice. Like he was trying to dull the fury…protect her from it. But he couldn't quite do it. "I have no idea where, though."

"Have you seen Monty?" She wasn't sure whether she wanted him to say yes or no.

He shook his head, the veins popping on his neck. "The asshole hasn't shown his face yet. He will."

Fear prickled across her skin. At what Monty had planned for them. At the way they were blind to everything that was coming.

It took all of her strength to not let hopelessness swallow her whole. To breathe through the pain, exhaustion, and fear. To not let the thrashing of her heart consume her.

"I've been working at these ropes for a while," Zane said carefully. "If I create a bit more room, I might be able to dislocate my thumb to get out, but then I'll need to work on my ankles."

Her stomach twisted at the thought of him dislocating his own thumb. There had to be another way.

She tugged at her bindings again, and as she did, her butt shifted…and she felt it. There was something digging into her. She gasped quietly when she remembered.

"Zane." Her voice was so low she wasn't even sure it carried across the space between them. "I think he left the knife in my pocket."

His brows flickered. "Can you reach it?"

"I'm not sure."

She lifted her butt and reached between the slats on the back of the chair. "I can feel it. I'm not sure if I can…" She forced her hand deeper into her pocket, the rope digging into her wrist, burning her skin. Suddenly, she gripped the pocketknife with her fingertips. "I've got it!"

Air rushed from her chest, the relief almost causing her to drop the weapon as she pulled it out.

"That's good," Zane said. "Watch your fingers as you cut into the rope."

She flipped it open with her thumb before blindly sawing at the material. The blade was sharp and when she nicked her skin, the pain almost made her flinch.

"Are you okay?" Zane asked, voice sharp.

Or maybe she *did* flinch. "Yeah. I think it's working."

The rattle of keys in a door at the top of the stairs suddenly sounded.

Bonnie froze.

Oh God. He was coming. Would he see the knife?

No. Her back faced the wall. She could keep sawing at the bindings. She could still get free. She just had to be subtle.

"Careful," Zane whispered, as boots sounded on the wooden stairs.

One rope popped. She tugged, but her wrists were still tightly bound together.

Dammit!

Monty appeared at the base of the stairs.

Air stalled in her lungs. He looked exactly like his photo. Dark hair and eyes. But also tall and broad and just *big* in every way. He looked every bit the former UFC fighter that he was.

He grinned at Zane. "Hey, cousin."

Fire burned in Zane's eyes. "You know you're a fucking dead man, don't you?"

"I'm the dead man? *You're* the one bound to a chair in my basement."

"Your basement? I doubt that."

"Well, it's mine now that the old recluse who lived here is dead." He grinned, as if killing people brought him joy. "It pays to do your research before pulling off something like this."

"And how exactly did you do that *research* from inside a prison cell?" Zane growled.

With Zane keeping the attention on him, Bonnie kept working on the rope. She was so close!

"Haven't you learned yet, Zane? Money can buy anything. Even prison privileges that I shouldn't be entitled to. It's not a question of, 'Can it be done?' It's 'How much?'" He shook his head. "This is why all that prize money was wasted on you. You never appreciated your fortune the way you should have."

"How should I have shown my appreciation? By killing someone and trying to cover it up?"

The hit from Monty came hard and fast, knocking Zane's head back.

Bonnie screamed. "Leave him alone!"

Monty turned his attention to her. "Hi. We haven't met. I'm Monty, the cousin. You know, originally, I was pissed at Ax for missing the shot and hitting that other bitch. But this turned out better."

Zane spat a mouthful of blood to the floor. "Don't you fucking talk to her!"

One side of Monty's mouth lifted. "Considering I'm standing here, and you're tied up there, I'd say I can do whatever the hell I want." He stepped closer to Zane. "How does it feel?"

"How does *what* feel?" Zane asked, body twisting as he tugged at his bindings.

Bonnie sawed at the rope around her wrists. Almost…there.

Monty lifted a brow. "Watching your future disappear."

Another growl from Zane.

"You took everything from me," Monty said, tone shifting. Darkening. Any hint of humor gone. "Now you can watch your future burn like mine did."

Zane twisted again. "What did you expect me to do? Let you get away with murdering that woman?"

"*Yes!* I expected you to have some fucking loyalty to the man who gave you *everything*. Instead, you tore my life out from beneath my feet!"

"You didn't give me anything, Monty. I won my own fights. And I didn't take your life. All I did was defend myself and hold *you* accountable for your actions."

Monty hit him again, and for the second time, Zane's head flew back.

"Stop it!" she shouted, heart racing.

"Shit, that felt good." Monty grinned. "Now, I promised the guys they could have some time with your bitch before we kill her, Zane."

Zane spat more blood, growls rippling from his chest, loud and fierce. "No one fucking touches her!"

"Oh, touch her they will. And you'll get a front-row seat." Monty turned to Bonnie. "Have fun, my darling. Or don't."

Her pulse raced, thin beads of sweat gathering on her forehead as she sawed blindly at the rope, not caring that her wrists were raw and bleeding, barely feeling when the blade sliced her skin.

Zane was visibly pulling and tugging at his bindings now, so aggressive his chair groaned and wobbled.

Monty disappeared up the stairs, and seconds later, more footsteps sounded before a new man appeared. She immediately recognized him from one of the photos.

The bald guy with the tattoos down his neck.

Come on, come on, come on.

Fear gnawed at her insides, making her entire body shake. She didn't hide her movements anymore. She couldn't afford to. She didn't have time.

The guy grinned at her. "Hey, baby."

"You touch her and I'll tear you the fuck apart!" Zane yelled.

Pop. The rope snapped.

The guy bent down to smell her neck—and she pulled her hands apart and thrust the knife into his throat.

He gasped.

She pulled the knife out as he stumbled back, grabbing at his neck.

Nausea tried to crawl up her throat, but she didn't let it. She didn't have time. She bent over and madly sawed at the bindings on her ankles but quickly realized it would take too long. She pulled at the knot.

"You've got it, Bonnie."

Zane's gentle words made the shake in her fingers still. In seconds, she was free.

She shot to her feet, pocketknife in hand. But she'd only taken a step when a body hit her. She fell to the floor hard, her cheek scraping against concrete, the knife slipping from her fingers.

"I'm going to kill you," the guy seethed.

"Get off her!" Zane yelled.

She bucked her hips, and as she did, he slipped an arm beneath her stomach. Immediately, she grabbed his arm and turned hard toward his shoulder, using her hips to drive the motion.

He grunted and rolled to his side.

She kicked her heel back between his legs, and followed up by smashing the back of her head into his face.

A crunch sounded, then a howl. He released her, and Bonnie crawled to the knife and shot to her feet, moving behind Zane and pulling at the bindings around his wrists.

Shit, his were tight. She switched to the knife, sawing at the rope.

The guy on the ground was groaning, and when he moved, panic dug its claws into her chest.

Come on.

The rope broke.

Zane pulled his hands free and bent over to work on his ankle bindings.

The man on the floor rose. Bonnie stood too, about to step in front of Zane to protect him—but the guy pulled out a gun.

That's when Zane shot up. He moved quickly, hitting the guy's wrist with one hand and grabbing the gun with the other.

Footsteps came from the stairs.

Someone else was coming.

Zane was throwing a fist at the bald guy as a man cursed from the stairs. He lifted his own gun, and Bonnie moved on instinct, screaming and lunging toward Zane.

The bullet hit her in the shoulder. The last thing she heard was Zane's shout before she fell.

* * *

ZANE THREW a hard elbow to the asshole's left cheek. The guy dropped, unmoving, eyes closed.

Bonnie's scream pierced the air. Zane's head shot up—but he saw the shooter too late. The gun fired but it didn't hit him. Bonnie dove to cover him.

Zane's world stopped. It just fucking halted at the sight of Bonnie going down, the bullet catching her in the shoulder.

"No."

He wasn't sure if the sound even made it to the air, but his growl sure as hell did.

Bonnie hadn't even hit the floor before he lifted the gun in his hand and fired, a bullet hitting the guy between the eyes.

Zane didn't wait to see him hit the floor. He dropped to Bonnie's side.

"Bonnie?" Fuck. There was so much blood. "Talk to me, honey! Open your eyes."

"Zane..."

Alive. She was alive. Thank God!

He pulled off his shirt and shredded it quickly, making it long enough to wrap around her shoulder. He pulled it tight then tied a knot. It wasn't optimal, but the pressure would slow the bleeding.

Before lifting her, he touched the pulse of the guy beside her. Blood pooled from the neck wound.

Nothing. He was dead. Good.

Carefully, he slipped his arms beneath her knees and back and lifted her.

She groaned.

"Sorry. I'm going to get us out of here, Bon, okay?" He needed to get her to the fucking hospital, and he needed to get her there fast. But fuck, Monty was still alive and upstairs somewhere.

Gun still in his hold, he moved up the stairs two at a time.

"Zane." Bonnie's voice was quiet. Almost breathless. "Put me down. You need two hands to get him."

He hated that she was right. He carefully lowered her to the floor just in front of the closed basement door, then crouched in front of her. "I'll be back in a second. I need you to stay awake. Okay?"

She swallowed, shutting her eyes tightly before nodding. "Stay safe. I need you alive."

He kissed her forehead, then slipped out of the basement into what looked like a hall.

Keeping his back toward the wall, he moved quietly down the hallway toward the living room. Where was the asshole? If he was inside the house, he would have heard the gunshots.

So was he outside? Or was he lurking in the shadows somewhere, waiting to shoot?

Zane slipped into the living room. There was a brown couch. An old TV. But no sign of Monty.

He crept toward the next door and only pulled it open slightly to peek inside. A kitchen. Not surprising that it was separated in an old house like this. There was also a back door.

He stepped inside just as the back door opened. But instead of a person stepping in, only a gun appeared around the doorframe.

Zane dropped behind the kitchen island as two bullets blasted into the cabinet above him.

"Zane? That you?" Monty called.

"Surprised?"

"A little. What happened? Did my guys get a little excited and your bitch castrate them?"

"Something like that. It's never smart to underestimate a woman."

He glanced around the island, and more shots fired, almost catching him in the damn face. He pulled back.

"But she's not with you, is she?" Monty called. "She dead?"

"No. But *you* will be." He aimed his weapon and fired through the wall beside the door.

Monty laughed. "One of us is going to die, Zane—and it won't be me. You see, rats like you eventually get what's coming. And today's your reckoning."

"You've forgotten something, cousin. I'm *better* than you.

Stronger. Smarter. I was better than you in the ring. And I'm better now."

Monty growled and started shooting, his footsteps loud as he entered the kitchen. Round after round, like the predictable asshole he was, trying to prove Zane wrong.

Without sticking his head out, Zane aimed and gently pulled the trigger once.

Monty grunted—and Zane quickly rose and fired again, nailing him center mass, right in the chest.

Straight through the heart.

Zane took two steps toward Monty, now on the floor, and waited for his cousin to take his final breath. When his chest finally stopped moving and he stared up at the ceiling, unseeing, Zane raced back to Bonnie. Feeling nothing but relief that his cousin was dead.

He opened the door to the basement and his world narrowed.

"Bonnie?" He dropped to his knees in front of her. Her eyes were closed, but she was breathing, brows tugged together. He cupped her cheek. "Bonnie, honey, open your eyes."

She didn't. And it set off a surge of panic in his body.

Quickly, he lifted her again.

On his way to the door, car engines roared outside. Not just engines. Sirens from patrol cars.

Jesse. The guys had figured out where he was. Thank God!

When he stepped outside, there were three patrol cars and two civilian vehicles. Guns pointed at him from people taking cover behind vehicles.

Jesse was the first to rise, then Noah beside him.

Noah's eyes went to Bonnie, face paling.

Zane raced to Jesse's patrol car. "We need to get to the hospital *now*!"

CHAPTER 30

Zane's fingers wrapped tightly around Bonnie's hand. Hours had passed since her surgery. *Hours.* And she still wasn't awake. It was killing him. Every minute that passed felt like ten. Every tick of the clock on the walls felt like a hammer in his damn head.

Come on, Bon. Open your eyes. Let me see those pretty hazel specks.

He lifted her hand to his mouth and kissed the back, letting his lips linger as he memorized the feel of her skin.

She'd taken a bullet for him. A goddamn *bullet*. He was so fucking angry. And frustrated and scared and a million other things, none of them good. He couldn't even feel relieved that Monty was gone. Not with Bonnie in a hospital bed.

Everything about the last twenty-four hours felt like a nightmare he couldn't wake up from.

The only good thing was that Jesse had run the car that had tailed Zane. It was the only gray Charger in Amber Ridge, and it had been owned by the old man who'd lived in the house Monty had taken over.

A knock sounded at the door. Before he could respond, it opened and Noah stepped in.

He looked at Bonnie, brow creasing, before shifting his gaze to Zane. "How is she?"

"I don't know. She hasn't woken up yet."

Noah crossed to the bed. "I hate that she was shot."

"I'm so angry I can barely breathe."

There was a short pause before Noah said, "You should go home and rest. I can stay with her."

He could have laughed. "There's no way I'm leaving her." And even if he did, even if he drove home and tried to sleep, there was no way he would.

Noah crossed his arms. "You know it's not your fault, right?"

Veins strained in his neck. "He took her because of her connection to me. Who else's fault would it be?"

"*His*. Monty's. And those idiots who helped him."

"They were *all* there because of me."

"No. They were there because Monty needed someone to blame for his prison sentence, and instead of blaming himself, he chose you. Because he was fucking weak and couldn't take responsibility for his actions."

And now he was dead. "She got shot because she jumped in front of a bullet for *me*." The moment played over in his mind again and again.

"Yeah. I'm pissed at her for that too. It must be a sister thing. But I'm sure she'd tell you that she'd do it again."

The muscles in Zane's arms flexed. No. She was *never* going to do it again. He wouldn't allow it.

"She's gonna wake up, Zane. She's going to come back to you."

He looked up at Bonnie's brother. "You *want* her to do that? Return to me when she wakes up?"

Noah lifted a shoulder. "Doesn't matter what I want. She's always been too stubborn to listen to me. But...yeah, I'm glad she has you. You love her. I can see it. And you got her out of that basement."

Zane shook his head. "That was all her. She broke out of her own ropes. She fought the guy who attacked her. Then she released me…and stepped in front of a bullet for me. She's the hero in this story."

"I'm not surprised. She's always been tough." Noah squeezed his shoulder. "I'm getting us both coffees."

Noah walked out and then it was just him and Bonnie again. He lifted her hand and pressed it to his forehead before closing his eyes.

"Wake up, Bon. Come back to me."

Suddenly, there was a squeeze of his hand. It was faint. Barely there. Then her voice…

"Zane?"

His head shot up. "Bonnie?"

Her eyes were half open.

And fuck, he was almost scared to breathe in case this wasn't real and she wasn't truly awake.

She frowned. "Your face…it's bruised."

He could have laughed. *She* was worried about *him*? "I'm fine."

"What…what happened?"

"What do you remember?"

"We were driving home from The Pit. There was someone following us and—" She gasped, her eyes widening. "The basement."

"Yeah." He slipped a lock of hair from her face, the gentleness in his touch in complete contrast to the anger that consumed him. "You found the pocketknife though. You got free, and then you freed me."

"But the guy came down the stairs with a gun."

Zane's back teeth ground together, his gaze going to the bandaging on her shoulder. "Bullet got you. But you're okay."

"Is Monty—"

"Dead."

Her sigh was loud in the otherwise quiet room. "Thank God. And thank you."

"For what? I didn't do anything."

She turned her head and looked at him. "You got us out of there."

"No, Bon. *You* did. You were unbelievable."

"No. I was desperate." One side of her mouth lifted. "It's over now."

Another knock sounded at the door, and this time Jesse stepped in. His eyes went to straight to Bonnie. "Hey, Bon. You're awake."

"Yeah. And I feel pleasantly numb."

"Good. I'm glad you're okay."

The smile slipped from her lips. "You've got all of them now, right? This is over?"

"That's all of them."

"So life can go back to normal?" she asked, hope weaving into her words.

"Almost. We haven't found the guy who decapitated the mouse and slammed you into the building yet," Zane said quietly, fucking hating that, after everything, they still had to look over their shoulders.

"I'm still hoping they'll stop now," Bonnie said.

And damn, he wished he shared her optimism. But he'd been witness to too much dark shit in the world for that.

"I don't want us to get complacent," Jesse said before Zane could.

Bonnie deflated a bit.

He tightened his grip on her hand.

"Do you need my account of what happened or anything?" she asked quietly.

"That can wait until tomorrow. I just came to check on you." Jesse squeezed her uninjured arm. "Rest up and call if you need anything."

She nodded.

When it was just the two of them, Zane swiped his thumb

over the back of her hand. "What can I do?"

"Get me home?"

"As soon as the doctor gives you the okay."

She studied his face, the quiet stretching out as tears gathered in her eyes. "You're okay."

"I'm okay."

"I was so scared we wouldn't make it out of there."

"We did." Zane frowned, something hard settling in his gut. "You can't ever do that again, Bon."

"Do what?"

"Step in front of a bullet for me."

"I saved you."

"You were *shot*. You could have died." Fuck, even saying that out loud tasted like acid on his tongue. "Promise me."

She cupped his cheek. "You would have done the same for me."

"Bonnie—"

"Would you promise that you wouldn't step in front of a bullet for me?"

His jaw clenched.

"Exactly." She swiped her thumb over his cheek. "I'll promise you something else. That I'll love you forever."

It wasn't the promise he'd been looking for. But fuck, it felt good anyway. "Forever's a hell of a long time."

"Thank God."

He lowered his head and kissed her. A gentle kiss. Only stopping when the door opened and Indie, Colt, Noah, and Addie stepped in.

* * *

BONNIE STROKED the back of Zane's head.

Finally, he was sleeping. Although, she wasn't sure how long he'd been out. She'd just woken to find his head on the bed beside her.

No matter how much she pushed, no matter how much *anyone* pushed, he refused to leave her side. A part of her loved that. She wanted him in arm's reach at all times. But she also knew he needed rest.

God, she loved him. Seeing that gun aimed at him…

Her heart stuttered, the fear still alive inside her, as if she were back in that basement. It would take a long time to recover. Or maybe she never would. Maybe the memory would live inside her forever, coming back to her in quiet moments, reminding her that Zane wasn't bulletproof.

She turned her head toward the window. Even though the curtains were closed, sun slipped through the gaps. It was morning. Good. The day from hell was over. It was in the past and she'd never need to live through it again.

Right now, her biggest problem was that she needed to pee.

Slowly, she slipped out from beneath the sheets, testing one foot then the other. Steady enough. And her IV pole could double as her walking stick. Win-win.

Zane didn't move as she stepped away from the bed. *That* was how tired he was.

He should have at least gone home for a bit of sleep. Noah would have stayed with her. But he'd refused. And she knew why. He blamed himself. But that was stupid. Everything that had happened was Monty's fault. And those other prison-escapee jerks. *They* were the ones who'd kidnapped them. *They* were the ones who'd tied them up and shot the bullet from the gun that had hit her. All the blame was squarely on *them*.

In the bathroom, she peed and washed her hands before noticing her reflection in the mirror.

Argh. She was a mess. Her unbrushed hair stuck up in every

possible direction, she was as pale as a piece of paper, and there were scrapes and bruises everywhere.

She tugged down the shoulder of her hospital gown to look at the bandage. She couldn't even remember the pain of the bullet hitting her. Maybe her body had gone into shock. It hadn't hurt then, and it didn't hurt now—thank you, medication.

With a sigh, she turned and stepped back into the hospital room…only to stop at the sight of the woman in the doorway. "Maisie."

The other woman spun toward Bonnie. She stood just inside the room, her hand still on the doorknob. "Bonnie. Hi."

Slowly—well, as fast as she could—she crossed over to her former best friend. "What are you doing here?"

"I, um, heard around town what happened. Word travels fast in Amber Ridge. I just wanted to check that you were okay and…" She lifted a bouquet of flowers. "I know this isn't much, but I couldn't come empty-handed."

"You brought me flowers?"

Maisie shuffled from foot to foot. "I was worried. We used to be friends. Good friends. And having you back here has reminded me of that. I know coming home hasn't been easy for you—"

"No. It hasn't. And you've done nothing to help that."

Maisie's eyes widened with what looked like authentic confusion. "What did you expect me to do?"

Was that a serious question? "The Whites hate me because they think I left Dean at that party while he was drunk, for no reason. You could tell them there *was* a reason."

She stepped back, face paling. "You know I can't do that."

"Why? It doesn't mean his death is your fault. It's neither of our faults. But it tells his parents that I wasn't selfish that night, stranding him there just because I'm heartless."

"They'd blame *me*!"

She was never going to do it. Unless Bonnie said something herself, she'd have to live with the White family's hate forever. "Does Damien know?"

Maisie swallowed, and for a moment, Bonnie wasn't sure she was going to answer. "He—"

"Bonnie."

They both looked at Zane, who was now on his feet and moving toward them.

"Hey," she said, "you're awake."

"You shouldn't be on your feet." He slipped an arm around her waist, and she leaned into him, letting him take most of her weight. He looked at Maisie. "What are you doing here?"

"I was just giving Bonnie these." She held out the flowers.

A part of Bonnie didn't want to take them, because she didn't want anything from this woman. And maybe Maisie saw that, because she set them on the counter behind her.

"I'm glad you're okay," she said quietly. Then she slipped out of the room.

Zane glanced down at Bonnie. "What was that?"

"I'm not sure. I don't understand why she came." She studied the pink roses. "It's like she wants things to be okay between us, but after what she did, that's not possible. I don't know why she can't see that."

"You're right. Things can't be okay between you two, because she doesn't get to hurt you and still be your friend."

"Yeah. And even if she hadn't done what she did with Dean all those years ago, she's now just standing back and letting her in-laws hurt me."

Slowly, he led her back to the bed. "Come on. Next time, wake me."

"You needed the sleep. You still do."

"No. I need to stay by your side."

She rolled her eyes. "I can go to the bathroom by myself."

He helped her into bed, but even when she slipped beneath the covers, her gaze returned to the door.

What exactly had Maisie been hoping to achieve by coming here? Had she really just been worried and wanting to check that Bonnie was okay? Was she trying to reconnect?

Or was something else going on?

Bonnie yawned and stared at the dark street outside the car as they drove. "Just so you know, I think it should be criminal to open the gym before the sun comes out."

Zane chuckled. "We're only open this early Wednesdays and Fridays, and because it's a gym. A lot of people like to work out before heading to their jobs."

"Crazy people," she muttered under her breath. "Those are people I have nothing in common with."

"I *am* those people. I usually get a session in before we open."

"This must be that whole 'opposites attract' thing."

"Well, I've certainly never been attracted to any six-foot-three men who like to hit a bag before work."

She laughed, then winced at the pain in her shoulder. Even though a week had passed since she'd been shot, it still hurt to move and laugh and do basically anything. It probably would for a while.

Zane took his gaze from the road to look at her. "You okay?"

"I'm fine."

"If you're not, we can—"

"Nope. I am not spending another day looking at the four

walls of the inside of the apartment." Absolutely not. She'd lose her mind. Hell, she'd already lost part of it being home for so long.

They'd moved back into Zane's apartment once she was out of the hospital. And Zane had been by her side the entire time, letting Stetson run the gym. He played it off like he wasn't bored as hell, but he was. He had to be.

"It's so unfair."

Zane frowned at her. "What is?"

Shit. She'd meant to say that in her head. "We were kidnapped. We fought for our lives, and we survived. In a fair world, we'd have earned our right to live in a safe small town without trying to figure out who else has it out for me."

He squeezed her thigh. "We'll find them."

"Maybe not. Jesse has no leads. None."

A muscle ticked in Zane's jaw, because he knew she was right. And it frustrated him as much as it frustrated her.

They pulled over in front of the gym. Zane frowned at the Hyundai parked in front of them. "Stetson's here. I told him to take the morning off."

"Maybe he forgot? He's probably delirious after all the hours he's worked this last week." She climbed out of the car, immediately wrapping her arms around her waist. Man, it was cold. Another reason not to wake up at this godforsaken hour.

Zane came around the car, scanning the street before setting a hand on her back and leading her toward the gym. "Any news on the shelter?"

Her lips curved into a smile. "Two more weeks and we should be reopening."

"Will it take time to get it back to what it was?"

She shook her head. "No. There are too many women who need a safe place. I'm sure they already have a list of people who've been assigned a spot." A new manager had been hired, and even though Bonnie hadn't met her, they'd chatted on the phone and she seemed lovely. Shelley's complete opposite.

Zane went to put his key into the lock, but as he grabbed the handle, the door opened. "I wonder what time he got here."

"Too early." She bumped his hip before stepping inside and flicking on the lights. The gym lit up. "Strange that he kept the lights off though."

Zane stepped in beside her. "Where is he?"

Good question.

Zane slipped his hand into hers and moved forward, his other hand hovering over where she knew he carried a concealed gun. The smile from moments ago slipped, and nerves kicked at her ribs.

Maybe something was wrong. A few things weren't adding up. Stetson's car being here. The lights that were still off.

Zane led her to his office. "Stetson?"

The room was empty.

Tension rolled off Zane's shoulders as he pulled his cell from his pocket and hit Stetson's number. A few seconds passed before he lowered the phone. "He's not answering."

Hand still in his, she trailed behind him as they moved to the back hall. After passing the bathrooms and equipment room, he tried the handle on the back door. "Locked."

She jumped at the ringing of Zane's phone.

Jesus. Calm down, Bonnie.

She glanced at the screen, expecting to see Stetson's name. It was Jesse's. And that made those nerves in her belly ripple.

Something was definitely wrong. Jesse wouldn't call so early if it wasn't.

Zane put his cell to his ear. "Jesse."

Bonnie breathed deeply, frowning. What was that smell?

"His parents can't get through to him?"

Her gaze returned to Zane. Was he talking about Stetson?

As he continued to talk, she turned back to the hall, the

strange smell making her nose wrinkle. What *was* that? Was it coming from the bathroom?

She took a few steps, about to push into the bathroom, when she paused. No. It was coming from the storage room.

She turned, her pulse speeding up.

The second she opened the door, she gagged. Good God, it smelled like something had died in here.

She flicked on the light and scanned the storage room, shelving lined with boxes. A shoebox immediately caught her attention. It was red and had a sticker in the corner. A sticker she recognized.

She'd given the box to Dean in high school. She'd put some dumb notes she'd written to him inside, and a few other keepsakes.

Suddenly, the nerves in her belly turned into a nausea that rolled and crawled, making her feel sick to her stomach. She shouldn't open it. She knew she shouldn't. Not here, not by herself. But her feet were moving before she could stop them, propelling her forward. A deep need to see what was inside squashing any and everything else.

With shaking fingers, she lifted the box. It took her three full breaths before she gained the courage to open it.

She screamed at what she saw, the boxing hitting the floor.

Loud footsteps sounded behind her. "Bonnie? What—" Zane cursed and gripped her shoulders, turning her away from the decomposing mouse head.

Her gaze caught on something behind Zane, hidden behind the storage room door. This time, her entire stomach dropped. "Oh my God…Stetson!"

Zane turned and saw what she did. He dropped down beside Stetson's still body. He had a black eye and lay on his side at an awkward angle.

"Is he alive?" she whispered, praying Zane said yes.

He touched Stetson's throat. "There's a heartbeat but it's

faint." His gaze shifted lower, the muscles in his back visibly tensing.

And that's when Bonnie saw the blood on his midsection, like he'd been stabbed or shot.

She stumbled back and pulled her cell from her pocket, about to call an ambulance, when something sounded from somewhere in the gym. A bang.

Zane stood and pulled Bonnie behind him, tugging his gun from the holster.

Someone had hurt Stetson. And that someone might still be here.

* * *

BEFORE STEPPING out of the storage room, Zane called Jesse back.

"Zane—"

"I need you at the gym *now*." He kept his voice low and quiet.

"What's wrong?"

"He's here." Two words…that's all he said before he hung up and shoved the cell back into his pocket. "Stay behind me."

He didn't want to take Bonnie out there with him, but he sure as hell wasn't leaving her alone.

He stuck his head into the hall.

Empty.

He reached behind him and gripped Bonnie's wrist, keeping her close as he moved down to the back door. He wanted out of here and he wanted out fast. There was a possibility someone was waiting out there for him. But better out in the open than boxed in here.

There was no safe option right now.

He slipped the lock and pulled the handle. It didn't move.

The fuck?

He tried again. Again, it wouldn't move. The asshole had done something to the door.

Shit.

He turned and headed the other way. When he reached the end of the hall, he stopped, Bonnie's warm body behind him. That and years of military training were the only things keeping him calm. He reached into his pocket and quietly pulled out his keys.

The second he threw them into the gym, the boom of a gunshot exploded through the room.

Bonnie flinched, her gasp cutting into the quiet.

"Come on," Zane yelled. "Don't you want to tell us who you are? Brag about trapping us in the hall?"

Zane didn't give a shit who the asshole was. He was a dead man walking. Zane just needed to waste enough time for backup to arrive.

"Why not? You'll be dead soon anyway."

Zane frowned. He knew that voice. Who—

"Damien," Bonnie whispered, disbelief mixing with fear in her voice.

Dean's brother. Of course it was. The fucker's wife had been in his damn storage room where the mouse head had been found. And he was Stetson's cousin. He'd probably tricked the kid into letting him in, then shot him to keep him quiet.

Zane opened his mouth to say more when Bonnie gasped. "Zane."

He glanced back and followed her gaze to a few feet away… where Maisie stood. Her right eye was bruised, like someone had hit her, and she held a gun that was trained solely on Bonnie.

"I've got her," Maisie yelled.

"Good. Come out, come out!"

Zane didn't move a muscle. Everything in him told him to stay exactly where he was.

"Do it," Maisie said, voice hushed. "Don't make me hurt her."

Were there tears in her eyes?

"I will," Maisie added. "You so much as start to move that gun my way and I'll have to shoot her."

Zane's jaw clenched as he stepped into the gym.

Damien stood a couple yards away, a smile curving his lips. "There you are."

"Maisie," Bonnie whispered. "Why are you doing this?"

"Don't talk to her!" Damien seethed. "This is all me. Drop the gun and kick it over here, Merrick."

Zane's fingers tightened around the Glock.

Damien lifted a brow before training his weapon on Bonnie.

"Fine." Zane lowered the gun to the floor and kicked it forward, leaving himself weaponless.

Damien bent and grabbed Zane's Glock, then slipped it into a holster.

"I'm sorry."

Zane frowned, not sure if he'd really heard the apology beneath Maisie's breath or not.

"Why?" Zane growled, not sure which one he was talking to. "What do we even have to do with you?"

Damien laughed. "Everything. The second this bitch came back to this town, it put a ticking time bomb on how long until the truth came out about the night my brother died. I can't have that."

"Really?" Bonnie said. "All this to keep people from knowing Maisie slept with Dean?"

"You think I want my family, the entire fucking *town*, knowing that my wife's a goddamn whore? Do you know what that would do to my reputation?" Damien shook his head. "And more than that, what it would do to my parents? If they knew Maisie slept with Dean the night he died, and that's why you left him behind? Then they'd inevitably find out that Maisie called me to pick him up, but I didn't because I was too busy getting high. They'd cut us both out of the Will."

Bonnie's head reared back as if she'd been slapped. "She called you?"

"You saw her on the damn phone that night," Damien yelled. "She told me you saw her. And now my darling wife feels bad that my parents and the entire town are being *mean* to you, and she wants to tell everyone the truth."

"And that's worth killing over?" Zane asked, incredulous.

Damien turned back to him. "Do you know what my parents are worth? You really think I'd risk them cutting me out because my wife can't keep her legs closed and I didn't pick up my cheating fucking brother that night? Because they *would* cut me out. They always loved that dumbass more than me."

"So we just don't tell anyone," Bonnie said quietly.

"Tried that. Caught Maisie sneaking out last night. Took a bit of convincing, but she eventually admitted that she was going to tell my parents everything. Decided I can't trust her until I get rid of you."

"How do you know you can trust her when Bonnie's gone?" Zane asked.

"You know the saying…out of sight, out of mind. Plus, there are always consequences for bad behavior—aren't there, honey?"

Zane shot a glance at Maisie. There was a mix of emotions on her face. Fear. Sadness.

But also a hint of anger.

"All right, let's get this over with. Maisie, you've got Bonnie. I've got Zane." Damien's smile widened. "Then she *really* won't say anything, because she'll have blood on her hands."

Zane eyed Damien's gun, calculating how much time it would take him to reach it.

Too long.

He needed to target Maisie. Shove Bonnie to the floor, get the gun, and kill the fucker. It wasn't optimal, but he was all out of good options. This was about survival.

"Any last words?" Damien asked, humor in his voice.

Zane's muscles coiled, ready to act.

But before he could dive for Bonnie, Maisie swung her gun away from Bonnie's head and fired.

The bullet hit Damien in the gut.

Maisie gasped and stumbled back, like she couldn't believe what she'd done. Zane lunged, grabbing Damien's wrist and forcing the gun down.

Movement sounded behind him, and he prayed that Bonnie was safe.

Damien growled and tried to knee Zane, but he immobilized him easily, knocking him to the floor and flipping him to his stomach before squeezing his wrist so hard, the gun fell from his hold.

The crash of the front door opening rang out, then footsteps. Zane looked up to see Jesse entering, his deputies behind him.

Then he shifted his gaze to Bonnie. She now held the gun and Maisie was on the floor.

Relief almost suffocated him. She was okay. Another gun had been aimed at her, but she was okay.

CHAPTER 32

Bonnie stood to the side of the gym, arms wrapped tightly around her waist. There was so much going on. Paramedics were with Damien, and more had run to the storage room for Stetson. Jesse was there and his deputy was cuffing Maisie.

Maisie. She'd pulled a gun on them but then shot Damien. Bonnie didn't know what to think. Damien had obviously been an abusive ass of a husband. But Maisie's participation today could easily have gotten her and Zane killed. She'd forced them out into the open, where Damien could have shot them at any second.

Zane's arm tightened around her waist as deputies passed her with Maisie in cuffs.

Maisie's cheeks were wet, and when she looked at Bonnie, more tears spilled from her eyes. "Bonnie. I…I'm sorry. He made me do it. He… I was scared. Our marriage was a mess. I thought I didn't have a choice."

"Come on." The deputy tugged her out of the gym.

"What are you thinking?" Zane asked gently once Maisie was gone.

"I'm not sure. A part of me feels so angry at her, but another part just feels sorry for her." She lifted a shoulder. "I'm glad it's over but…I wasn't expecting it to be Damien. And even if I was, I didn't think he'd go so far as to try to kill me. Us."

"Greed. It makes people do unthinkable things."

She nodded almost absently. "You're right. It just makes me so angry."

The paramedics came out of the hall with Stetson on a stretcher. Zane straightened. "If I go talk to the paramedics, will you be—"

"I'm fine. Go."

He kissed her head before following the paramedics out. A second later, Indie rushed into the gym, Noah behind her.

Her sister pulled her into a hug. "Oh my God, Bonnie!" She pulled back, still gripping her shoulders. "Are you okay?"

"I'm not hurt."

Noah wrapped his arms around her next. It was a tight hug. One of those all-encompassing embraces. He didn't speak until he moved back. "What happened?"

"It was Damien. He was the one harassing me. He was afraid his parents would find out Maisie had slept with Dean the night he died. Also, that she called Damien to pick up his brother, and he didn't."

Indie frowned. "Maisie and Dean slept together the night of the graduation party?"

"Yeah. I found them together. It's the reason I fought with him and left."

"Why didn't you tell anyone?" Noah asked, shock clear on his face.

She lifted a shoulder. "At the time it seemed inappropriate. Dean had just died, and I fell apart. Then Mom and Dad were in that crash. It all felt like too much for me, and I just had to leave. And when I got back—I don't know. Maisie hadn't said anything and I didn't either. Maybe deep down I didn't want anyone, not even her, to go through what I was going through."

"Was she working with Damien?" Indie asked.

"I think Damien coerced her. Then she was the one who shot him." In a way, she'd saved them. But she'd also put them in the situation where they'd needed saving.

Noah glanced at the ambulance through the gym window before turning back to her. "Thank fuck they have him."

"And maybe we can finally move on now," she added quietly, almost scared to feel hopeful. "Not just from the danger, but maybe the town will finally leave me alone."

Noah slipped an arm around her and kissed the top of her head. "You deserve peace, Bon."

Indie rubbed her back. "You really do."

The next hour went slowly. She spoke to a couple of deputies and so did Zane. They both gave their version of events. She learned from Zane that Maisie had been caught in the storage room a few weeks ago, which was likely when she'd left the box. He'd said that because the place had been closed for a while, and they had the equipment boxes on the gym floor, they hadn't gone in there often enough to see it. Plus, it was in a brown box like a whole lot of other stuff. It had just been another means for Damien to torture Bonnie out of town.

When it was finally time to leave, Zane slipped an arm around her waist. "Ready to go?"

"Back to the four walls of your apartment?" Not that she was complaining anymore. It wasn't even lunchtime, and she was exhausted. But then, she'd woken at the ass crack of dawn. "You know what today has taught me?"

"To trust no one?" Zane asked through gritted teeth.

"No. That nothing good comes from waking before the sun."

He chuckled. "I'll keep that in mind, Bon."

* * *

ZANE SHOT a glance at Bonnie on the couch from the kitchen as he made coffee. She was on the phone with the new shelter manager. He'd told her to leave work stuff until another day, but she'd wanted the distraction.

He sure as hell wished something would distract *him*. The shower and rest hadn't worked. He'd barely stomached food all day.

Today had been too damn close. If Maisie hadn't had that last-minute change of heart, he wasn't sure they'd have made it out unscathed. And that made him so damn angry he could barely breathe.

He was about to lift the mugs when his phone rang, Ethan's name on the screen.

He leaned his hip against the counter and put the cell to his ear. "Ethan."

"Hey, I've been trying to hold off calling to give you guys time to recover. You both okay?"

He'd texted his friend the CliffsNotes of what had happened. "We're fine. Last I heard, Damien's cuffed to a hospital bed, with deputies posted outside his room, and Maisie's in a jail cell. I haven't received an update on Stetson since he was taken into surgery." But damn, he hoped the kid was going to be okay.

"Jesus. Did you have any clue it was the brother?"

"None. I was so sure the entire time it was the dad."

"What do you need from me?"

"Nothing. You've done enough, Ethan. I really appreciate your friendship."

"Of course."

"It better be fucking over now." He sipped his drink, eyes still on Bonnie. "How's Deep River?"

Ethan chuckled, but there wasn't a lot of humor in the sound. "You do not want to hear about my small-town drama. Another day. I'm glad you and Bonnie are safe."

"Me too. Thanks, Ethan."

When the call ended, he set his cell on the counter before taking the coffees into the living room. Bonnie smiled as she took the mug from his hand, cell still to her ear.

"Absolutely," she said to her new boss. "I'm really looking forward to it."

He lowered to the couch beside her, hand going to her thigh. He had a feeling too close wouldn't feel close enough for a long damn time, not after the last several weeks they'd had.

"Thanks, Mia." She hung up and sighed, leaning her head against the couch and looking at him, fingers wrapped around her mug. "Hi."

"You doing okay?"

"Yeah, the distraction of work is good. I think I'm going to like the new manager."

"You deserve some good." He swiped his thumb against her thigh.

She glanced down at her coffee. "I'm sorry that what happened today happened in your gym."

"Why are you sorry? You're not the asshole who pulled a gun on us."

"I know. I just...I feel guilty." She frowned. "And I keep thinking...what if Maisie hadn't had a change of heart and shot him? A second longer and he would have—"

"Bonnie. I would have found a way to murder the asshole. There is no scenario where either of us died today. I wouldn't have allowed it." Yeah, he couldn't guarantee that. He'd been a fraction of a second away from shoving Bonnie to the floor and diving at Maisie, and he liked to think he would have found a way to end Damien, because losing Bonnie wasn't an option.

"Today was a close call," she whispered.

He grabbed her mug and set both their drinks on the coffee table before gripping her waist and pulling her onto his lap. He slipped a piece of hair off her cheek and behind her ear. "It was. And I'll have nightmares about it for a long time. Never again."

"Never again," she repeated, palm pressing flat to his chest.

She lowered her head and kissed him for long seconds before touching her forehead to his. "Thank God we're good at getting out of dangerous situations alive."

He couldn't even laugh. "Thank God."

CHAPTER 33

*B*onnie swiped the paintbrush across the stark white wall of The Pit. Gray. Or dark gray, to be more exact. She'd argued for a pretty yellow similar to a sunflower, to brighten the place up, but Zane had been a firm no on that. Well, actually, his exact words were, "The Pit is not having yellow fucking walls."

He'd said it like it was a crime. Then, of course, he'd grabbed her and kissed her. It softened the no.

And it was his gym. She was just the help, much like her family.

She glanced around the room. At Noah and Indie. Ethan. Her cousins. Everyone's partners. Even Pam had rolled up her sleeves to help freshen the place up.

The room was busy and noisy and filled with all her favorite people.

She paused, her gaze on Zane, who was deep in conversation with her aunt and Ethan. He was smiling, and Pam was touching his arm as she laughed. How was he so good at just slotting right into her family? Like he was always meant to be here. Like they were *both* meant to be here.

Indie came to stand beside her, a blob of paint on her nose from where Colt had gotten her a few minutes ago. "Penny for your thoughts?"

"I'm having one of those moments. You know, the ones where you just feel really grateful for everything."

Indie rubbed her belly, her smile softening. "I have them a lot. Especially since you got back. It's that feeling of things being so perfect you almost don't want to move in case you disturb the world around you and it changes."

That's exactly what it was. A deep happiness combined with a slight fear of things being taken away.

Indie bumped her hip. "I heard the shelter reopened this week?"

"It did. We've got eight women and two children right now, and my new shelter manager is just beautiful."

"Does she know what you've been through?"

"She does. And she was really pushing for me to work fewer hours with the same pay for the first couple of months, but I assured her I was okay."

"She sounds great." Indie's voice softened. "You deserve to be happy, Bon."

A strong arm suddenly slung over her shoulders. "What about me? Do I deserve to be happy?"

Bonnie laughed at Noah, while Indie just rolled her eyes and said, "Most of the time. Sometimes you deserve a swift kick to the midsection."

"You're lucky you're pregnant, woman," he said jokingly.

Two familiar figures passed the window outside, and the smile dropped from Bonnie's lips. Indie and Noah's gazes followed her own.

Noah's arm dropped and he stepped toward the door.

"No." Bonnie grabbed his arm. "I'll do it."

"Bon—" he started.

"I'll be okay. I've actually been wanting to talk to them." She needed to know if things had changed since they'd learned the truth. She wasn't sure why. She probably shouldn't care. But she couldn't close the chapter on any of this until she at least spoke to them.

Her brother didn't have a chance to argue anymore because she was already moving across the room. The skin at the back of her neck prickled when she felt Zane's eyes on her. But she didn't stop or turn.

Outside, she met them by the door.

Jane's brows rose. "Bonnie."

Bonnie wrapped her arms around her waist. "Do you have a second?"

The older woman swallowed. "Yes. We, um, were actually coming to see you. We've been wanting to talk to you for a few days now."

"Okay. You can go first." She wasn't being easy on them. After everything they'd both put her through, they didn't deserve easy.

"We're sorry," Carlos said, his tone softer than he'd ever used with her.

"For what?"

"Everything," Jane replied, tears building in her eyes. "The text I sent you. The way we both spoke to you and shamed you. We… we know what really happened that night, now. With Maisie, and then Damien not going to pick up his brother." Her voice cracked. "But even if it hadn't happened that way…we should never have put the blame for Dean's death on you. Maybe if we hadn't, none of this would have happened."

"We were angry," Carlos said quietly. "We needed someone to blame for our son's death, and we unfairly targeted you because you were the easy option."

"And not letting any of it go when you got back…it was wrong," Jane added. "You being home dredged up our grief again, but that was *our* problem, not yours. We're so sorry about what Damien did."

"You're right. It wasn't my fault. And you shouldn't have placed the blame on me. Not when I was eighteen years old and basically a kid. And not thirteen years later."

The door to the gym opened and Zane walked out, his arm immediately slipping around her waist and tugging her against him. "Everything okay out here?"

Carlos straightened. "We came to apologize."

"You think an apology is going to fix anything?" he asked.

Bonnie touched his chest before looking back at Jane and Carlos. "I appreciate the apology. I don't want to hold on to any of this anymore. We won't be friends anytime soon, but I also don't want to be enemies. You've lost both your sons now. You've lost too much. We all have."

More tears built in Jane's eyes, and she swiped them away.

"This is my home," Bonnie continued. "And all I want is to live in it peacefully."

Carlos dipped his head. "You have our word that you won't get any trouble from us."

"Good."

They were about to turn when Bonnie spoke again. "Have you heard from Maisie?"

Jane's chest rose on an inhale. "Yes. Apparently—" She stopped abruptly, like her next words caused her physical pain. "Damien was quite controlling and abusive throughout their marriage. We missed it. We missed a lot."

Carlos took his wife's hand, and they walked away.

Zane stepped in front of her. "You don't have to forgive that family for anything they've done to you."

"I don't want to hold on to any of it. Letting it all stay in the past is more for me than them. It will weigh me down otherwise." She touched his chest. "And I think that them acknowledging they were wrong was the closure I needed."

"Okay...but I'm not forgiving them."

She cupped his cheek. "And that's why I love you. Because you are my biggest protector."

"Is that the only reason you love me?"

She pretended to think about it. "I also love to beat you in the ring. I get a lot of joy out of that."

He growled before pulling her closer. Then, with one hand cupping her cheek, he lowered his mouth to her ear. "I love *every-thing* about you."

A shudder rolled down her spine. "Even my overprotective brother and cousins?"

"Everything. You coming back to Amber Ridge was the best damn thing that happened to me."

"It was a pretty good decision, wasn't it?" She had a great family. A great job. And Zane. She had more than she ever thought possible.

"The best decision." Then he kissed her.

She hadn't just gained freedom from her past in coming here. She'd gotten an entire life.

* * *

THE SECOND ZANE'S lips touched Bonnie's, he felt it. The peace that came with knowing the woman he loved was his. The calm of knowing she was safe, and he had the rest of his life to love her.

He wasn't sure what the hell he'd done to deserve Bonnie, but he wasn't questioning it. He was accepting all her love for as long as she'd have him.

When she separated from him it was too soon, the yearning to pull her back so strong he had to physically fight it. But then he saw her smile. Wide and so radiant that he couldn't look away.

"I love you so much, Zane Merrick."

Air hissed from his throat. "I'm *in* love with you, Bonnie. Always will be."

She sighed and leaned her head against his chest.

When they stepped back into the gym, he took in Bonnie's family. People who had welcomed him with open arms. He'd come to this town with nothing. No family. No one to love. And fuck, he'd gained so much in such a short amount of time.

Bonnie squeezed his hands before returning to Indie and Clara and picking up a paintbrush.

Noah came to stand beside him, but Zane didn't take his gaze off Bonnie. Because Clara had just said something to make her laugh, and with her head thrown back and that big smile on her face again, his gaze was totally stuck.

"I like it when you look at her like that."

Zane's lips twitched at Noah's words. "Finally ready to admit you were wrong about me?"

Noah scoffed. "I wouldn't call it wrong. I'd call it being cautious."

Finally, he dragged his gaze from Bonnie to look at her brother.

"But," Noah added, "I shouldn't have thought I knew better. She's an adult. Even if I remember her as a teenager. She can make her own decisions. And her decision to choose you seems to be a pretty good one so far."

"I'm glad to have you on my side."

Noah grinned at him. "You know you're part of this big, crazy family now, right?"

Zane glanced around the packed gym. At Bonnie's siblings and cousins and partners and aunt. "I've gained more than I thought I would, coming to Amber Ridge."

Noah chuckled. "I did the same. There's something about this town that does that."

Jesse crossed the gym to them, phone to his ear. "Thanks, Claudia." When he hung up, he looked at Zane. "Good news. Stetson's out of the hospital."

The last weight lifted off his chest. He'd been worrying about the kid.

Apparently, the morning Stetson was shot, Damien had shown up at his place, asking to do an early morning session at the gym.

Thank God Stetson was okay. With no reason not to trust his cousin, Stetson opened the building for him and got betrayed for his trouble. Damien was behind bars without bail until his trial. And the prosecutor had agreed not to press charges against Maisie in exchange for her agreement to testify against Damien, because it was deemed that she was acting under duress.

"You guys helping here or what?" Becket called from the far wall, paintbrush in hand.

Noah and Jesse grinned before crossing the gym.

Zane joined Ethan, who was pulling on his jacket at the desk. "Leaving?"

"Yeah. Told Ferris I'd come to his office to talk."

Zane frowned. "The mayor of Deep River wants to talk to you?"

"Yeah. I'm guessing it will be another rant about Ward not doing his job as sheriff."

Zane shook his head. "I can't imagine having a town sheriff who doesn't do his job." Especially when they had such a damn good one here in Amber Ridge.

The problem was, no one had ever run against him, and the last election had been just before Ethan had gotten home, so he hadn't had the chance to oppose Ward.

"Unfortunately for me, I don't have to imagine," Ethan said.

"I'm sorry." Zane walked him out. "Thanks again for everything, Ethan. You've been a good friend these last few months."

"Just these last few months?"

Zane chuckled. "I owe you. Anything you need, I'll be there. I'll even come to Deep River and search those mountains with you."

"You could also come just for a visit."

"To visit the black-and-white theater and the self-proclaimed psychic?"

"Hey, I hear Maureen accurately predicted Ward's microwave lasagna starting a fire at the station."

Zane scoffed. "That probably happens weekly."

Ethan just grinned, because Zane was right.

"So..." he started. "Any more dates with that woman? What was her name? Nel?"

A muscle ticked in Ethan's jaw.

Zane frowned as they stopped at his friend's car. "What happened?"

"Nothing. I just..." He blew out a breath. "The day after our second date, I went to Bloom for coffee."

The coffee shop was called The Wandering Bloom, but locals referred to it as Bloom. It was a combination coffee shop, book-store, and florist. "And?"

"And...Polly was on the phone in the back. Her call was on speaker, and I heard..."

Shit. Ethan didn't need to finish his sentence, because Zane knew. Polly had been best friends with Maggie in school, prob-ably still was, even though Maggie didn't live in the town anymore. And Maggie and Ethan had dated in high school. Hell, they'd dated *after* school too, and done long-distance for a while...until she'd broken up with him.

The breakup had shocked the hell out of everyone, including Ethan. They were one of those unbreakable couples that you just assumed were a forever kind of thing.

"You heard Maggie," Zane finally said quietly.

Ethan rubbed the back of his neck. "Her voice shouldn't affect me so much. We broke up over a decade ago. I should be over her. But hearing her...dammit, I don't know. It did something to me."

"Maybe..."

Ethan frowned. "Maybe what?"

"Maybe she'll return to Deep River."

The reaction was subtle. A small flaring of Ethan's eyes. A tiny twitch of his jaw. Then he shook his head. "No. Her aunt still lives there and she's awful. Anyway, I should go. I'll see you next time." Ethan squeezed Zane's shoulder before lowering into his car.

When Ethan was gone, Zane went back into the gym. Bonnie was the first person he saw. For a moment, she was the *only* person he saw. And Zane was reminded of just how damn lucky he was. Not everyone got their happy ending with the person they loved. But he did.

Why the fuck had he brought up Maggie? Jesus Christ. He'd been twenty-two when she'd broken up with him. That was eleven fucking years ago.

Ethan Moore took a hard right.

Not only had they not dated in eleven years, but he hadn't seen her for just as long. So why had hearing her voice one time —one fucking time—caused him to stop seeing Nel, a woman he'd taken on two dates? *Good* dates. But suddenly the thought of going on a third felt…hell, he didn't even have words. Wrong? Dishonest?

He blew out a breath as he turned onto the highway, driving toward Deep River, forcing Maggie out of his head.

But the second he stopped thinking about her, he started thinking about Ward.

His fingers tightened around the wheel. In the year he'd been home from the military, he'd realized the sheriff had gotten even worse. Become lazier. Just a general not-giving-a-shit attitude.

It was pissing Ethan the fuck off, because he loved his town. He loved The Pancake Bar, which had been awarded the "best pancakes in the world" in 1990 by some small magazine, yet Basil still advertised it like it was yesterday. He loved the black-and-white theater that had missed the memo that color was introduced to film in the early nineteen hundreds. He even loved the eighties-themed bar with the old-school TV.

So Ward failing to do his job to keep the town safe, while also refusing to give up the badge, was making Ethan mad as hell. There were still three years left on Ward's term as sheriff, and it felt too long.

He pulled into a gas station to fill the truck. When he got back in, a text came up on his phone.

His mouth stretched into a smile. It was the group chat with his old team.

Joel: The neighbor's dog ate my glacier lilies.

What was a glacier lily? But Ryan got the text in first.

Ryan: What the hell's a glacier lily?

Joel: It's a flower, jackass.

Connor: I just Googled it. Glacier lilies can be toxic for dogs. Is your neighbor's dog dead?

Joel: Going by the vomit on my front porch this morning, I'd say no.

Ethan's lips twitched. He fucking loved his friends. He'd loved them when they'd become a SEAL team, and nothing had changed. Although, living across the country from one another was fucking hard. Five of them were out, three still in.

Ethan typed out a reply.

Ethan: There you go, the dog got sick so they paid the price.

Joel: The mutt ate my flower and threw it up on my porch. I paid the price.

Ryan: Your neighbor obviously hates you. What did you do?

Joel: Existed. I just existed.

Ethan: Obviously, you're in the wrong town. You should come to Deep River.

Joel: Any dogs there?

Ethan: We'll find you a dog-free street.

Joel: Don't tempt me.

Zack: Hey, do I get an invite?

Ethan: You can all get your asses here. But I'll put you to work. God knows we need the help.

Connor: Still no luck on the missing tourist?

Ethan: None. It's a mess. But you're right, your dog problem's bad too.

Joel: Hey. It's a flower problem. I grew those babies with my bare hands.

Connor: You're calling flowers your babies?

Ryan: You start knitting hats and we're calling an intervention.

The smile remained on Ethan's face as he pulled out of the station.

Damn, he missed the guys. They'd gone from seeing one another every day, saving each other from goddamn bullets, to being scattered across the country.

They'd only gotten together once in the last year, and Tate, Lincoln, and Kolbe, the three who were still active-duty SEALs, hadn't been able to make it.

The phone kept lighting up with texts. It would probably do that for a while.

As he drove, his mind went back to Maggie again. To the soft sound of her voice. Her lyrical laugh over the line as she talked to Polly.

The beats of his heart did that thing where they sped up and stumbled over one another.

Once upon a time, he'd been so sure he was going to marry the woman. That was before she'll pulled the floor from beneath his feet and broken up with him.

He gritted his teeth and turned the radio on loud, trying to fill his head with anything but her. He was an hour into the drive when his phone rang, the town mayor's name on the screen.

Ethan frowned before hitting the Bluetooth on his wheel to answer the call. "Ferris. I'm an hour out. Everything okay?"

"Okay? Son, I just had the least-productive call I've ever had with our sheriff about the crime rate in this town."

"Is a talk with Ward ever productive?"

"No. And it's making me angry as hell. But not five minutes after the meeting, I got a call from someone who turned my day around."

Ethan lifted his brows. "Sounds intriguing. Care to share?"

"Actually, I'm calling a town meeting next week. Wednesday evening at six thirty. I need you there, son."

"You need me, specifically?"

"Yes. Can you make it?"

"Can you tell me what the meeting will be about?"

"I can do better. I'll tell you *everything* at our meeting later today. I think we'll both benefit from this. Your SEAL friends too."

What the hell did his team have to do with anything?

Ferris was being cryptic. But that wasn't a surprise. The mayor liked to keep his cards close to his chest, but unlike their sheriff, Ferris actually cared about the town and was good at his job.

"I'll see you in an hour then."

"Great. Talk soon, son. I'm going to turn this town around. And you're going to help me."

When the call ended, Ethan was still frowning. What the hell did Ferris have planned? And how did it involve him and his team?

Order Ethan and Maggie's story—book one in the Deep River series, titled WHISPERS IN THE WATER, now!

ALSO BY NYSSA KATHRYN

PROJECT ARMA SERIES

Uncovering Project Arma

Luca

Eden

Asher

Mason

Wyatt

Bodie

Oliver

Kye

BLUE HALO SERIES

Logan

Jason

Blake

Flynn

Aidan

Tyler

Callum

Liam

MERCY RING

Jackson

Declan

Cole

Ryker

BEAUTIFUL PIECES

Erik's Salvation

Erik's Redemption

Erik's Refuge

SHORT CHRISTMAS STORY

Hidden Shadows

RECKLESS SERIES

Reckless Hope

Reckless Trust

Reckless Fall

Reckless Faith

Reckless Love

AMBER RIDGE SERIES

Unafraid

Unraveled

Untouched

Unbroken

Unchained

Unfinished

DEEP RIVER SERIES

JOIN my newsletter and be the first to find out about sales and new releases! CLICK HERE

ABOUT THE AUTHOR

Nyssa Kathryn is a romantic suspense author. She lives in South Australia with hubby and two daughters and takes every chance she can to be plotting and writing. Always an avid reader of romance novels, she considers alpha males and happily-ever-afters to be her jam.

Don't forget to follow Nyssa and never miss another release.

Facebook | Instagram | Amazon | Goodreads

www.ingramcontent.com/pod-product-compliance
Lightning Source LLC
Chambersburg PA
CBHW050556190726

48283CB00007B/2160